When A Heart Cries

KIM VOGEL SAWYER

Mountain Lake, Minnesota Trilogy

A Seeking Heart

A Heart Surrenders

When a Heart Cries

Mountain Lake, Minnesota Trilogy
· Book Three ·

When A Heart Cries

KIM VOGEL SAWYER

HENDRICKSON
PUBLISHERS

When a Heart Cries

Hendrickson Publishers Marketing, LLC
P. O. Box 3473
Peabody, Massachusetts 01961-3473

ISBN 978-1-59856-927-8

First Hendrickson Edition Printing — October 2012

Dedicated to
Kristian, Kaitlyn, and Kamryn, of course—

You fill my heart
with love and laughter every day!

"Every good and perfect gift is from above,
coming down from the Father of the heavenly lights,
who does not change like shifting shadows."
James 1:17 (NIV)

A Note to Readers

Thank you for choosing to spend time with Samantha and Adam and the residents of Mountain Lake. This story is particularly dear to me because it is loosely based on my family history. I still remember with deep appreciation my visit to the Mountain Lake community years ago.

The Mennonite Brethren referenced in the Mountain Lake, Minnesota Trilogy originally resided in Germany. Persecuted for their faith, which included resistance to taking human lives even in times of war, they accepted the invitation of Catherine the Great to settle on the *steppes*, those grassy plains of Russia, and live their beliefs without government interference. They built colonies and settled the untamed land, living peacefully for a century before new political leaders once again demanded their sons serve in the military and otherwise intruded upon their peaceful village life. Consequently, a number of the families chose to leave Russia and immigrate to the United States of America, where they could practice their religion freely, without fear of those terrifying knocks on the door from soldiers with official documents and weapons.

My great-grandparents, Bernard and Maria Klaassen, were part of a large number of German Mennonites who left Russia in the 1870s to start a new life in America. They established a farmstead near Mountain Lake where they raised their nine children, including my grandmother, Elizabeth. My grandmother's caring, giving spirit is captured here in the character of Laura, and it gives me great pleasure to honor her tender heart and deep faith.

May God bless you richly as you journey with Him,

Kim Vogel Sawyer

Contents

Klaassen Family Tree

Simon James Klaassen (1873) m. Laura Doerksen (1877), 1893
   Daniel Simon (1894) m. Rose Willems (1892), 1913
      Christina Rose (1915)
      Katrina Marie (1916)
      Camelia Ann (1921)
   Hannah Joy (1895–1895)
   Franklin Thomas (1896) m. Anna Harms (1900), 1918
      Laura Beth (1920)
      Unnamed baby boy (1922–1922)
      Kate Samantha (1923)
   Elizabeth Laurene (1898) m. Jacob Aaron Stoesz (1897), 1915
      Andrew Jacob and Adam James (A.J.), (1917)
      Amanda Joy (1921)
   Adam Earnest (1899) m. Samantha Olivia O'Brien (1900), 1918
   Josephine Ellen (1900) m. Stephen Koehn (1896), 1918
      Simon Stephen (1920)
   Arnold Hiram (1903)
   Rebecca Arlene (1906)
   Theodore Henry (1909)
   Sarah Louise (1911)
Hiram Klaassen (1872) m. Hulda Schmidt (1872), 1898

O'Brien Family Tree

Burton O'Brien (1870) m. Olivia Ruth Stanton (1873–1900), 1891
   David Burton (1894) m. Priscilla Millicent Koehn (1900), 1918
   Samantha Olivia (1900) m. Adam Earnest Klaassen (1899), 1918

amantha Klaassen gazed in wonder at the tiny bundle in her arms. Jenny Millicent O'Brien was absolutely beautiful. The baby's fine dark hair stood out like a halo around her perfectly shaped head, her dark eyes wide lined by nearly invisible lashes and a tiny button nose tilted impishly. When the newborn's mouth stretched into an adorable yawn, Samantha laughed softly.

She lifted the infant higher to press the soft cheek against her own and breathe in the sweet milky smell that said *baby*. "Oh, Pris . . ." Samantha spoke to her sister-in-law but lilted her voice for the baby's ears, "you must be so proud."

Priscilla shifted herself higher against the pillows in her tall bed. Her tangled hair, black as midnight, spread across her shoulders, and she pushed it aside. "Proud but tired. Whatever doctor attached the label 'labor' to describe giving birth wasn't just joking! It's the hardest work I've ever done. You'll find out one day—mark my words!"

Samantha felt her heart lift. "Oh, I hope so." Samantha gently placed her new niece into Priscilla's waiting arms. She watched as little Jenny immediately nestled against her mother, as if sensing she was back where she belonged. Samantha's chest filled with longing for her own sweet baby to cuddle.

Priscilla smoothed the blanket away from Jenny's face. "Where's Joey? It's too quiet out there."

Samantha smiled, picturing her brother David and Priscilla's firstborn, a son named Joey. At two and a half, the toddler

was a never-ending cyclone of activity. Under the best of circumstances, he was a challenge. Now that Priscilla had a new baby to care for, how would she keep up with the little boy? Samantha answered, "David took him to the mercantile for a while so you could get some rest."

"Oh, bless his heart," Priscilla sighed and shook her head. "I know he took Joey with him to help me out, but my poor husband always comes home grumpy after he's had to battle with Joey at the store."

"Well, he'll only have Joey there a short time." Samantha leaned over to stroke Jenny's soft cheek with one finger. "He said Josie would pick him up to spend the afternoon playing with Simon, so maybe it won't be so bad." Only two months separated cousins Simon and Joey, and the two little boys got along famously.

"That's a relief." Priscilla sighed again. "If I could just regain my strength, I could be more helpful around here, but it seems—" The tears that were always just below the surface these days spilled over again. Priscilla hid her face in the crook of her arm. Samantha sat back, feeling so helpless at the depression that had taken hold of Priscilla days after Jenny's birth.

Wanting to provide some sort of assistance, Samantha offered, "Why don't I plan to pick up Joey from the mercantile and take him home with me for a few days? Auntie Sam can spoil him a bit, then bring him home. You could use the rest, and I could use the company. With harvest in full swing, I hardly see Adam during the day. I'd enjoy having someone to keep me occupied." Samantha's husband, Adam, would be gone from dawn to dusk for several more weeks, working with the community members to harvest wheat and corn. Even with the help of gas-powered machinery, it was a long process and required the participation of every area farmer.

Priscilla blinked at Samantha with eyes red rimmed and raw from all the tears that had been shed in the past two weeks. "Oh, Sammy, I appreciate that, really I do. But I don't know what David would say. He seems to think if I'd just get up and get moving, everything would go back to normal, but—" She sniffled.

Samantha sat on the edge of the bed and patted Priscilla's hand. "I'm sure it's just that David is worried about you. This birth was harder on you, and it will take a while to get back to your old perky self. I tell you what: I'll talk with Davey and make sure he knows it was all my idea to take Joey. I'm sure I can make him see the sense of it. Would that be all right?"

Priscilla sent her sister-in-law a grateful look. "Oh, would you, Sam? I'm sure I can get my strength back if I don't have to chase after Joey for a day or so."

"I'll go talk to him right now." Samantha leaned forward to place a kiss on Priscilla's wan cheek. "You rest while Jenny's still sleeping. I'll check in on you tomorrow."

"Thank you." Priscilla's eyes were already closed.

Samantha paused in the doorway for a moment, capturing the scene of mother and child snuggled together beneath a bright patchwork quilt. The sunlight slanting through the lace curtain at the window created a weblike pattern across the foot of the bed. Priscilla and little Jenny were a picture of contentment. Samantha couldn't help the envy that rose inside, and she turned away.

As she drove her wagon to the mercantile, she reflected on all the changes in the family over the past three years. Priscilla and David had Joseph and now Jenny; Priscilla's brother Stephen and his wife, who was Adam's sister, had Simon; Adam's brother Frank and his wife, Anna, had Laura Beth and were expecting another child before Thanksgiving; Adam's sister

Liz and her husband, Jake, already had three little ones running around the house—the twins, Andy and A.J., and now
little Amanda; and Adam's oldest brother Daniel and his wife,
Rose, had added a third daughter, Camelia, to their family the
same year Amanda had been born. Everyone's families were
growing . . . except Samantha's and Adam's.

It wasn't fair, Samantha mourned. She and Adam had been
married longer than David and Pris, Josie and Stephen, too!
When would it be her turn for the congratulations and gifts of tiny
gowns and teasing comments about her expanding waistline?
Everyone told her to be patient, that her time would come, but
Samantha's patience was spent. She wanted her time to be *now*.

When she entered the town's mercantile, which David managed, she was still feeling resentful and swung the door harder
than necessary. The cowbell above the door clanged angrily,
and she grabbed it to still the sound. Another noise reached
her ears from the storeroom at the back—Joey's plaintive cry
and David's scolding voice.

"Joey, I don't know how many times I've told you: you can't
climb on the shelves! Look at the mess you've made for Papa
now." It seemed David's patience was spent as well, but for a far
different reason, she thought.

Samantha pulled back the curtain over the storeroom door
and peeked in. Startled, her hand clapped her cheek as she
gaped at the fiasco. The wooden shelves that had been secured
to the wall hung crazily. David stood knee-deep in overshoes
and work boots. He held Joey, who was hollering and doing his
best to free himself from his father's grasp. Samantha immediately knew what had taken place—and what else would soon
take place if someone didn't intervene.

Although Samantha tried not to butt in to her relatives'
child rearing, she hated to see Joey punished for what she

considered to be normal curiosity. What little boy didn't like to climb? Besides, it seemed like a perfect time to borrow Joey for a few days. "David?"

David turned to the doorway, exasperation creasing his narrow face. "Oh, Sam."

When the wailing Joey spotted his Auntie Sam, he reached his chubby arms for Samantha. She waded through the mess to take him. "Looks like Joey's been busy," Samantha offered with a wry smirk as she lifted him into her arms.

David threw his hands upward. "When isn't he?" David surveyed the disorder. "I declare, Sammy, I can't keep up with that child! He goes from one thing to another, and another, and another. . . . And he leaves messes behind wherever he's been." Her brother blew out his lips in disgust.

Samantha found herself unable to generate even a wee bit of indignation at Joey's mischief making. "At least you'll never lose track of him," she quipped.

David shook his head. "You never lose patience, do you, Sam? It's too bad—" He broke off, but the unspoken words, *it's too bad you don't have any children of your own*, hung in the air between them.

Samantha steered the conversation elsewhere. "I thought Josie was going to pick him up."

"She was—she is—but not till noon. If I last that long." David gave his sister a look that told her he'd had enough.

"Well," Samantha said with forced brightness, "given my penchant for patience, I have a request."

"What's that?" He had started sorting through the jumbled pile of shoes, trying to pair them up again.

"I'd like to take Joey home with me for a few days. Would you like that, Joey?" Samantha noticed David's sharp gaze settle on her, but she ignored his stern expression. "I'm so lonely with

Adam gone all day, I would very much enjoy the company. Plus Priscilla seems to need some extra time to rest, to get back on her feet."

"Did Priscilla put you up to this?"

"No, it was all my idea. But she didn't oppose it, if that's your next question."

"It was." David high stepped through the chaos to his sister and placed a hand on Joey's dark head.

Joey had laid his head on Samantha's shoulder and was sucking his fingers contentedly. Samantha rocked him back and forth. She loved the feel of Joey's hair against her cheek. Samantha looked up at David. "It was my idea, and I think it's a good one. Pris is really washed out from the difficult delivery. Joey is just too much for her right now. And I don't see how you can expect to keep him here and still pay attention to the store. I'm serious about wanting the company." She paused, tipped her head and asked in her best pleading voice, "Please, Davey?"

David lost his stern expression, the lines around his eyes turning into a smile. But to Samantha it looked like a sad smile. "I can't say no to you when you look at me that way, Sammy."

"Good!" Samantha whispered in Joey's ear, "You get to come home with Auntie Sam for a few days, Joey!" Joey continued sucking his fingers, but his dark, fine eyebrows shot up in happy speculation. She looked up at David. "I'll stop by the house and collect a few of his things on my way home. I'll check on Pris too once more."

"Thanks, Samantha." David perched on the edge of a crate and ran a hand through his wavy hair. "It's been rough since Jenny was born. Priscilla just sits and cries and practically ignores Joey. I guess it's small wonder he's been into more mischief than usual. I can't figure out what's wrong with her."

Samantha didn't have much advice to give. She couldn't begin to understand all of the emotions that might accompany childbirth. But she could offer sympathy. "I'm sure Pris is just tired, David." She placed a hand on David's wide shoulder. "Wait and see—a few days of relaxation, and she'll be back to her same sassy self."

"I hope so." David shook his head. "These constant tears and melodramatic sighs are wearing me down."

Samantha left David to his mess. As she held Joey's small hand and walked to the waiting wagon, she told the little boy, "What fun we're going to have, Joey! For a while we'll pretend you're my little boy and forget all about everybody else! Yes?"

Joey blinked up at her innocently and echoed, "Yes."

For the moment, her joy would be in pretending.

Chapter Two

*A*dam Klaassen lowered the crossbar on the barn door and ambled toward the house, the warm glow from the windows a beacon of welcome. The aroma of supper—vegetable soup, if his nose was correct—drifted across the yard, and he hurried his steps. Although he'd eaten a hearty noon meal and an afternoon snack as well, he'd never turn down Samantha's well-seasoned soup made from vegetables from their own garden. His heart gave a bit of a leap, as it always did, when coming home to his wife. How he loved her . . .

"I'm home!" he called as he entered the kitchen. Surprised, he saw Samantha in her favorite, scarred rocking chair with their nephew Joey squirming in her arms. When Joey spotted Adam, he wriggled all the harder, and Samantha released him with a sigh.

"Unc'oo Adam!" The little boy galloped barefoot across the floor, his nightshirt flapping. He threw pudgy arms around Adam's legs.

"Hey there, big guy." Adam scooped up the giggling toddler and hoisted him high onto his shoulder. "What brings you here?"

"Joey tum home wif Auntie Sam." Joey grabbed two fistfuls of Adam's hair for support. "We betendin' I Auntie Sam's widd'oo boy."

Adam wasn't sure that was a healthy pastime for Samantha, but he chose not to broach the subject. He carefully dislodged Joey's hands from his hair and set him back down on the floor. Joey kept a two-handed grip on Adam's wrist, suspending himself happily, while Adam leaned over to receive a kiss from his wife.

"I hope you don't mind if we have Joey for a couple days." Samantha lifted Joey into her lap and set the rocker in motion. "When I visited Priscilla this morning, she looked so worn out, and David was at wit's end, trying to keep track of Joey at the mercantile. I felt sorry for them both and on the spur of the moment offered to help out. I didn't think about checking with you before it was all settled."

Adam pulled over a pressed-back chair from the table and seated himself backward, stacking his arms on the top to prop up his chin. He grinned at Joey, who continued to wiggle in Samantha's embrace. "There was no need to check with me, honey. Besides," he chuckled, "watching him will be your responsibility, since I'll be gone all day." He grinned as he observed Joey's constant wriggling. "Looks like you'll have your hands full."

Samantha leaned forward to give Adam another kiss, and Joey said, "Ooooh! Tisses!"

Adam joined Samantha in a laugh. He reached out to poke Joey's tummy. The boy giggled and pulled up his knees to protect his ticklish belly. Samantha wrapped her arms around him and held him tight. "Shhh now, Joey. It's time for sleep." She began humming a lullaby.

Adam got up, poured himself a cup of coffee, and leaned against the kitchen counter to watch Samantha play mommy. She rocked and sang softly, stroking Joey's dark curls back from his forehead in a rhythmic gesture that appeared to relax him. Joey's fingers went to his mouth as his eyelids dropped. Samantha rocked, her face wearing an expression of bliss.

Adam swallowed hard. "It feels good holding him, doesn't it?" Adam asked quietly.

Samantha nodded. She pressed her lips to Joey's temple, her eyes sliding closed. The beauty of his Samantha cradling a child made Adam's chest ache. Tears pricked his eyes. Yet he couldn't look away. He remained across the room for several minutes with only the squeak of the rocking chair runners against the wood floor and the measured tick-tick, tick-tick of the mantel clock providing homey intrusion.

When Joey's fingers slipped from his mouth, Adam put down his cup and crossed to the chair. He held out his arms. "Let me put him to bed now."

Samantha's grip tightened for a moment, but then she transferred Joey to Adam.

Adam whispered, "Which room do you want him in?"

Samantha's forehead creased. "The nursery."

Adam cringed. He wished she'd stop referring to the small bedroom at the right of their own as the nursery. The room, away from the head of the stairs and with a door connecting it to theirs, would make a perfect nursery. But it contained no cradle and no baby, so using the term only served to hurt her. And him.

She added in a raspy whisper, "I made a pallet on the floor for him."

Adam carried the slumbering little boy upstairs. The child's weight in his arms felt good. Right. He knelt and carefully placed Joey on the folded quilts. Joey snuffled, wrinkling his nose, then rolled onto his tummy and hiked his bottom in the air. A chuckle rose in Adam's throat, but he held it inside as he eased a blanket over the little boy and tucked it in around him. He remained crouched beside the pallet for a few moments, gazing down at Joey's peaceful face, before leaning over to deposit a kiss on the child's round cheek.

He closed the door silently behind him and tiptoed downstairs. As he reached the bottom, Samantha rose from the rocker to meet him. Adam beamed at her. "He rolled over, stuck his little behind in the air, and started snoring."

Wordlessly Samantha stepped into him, wrapping her arms around his middle and burying her face in the hollow of his throat. He closed his arms around her and rested his chin on the top of her head. "When, Adam?" she asked, her voice muffled by his collar.

He knew what she wanted to know. But he had no more answers than she, so he could only say, as he had many times before, "Give it time, Sammy."

She pushed against his chest, freeing herself from his embrace. "Please stop saying that."

He reached for her, but she stepped away from his touch. "Samantha . . ."

On the other side of the table, she planted her feet and sent him a dismissive look of frustration and hurt. "I mean it. I'm tired of hearing it. Everyone keeps telling me, 'Give it time.' I've given it time, Adam! I've given it five years!" As quickly as her temper flared, it sputtered and died. She dropped into a kitchen chair, her head in her hands. "Oh, Adam, when we built this house we had such hopes of also building a family. Four bedrooms upstairs. Three of them unadorned, furnitureless, *childless* rooms."

Adam inched forward and seated himself at the table, placing his hand on her shoulder. She remained in her hunkered-down position. His heart ached with hers. The empty rooms upstairs echoed a hollowness in his own chest. He too longed to fill those rooms with children.

With a sigh, she raised her head. Tears swam in her pale blue eyes. "For the first year, it didn't matter so much. I was so busy being a wife and homemaker, learning to accomplish everything a farmer's wife needs to do. I enjoyed visiting our family and playing with our nieces and nephews and dreaming about the day we'd have our own little one. It wasn't a pressing need then, because we'd only been married a year."

One tear trailed down her cheek. "But then Priscilla and Josie announced the impending arrival of little ones before a full year of their marriages had passed. And it didn't seem fair. We'd been married longer; we deserved to start our family first."

Adam winced, recalling how he'd teased her about getting busy and adding a new member to their family since they were getting left behind. He hadn't meant to be hurtful, but no doubt his comment had stung. As did the rambling size of their house.

When they were first married, they'd lived in the dugout Grandpa Klaassen had built for his own bride. The tiny home carved out of a hill toward the back of the farm was primitive but cozy, and they'd been happy there. But Adam, eager for their own family and wanting space to spread out, had decided to build this big farmhouse. There was never any doubt, as the house plans were drawn and the two-story frame home was erected, that they'd soon fill the house with a whole passel of little Klaassens. But Adam and Samantha's recent fifth wedding anniversary had passed, and it was still just the two of them.

Adam took Samantha's hand and gave it a gentle squeeze. "Don't lose heart, honey." He forced his lips into a smile. "Who knows? You might be expecting right now, and—"

She pushed away from the table. "I'm not expecting. Not now." Her lips pursed into a tight line for several seconds, her chin quivering. "I'm beginning to understand why some women refer to their monthly time as a curse. It's certainly that for me, dashing my dreams month after month, year after year. . . ."

Adam rose and came around the table to embrace her. If only he could remove the pain she carried. He rubbed his palms up and down her back, then gently set her aside. "Go on upstairs, honey. I want to eat a bowl of your soup"—although his appetite had fled—"and then I'll be up."

She flicked a look of hurt betrayal in his direction that cut him to the core. Who did she feel was betraying her—himself or God? He reached out to stroke his thumb across her cheek and gave her a smile meant to convey his understanding.

Samantha simply turned away and trudged up the stairs, her eyes downcast and her shoulders slumped. As Adam watched her joyless ascent, his heart ached for the desire to fulfill her dreams. They were his dreams, too. He wanted the babies Samantha longed for as much as she did.

Clenching his fists, he turned his face heavenward and repeated Samantha's question. "When, Lord?" But he heard no reply.

⁓◯

"Oh, Joey, sweetheart, no no!"

In the less than ten minutes Samantha and Joey had been in the vegetable garden, Joey had managed to pull down three tomato vines and stomp what was left of the carrots. Samantha scooped him up and set him outside the garden fence. "Joey, you stay right here where Auntie Sam can see you," she said with as much enthusiasm as she could muster. "Play with these little soldiers." Joey swept his hand across the painted tin soldiers Samantha had lined up in the dirt. "I hewp!"

"But, sweetheart—"

Joey's lower lip poked out and two tears formed in his blue eyes. He tilted his head. "I hewp?"

Samantha melted. She pulled Joey into her arms and hugged him for as long as the active little boy would allow.

When he wiggled loose, she had to laugh. "All right, little monkey, you come help. But you stay close to Auntie Sam. And don't pick anything unless you ask first, all right?"

"Aw right!"

They spent the better part of an hour with Joey trotting back and forth, depositing dried cucumber vines into a big pile at the corner of the garden and scooping up dirt from the potato mounds with a trowel. By the time Samantha finished her tasks, Joey was filthy and required a bath that took nearly another hour.

Samantha enjoyed Joey's bath much more than Joey did—and Joey had a pretty good time. What joy she found in lathering the little boy's sturdy back, arms, and legs, blowing bubbles through her fist to make him laugh, pouring cups of water through his open hands, then holding out her own hands for Joey to pour water over. Samantha was nearly as wet as Joey by the time he'd finished splashing, but it was worth every minute of the time it took to clean up the water mess and change her clothes.

After a simple lunch, Samantha put Joey down for a nap and laid down with him on the pallet, stroking his back until he finally fell asleep. She stayed beside him, listening to him breathe for a long time after he dropped off.

A knock on the front door brought her quickly tiptoeing downstairs. She peeked through the oval cut glass opening, surprised to find David on the other side. She swung the door wide, and he stepped in, catching her in a quick hug. "Hi, Sammy, where's Joey?"

Samantha placed a finger against her lips. "He's upstairs napping." She closed the door with great care.

David's eyebrows shot up. "You got him to take a nap?" He whispered too. "How'd you do it?"

Samantha grinned. "Laid down beside him and rubbed his back. He went out like a light." She snapped her fingers.

David shook his head. "Sammy, you'll spoil him. You know Pris and I don't have time to coddle him that way." His kind tone softened the reprimand.

Samantha shrugged. "Well, I do. Besides, I did it as much for me as for Joey. We're having a wonderful time." She drew her brows together. "You haven't come to take him home already, have you?"

"No, actually I came to check on you, to see how you were holding up. Joey can be a handful, to put it mildly."

"A delightful handful," Samantha insisted. "He helped me in the garden"—she ignored David's smirk—"and then he had a bath—"

"—which I'm sure he needed—"

"—and some lunch—"

"—which he probably wore—"

"—and now he's napping. So there!"

They laughed and Samantha turned toward the kitchen. "I baked carrot cake yesterday. Come sit and have a piece with me."

"You don't have to ask me twice." David followed her to the round table in the center of the kitchen. He noted matter-of-factly, "Pris never has figured out that it's nice to have sweets around. Any kind of cake is a treat to me."

Samantha laid a large piece of cake on a plate, poured a glass of milk, and carried the treat to the table. He dug in immediately and complimented her with a smiling "mmmm."

Samantha sat opposite him and propped her chin in her hands with a smile. "Now I know where Joey gets his sweet tooth. I had to promise him cake to get him to eat his green beans last night."

"And it worked?"

"Yep. He ate all two of them."

"Two!" David's fork stopped midway to his mouth. "That's all you gave him?"

"Well, it seemed fair—one for each year of age."

David put down the fork and pushed the plate aside. "Sammy, we've got to talk."

Samantha's scalp prickled at his tone. "About what?"

David folded his hands on the tabletop. "I know you love Joey, but it isn't fair to him—or to us—for you to give in to him so easily."

She sputtered, "I don't give in to him. He ate his vegetables, and I got him to take his nap, and—"

"Yes, you did," David said, "but in both instances bribery was involved. Joey is a very strong-willed little boy, and I know how difficult it can be to get his cooperation. Priscilla and I are trying to teach him he has to obey simply because we know what is best for him. If you offer sweets and extra attention to get him to obey, then you undermine what we're trying to do."

Samantha bristled. "Have you considered I have the time and patience to work with Joey? Besides, I'm his aunt, not his parent. I don't want to be the disciplinarian."

David sighed. "Samantha, I think I know why it's so hard for you to say no to Joey or to any of your nieces and nephews. Pa always said no to everything we asked because it took less effort. I know how many times your feelings were crushed by his negative reaction."

Memories—none of them pleasant—flooded through Samantha's mind. She turned her face away.

David continued in a reasonable tone. "You can't compensate for Pa's harshness by being overly indulgent with the children in the family. Of course all the little ones adore their

Auntie Sam. But wouldn't it be better for the children if you exercised control? As they get older, they might begin to take advantage of you."

Samantha refused to answer.

"Sammy, listen to me, please?" David took Samantha's hand and tugged it until she shifted her gaze to meet his. "I'm not saying this to hurt your feelings, sweetheart. But children need structure and discipline so they can learn to discipline themselves. You're going to spoil them if you're always offering sweets or some other reward for appropriate behavior, and we both know there's nothing less attractive than a spoiled child."

Samantha gave a small nod of acknowledgment. David's wife, Priscilla, had been spoiled shamefully by her father. For years she made people miserable with her willful, selfish behavior. Samantha wouldn't want Joey or any of the others to behave in such an unpleasant manner.

David continued, "Someday you will have children of your own, and—"

Samantha shot out of the chair so fast it balanced on two legs for five seconds before crashing against the floor. She fled to the pantry and stood with her back to the kitchen. Pressing her fist to her mouth, she held back sobs of anguished fury.

Strong hands descended on her shoulders and turned her around. David gazed down at her in confusion. "Sam, what's wrong?"

The frustration welling inside erupted, and she thrust her fist against David's chest. "I'm so tired of being told *someday* I'll have children of my own. Doesn't it occur to you that I want someday to be now? I'm tired of being just Auntie Sam! I want to be a mama!" Mingled hurt and fury propelling her, she pulled her fist back for another swing.

David's eyes wide in shock, he caught her wrist and wrestled it downward. "Samantha, stop! What's gotten into you?"

Samantha froze and stared at him, startled by his heartless question. Slowly, realization dawned. He didn't understand. How could he? He had his family—an adorable son and a sweet little daughter. He had *everything*. And he couldn't see how special the gift was. Distress washed through her, and she forced herself to calm down. When she relaxed her fist, David released her. She left the pantry in silence.

She moved to the table and began sweeping nonexistent crumbs into her hand. "I'm sorry, David, I shouldn't have turned on you like that. And I'll try not to be so lenient with Joey, if it will please you." She turned to face him again. "But don't expect me to be as strict as you and Priscilla are. It's not my place as Joey's aunt."

David stood several feet away, examining her face. He seemed afraid to approach her. A hysterical giggle built inside her at his obvious consternation. "All right, I won't strike you again," she promised.

Finally his head bobbed in a slow nod. "All right, Sammy." He paused. "Are you sure you're . . . up . . . to keeping Joey?"

Samantha gave a brief huff of laughter. "Yes, Davey, I am definitely. . . up . . . to keeping Joey." She made it a point to imitate his vocal tone.

"Well, all right," he said, still sounding uncertain. "But Pris misses him. Would you take him into town to see her when he wakes from his nap?"

Samantha nodded. "That would be fine."

He pulled out his timepiece and flipped open the cover. "I've got to get back. I've left Arn alone at the mercantile far too long." He gave Samantha a kiss on the cheek and headed for the door. "Thanks for the cake. I'll see you later."

When he had gone, Samantha crept upstairs to peek in at Joey. The little boy still slept—flat on his back with his arms stretched above his head. She smiled. No matter what David thought, a little indulging wouldn't ruin Joey for life. While she had him, she intended to pamper him silly.

Chapter Three

*M*uch to Samantha's disappointment, David and Priscilla chose not to have Joey stay another night with his Auntie Sam. Priscilla claimed she missed him too much, and David stated it was taking unfair advantage of Samantha. Samantha thought they were being unreasonable, but what could she say? They were Joey's parents and had the final word.

She stayed at David and Priscilla's past the supper hour, building block towers with Joey and cuddling little Jenny. The sun was a thin magenta slice of brightness along the horizon when she arrived home.

Adam met her at the back door. "Sam, where've you been? You didn't leave a note or anything. I've been worried sick, wondering what happened to you and Joey."

Normally Samantha would have apologized for worrying her husband, but her pride still stung from the notion that she wasn't capable of handling Joey correctly. Adam's lecture seemed to underscore her lack of responsibility. "In case you hadn't noticed," she shot back, "you've not been getting home before dark, so I assumed I would be back long before you were. If I'd known you would beat me home, I would have left a note, but I didn't know." She whirled away from him. "I am a grown woman, and I don't need to be told what to do!"

She yanked off her bonnet hard enough to dislodge the knot of hair twisted on the back of her head and flung it on the kitchen table. Adam stood gaping in stunned silence as she stomped over to her rocking chair, sat down, and began to rock much faster than necessary.

Adam approached slowly, stopping in front of her. In an even, unruffled voice he said, "Do I dare ask what brought that on?"

Samantha gave him another hard stare that lasted only seconds before she gave a sigh and let her head drop against the back of the rocker. "I'm sorry, Adam." She aimed her gaze toward the ceiling. "You had every right to be concerned when I wasn't here, and I shouldn't have yelled at you."

Adam bent down on one knee and sandwiched her hands between his. "David said you hollered at him today too."

She tilted her face to look at him. Her throat went tight. "When did you see David?"

"He stopped by the Voth farm on his way back to town this afternoon."

Samantha pulled her hand away and covered her face, mortified. "I can't believe he went and tattled on me!"

Adam tugged her hands downward. "Don't be unfair, Sam. He wasn't tattling. He was concerned for you; you weren't acting like yourself."

Hurt and embarrassed, she retorted, "And that's why he kept Joey?"

"I wondered if they would insist you bring Joey back home." He rubbed his thumbs back and forth over Samantha's knuckles, the touch soothing. "He said you were . . . highly emotional."

Samantha gave a little snort.

Adam raised one eyebrow. "I have to admit, just a minute ago you reacted very differently than I would have expected."

Samantha pulled her hands free. "Well! You tied into me the minute I came through the door! Questioned me like I don't have enough sense to take care of myself, and David insinuated that I spoil Joey and undermine their attempts to discipline him. And I'm not supposed to be upset?"

"I'm not convinced, Sammy, that what David said is what's upsetting you right now."

Samantha's pulse tripped hard and fast. She glowered at Adam with narrowed eyes. "Oh? And what is it you think is upsetting me?"

"Those bedrooms upstairs, Samantha. Those empty bedrooms."

*

Adam watched Samantha fight for control. Her chin quivered, her eyes filled, but she didn't cry. She set her jaw tightly and simply stared, wide eyed, at him. Suddenly she bolted out of the chair, pushed past him, and stood before the kitchen window, her arms crossed and shoulders stiff.

Adam let his head hang low for a moment, remaining on one knee in front of the rocking chair. The same one in which Samantha's great-grandmother had rocked baby Samantha to sleep. The rocking chair in which Samantha had planned to rock her own babies to sleep.

He lifted his head to look across the room at his wife. He'd never seen a sadder sight, Samantha with her silent sorrow pulling her down from the inside. Slowly he pushed himself to his feet and walked up behind her, placing his hands on her shoulders and pulling her against his chest. She allowed his comforting embrace, but offered nothing of herself to it—standing stiff and unyielding against him.

In time Adam said gently, "Sammy, it's been more than five years."

He heard her sharp intake of breath. "I know, Adam. I've counted each and every one of those years, months, weeks, days—my heart breaks a little more with each new month that passes childless for me. . . ."

He tightened his hands on her shoulders. "I think it's time we saw a doctor. Maybe there's something—"

"Maybe there's something wrong with me—" she jerked away from him—"that's what you were going to say?"

Adam came after her, wanting to hold her, but she held up her hands as if to ward off a blow.

"No, Sammy. I was going to say maybe there's something a doctor could do to help us."

Samantha's expression softened, and her arms lowered until they hung limply at her sides. "I'm afraid." Her words were almost a whimper.

This time when Adam reached for her, she came willingly, clinging to him like a drowning person clings to his rescuer. Adam admitted, "I'm afraid too. But we have to find out. We can't go on wondering and wishing . . . and letting the desire for children dictate everything we do. We have to find out if there's a problem, and if there is, then find a way to solve it."

Samantha lifted her head from Adam's chest. The fear in her eyes made his pulse race in apprehension. "What if there is a problem, Adam? What if—?"

He placed two fingers against her lips, then pulled her snug against him and whispered in her hair, "We'll cross that bridge if we come to it. Let's try to think positively, yes?"

Samantha nodded. She relaxed against him, and he circled her with his arms, seeking to provide security with his embrace. His entire body ached with the desire to give her all she longed for. If love could make everything right, their child would already be in their arms.

With her face pressed against his dusty plaid shirt, she said, "We'll pray too, Adam. Won't we?"

"Of course we will." Adam planted a kiss on her tousled russet hair. "We'll put it all in God's hands." For the first time since he was a little boy, Adam discovered no sense of peace in handing his problems to his heavenly Father. The realization frightened him even more than what the doctor might discover.

～ↄ

Mountain Lake had only one physician, Dr. Robert Newton. Samantha trusted him completely. He'd delivered several of her nieces and nephews, had been there for simple things like earaches and stomachaches, along with more serious things like David's near-drowning accident and Teddy's broken arm. She had already talked with the doctor once about her desire to conceive a child, so visiting with him a second time was easier than she might have thought. Although she found it difficult to admit her fears, at least she was sharing them with someone she knew.

After a cursory examination, Dr. Newton instructed Samantha to dress and meet him in his small office. She hurried into her clothes and then joined Adam on a narrow bench which faced the doctor's scarred, cluttered desk. Dr. Newton leaned back in his squeaky chair, very much at ease. Samantha perched stiffly beside Adam, very much on edge.

"Samantha, Adam, I wish I could give you the answers you're looking for, but I'm afraid I'm simply not well versed in the medical field of reproduction. I am a family practitioner, not a specialist. Samantha, when you came to me two years ago, I gave you special instructions on how to determine the best time of the month for conception. I assume you followed my directives?"

Samantha gave a little nod. "It means so much to both of us to become parents. Of course I did what you instructed."

Dr. Newton sighed, pushed his spectacles toward his forehead, and rubbed his eyes with the pads of his thumb and first finger. When he'd settled his wire-rimmed glasses back in place, he said, "Then that's as much as I can do for you."

Samantha sent Adam a confused look. Were they just to give up their dreams?

Adam held his hands out to the doctor in query. "Then what do you suggest *we* do?"

The doctor leaned forward, resting his elbows on the desk top and pressing his interlaced fingers against his chin. "I suggest you see a specialist."

Samantha's stomach flip-flopped. "A specialist? But . . . but . . ." How could she speak of such intimate matters to a stranger?

Dr. Newton nodded solemnly. "There's a hospital in Rochester called the Mayo Clinic. It's a wonderful facility. They have specialists in all fields of medicine, including reproductive medicine. I'm sure they would be able to give you the assistance you need."

"Rochester?" Samantha clutched for Adam's hand. "We don't know anyone there!"

Adam laced his fingers through hers. "Dr. Newton, do you believe someone there can help us?"

"They know all there is to know, Adam. If anyone can help you, they can."

"Then we'll go. We'll do whatever is necessary to have the children we want."

Adam's lack of hesitation spurred Samantha's courage. She nodded resolutely. The decision was made.

wo weeks later Samantha and Adam entered the office of Dr. Phillip Zimmerman, Women's Specialist. Samantha couldn't help but think of Dr. Newton's small office back home. Its typically disorganized interior was the opposite of this white, sterile, a-place-for-everything-and-everything-in-its-place room.

And Dr. Newton was small of stature. Dr. Zimmerman stood taller than Adam and twice as big around. Dr. Newton was uncombed and rumpled, but Dr. Zimmerman looked—and smelled—as if he'd just stepped from a barber's shop. Dr. Newton always seemed relaxed and informal; Dr. Zimmerman's approach was brusque and business-like. But from the moment of introduction, Samantha sensed this man held a great deal of knowledge. How she prayed he would have the answers they needed.

"Mr. and Mrs. Klaassen, please sit down." The burly doctor gestured toward two upholstered chairs. He settled his rather impressive frame on a wheeled, wooden chair, crossed right leg over left, and balanced on his knee a slim board that held a writing tablet. He fixed Samantha with a serious gaze and angled graying brows low. "Now—I understand you have been married for five years, four months. Mrs. Klaassen, you are twenty-three years of age?" At Samantha's nod he turned to Adam. "And you are twenty-six, correct, Mr. Klaassen?" Adam, too, nodded. "Mm-hm, certainly of child-bearing age."

Samantha flicked a brief sidelong glance at Adam. He offered an assuring smile.

"Mrs. Klaassen . . ." Dr. Zimmerman began a series of questions that would have been embarrassingly intimidating had they not been stated with such forthrightness. Although Samantha had to swallow a couple times, and her voice quavered hesitantly, she managed to answer everything he asked. In a matter of minutes the doctor had scribbled down a long list of notes that seemed to have meaning for him. He reviewed them, his lower jaw thrust out and his eyes narrowed thoughtfully. Then he looked up, the pen paused above the paper. "Have you conferred with a doctor before?"

Adam cleared his throat and leaned forward. "Samantha went to our town doctor a couple of years ago, then again recently. He recommended we come to you."

The doctor made a checkmark on the paper. "What did he tell you?"

"He told her women can only conceive during certain days of the month, and he explained how to know when those days were."

"And you followed his guidance?"

Samantha squirmed in her chair, and Adam turned a bit pink around the ears. He said, "Yes, sir."

"And you've charted your fertile days for over two years without a pregnancy. . . ." The doctor stroked his chin with his thumb and first finger, staring at his notepad. He then sat forward abruptly and wrote something else. Samantha tried to get a peek at the pad, but she couldn't read a word of his messy-looking handwriting. He leaned back, reaching behind him to slap the pad onto his desk top. He capped his pen, dropped it on the pad of paper, and then offered the first hint of a smile since she and Adam had entered the room. "I will need to do a thorough examination. If you will follow me, I'll take you to an examination room."

Fear swirled through Samantha's stomach, bringing a rush of nausea. She gripped Adam's hand. He rose, tugging her up with him and whispered, "It'll be all right, Sam. Go on now. I'll wait for you here, and I'll be praying."

Samantha took a deep breath to gather courage. With one last look at Adam, she followed Dr. Zimmerman down a long hall filled with many bustling, gray-garbed women and men. They all appeared so filled with purpose! Eyes aimed straight ahead, feet moving briskly, their faces a study in determination. Samantha found herself wishing that just one of them would look at her—really *look* at her—and recognize her misgivings, offer some reassurance.

The doctor opened a door on the right side of the hall and held out a hand, indicating she should enter. Samantha looked around nervously. Directly in the middle of the small, square room sat a table—tall, flat, and covered with a white sheet. A shelf along the back wall held all sorts of unrecognizable metal instruments, toweling, and glass jars filled with everything from white cotton puffs to small wooden sticks.

In one corner a white cotton curtain hung suspended from the ceiling, creating a small cubicle. Dr. Zimmerman crossed to it and pushed it aside, revealing a short bench and two silver hooks on the white-painted wall. The doctor said, "You may undress back here, Mrs. Klaassen. Please remove all of your clothing. Then lie down on the table, and cover yourself with the sheet. In a few minutes, a nurse will check on you. When you are ready, I will begin my examination."

Samantha pressed her hands against her queasy stomach. She licked her lips, battling a fierce desire to escape.

Dr. Zimmerman had headed for the door but glanced back. His expression softened. He crossed to her and placed a hand on her shoulder. "I realize this is all new to you, Mrs. Klaassen, but please trust me when I say we are here to help you." His fingers briefly tightened. "However, I cannot help you unless you cooperate with me. Will you do what I've asked?"

The kind contact, however brief, gave Samantha the courage she needed. But her mouth felt dry, so she simply nodded.

"Good." He turned brisk again. "I will return when you are ready." He left her alone in the small room that smelled of strong disinfectant.

Samantha paused for a moment, realizing the great significance of the next several minutes. Soon her greatest desires or her worst fears would be realized. Her eyes rested on the tall, stark table, and her heart leaped into her throat. *Oh, Lord, please let him give me good news.*

The exam, which the doctor had promised would be thorough, took a little less than an hour. But Samantha felt she aged a year for every minute spent on the table. Tense and expectant, she waited for the doctor to suddenly cry out: "ah, ha!" and give her a miracle cure. But of course he didn't. When he finished, the attending nurse waited while Samantha dressed and then escorted her to the doctor's office.

Adam greeted her with a kiss on the temple. "Dr. Zimmerman told me he'll need time to go over the information before he can make a diagnosis."

Samantha sucked in a nervous breath. "How much time?"

"He wants us to come back tomorrow afternoon at two o'clock. He'll discuss his findings then."

Every muscle in Samantha's body wilted. She leaned into Adam's arms. "The waiting is so hard. . . ."

Adam offered a sympathetic frown. "I know, honey. But tomorrow's not so far away. And while I was waiting for you, I asked a receptionist about good places to stay. He recommended a hotel nearby. Let's go get a room, shall we?"

Despite everything, the prospect of staying in a hotel for the first time in their married lives seemed an adventure. Samantha nodded, and soon she and Adam checked into the Kahler Hotel.

"Well, this is all rather exciting, isn't it?" Adam smiled at her as he dropped their small valise on the dark-green chenille spread that covered the brass bed.

Samantha stared in awe at the heavy velvet draperies and fine, velvet upholstered furnishings. "This room is like a palace." She turned to Adam, feeling guilty. "How can we afford a place like this? And all because I—"

Adam stilled her words with a gentle kiss. "Sweetheart, the expense is nothing compared to our peace of mind. I have every confidence in Dr. Zimmerman. I'm glad we came. Aren't you?"

Samantha closed her eyes for a moment, trying to put aside her anxieties for Adam's sake. "Yes, I'm glad we came. And I trust him too."

Adam kissed her again, a little longer this time. Then he released her to slap a hand on his belly. "I don't know about you, but breakfast was a long time ago, and I'm hungry. What say we find a fine restaurant and dine like kings?"

"Do we have enough money?"

Adam grinned at her. "Thank you for being so frugal, my sweet. That's a sign of a good wife, but I do believe we indeed have the funds for two steak dinners." Samantha sent him an uncertain look. He laughed and said, "Darlin', we have to eat. Will you please believe me when I tell you we won't need to wash dishes to pay for the meal?"

Samantha laughed at herself. This was the first time she and Adam had been away from their home alone since they'd gotten married. Why shouldn't they relax and enjoy a bit of fun as long as they were here? She assumed a bright smile. "All right, let's go. But a walk first, please, to relax. And instead of steak, may I have shrimp? I've heard it's wonderful."

"Shrimp it is!" Then he teased, "But I think you only want to walk to save us the cost of a taxi cab."

How well he knew her! *Oh, Lord, I don't deserve a man like Adam. Thank You for giving him to me anyway.* Adam gallantly held out his elbow, and Samantha took it with an exaggerated flourish.

They walked in proper fashion through Rochester's finest housing district. Arm in arm, relaxed and happy, they enjoyed the sight of tall, Victorian houses with gingerbread millwork, cut-glass windows, and neatly manicured yards. The shrubs on the lawn of one particularly grand house were trimmed to resemble a bear, a swan, and an elephant.

"Oh, Adam, look!" Samantha pointed, as excited as a child. "Isn't that unique? I wonder how they did it."

"Yes, it is something. Someone is certainly talented."

They came upon a green, flower-filled park sporting a marble fountain. In the center of the fountain's pool, a marble cherub stood frozen in a delicate pose with its hand upraised, spewing water from its mouth. Samantha leaned to dip her fingers in the sparkling water, and she noticed a scattering of coins across the bottom of the pool. "It must be a wishing fountain. May I have a penny, please?"

Adam gave it, and Samantha closed her eyes tight. She didn't need to form the wish—God already knew what she longed for the most. Opening her eyes, she sent the copper coin sailing to the fountain's bottom. Then she flashed a smile at Adam, and she sensed in his tender gaze his desire to see her wish come true.

At last they entered a restaurant with an entrance bigger than their parlor at home and containing more stained glass than any church she'd ever seen. A gentleman wearing a black swallow-tail coat escorted them to a linen-draped table. The man had very large ears and walked with his hands clasped at the base of his spine and his head held high. His stiff stance gave him a swaying gait. Adam caught Samantha's gaze and imitated the man's posture, and she covered her mouth to stifle a giggle. The man seated Samantha with somber solicitude, informed them that a waiter would be with them shortly, and walked away in the same dignified way he had come.

Adam leaned across the round, candlelit table and said, "Didn't he look like a penguin?"

Samantha whispered, "No. Penguins don't have ears."

Then followed a lively conversation on whether penguins were truly earless or if they had ears that didn't show. By the time the waiter arrived with the elegant menus requiring two hands to hold them up, both were in a state of hilarity that was impossible to squelch.

After a brief perusal of the choices, Adam formally ordered steak for himself and the promised shrimp for Samantha. But his lips twitched and his eyes danced as he obviously stifled amusement. Samantha bit the insides of her cheeks to keep from laughing at her husband's antics. Their stern-faced waiter didn't seem the type to appreciate levity.

"I shall bring your drinks posthaste, sir," the waiter said with great dignity.

Adam responded, "Yes, posthaste would be just fine."

Samantha dissolved into giggles when the man walked away. She reached across the table to hold Adam's hand and smiled a genuine, down-to-her-toes smile. "Oh, Adam, this is wonderful."

Adam agreed. "Yes, it's just what we needed."

For the next few hours, they did their best to be lighthearted and unburdened, the way young people in love should be. And for those few hours, Samantha even managed to forget the purpose of their excursion.

Chapter Five

*E*ven without a rooster's crow or open windows beckoning the first rays of dawn, Adam awoke promptly at his normal time of five-thirty. He rolled over slowly to avoid disturbing Samantha. She had tossed and turned restlessly far into the night.

Gently he lifted the coverlet, slipped out without so much as a *ting* from a bedspring, and padded over to the heavily draped windows. He pulled the green velvet curtain aside enough to see that most of the sky was hidden by the city's expanse. But a space between two four-story buildings allowed him a limited view of the early morning sky. Even in Rochester, the sunrise was beautiful. He decided it was a hopeful sign to see that some things here in the city were like home in Mountain Lake.

Creaking of the bedsprings alerted him, and he looked over his shoulder to see Samantha stretching beneath the covers. She sighed, balling her fists to rub at her eyes. Her gaze met his, and she smiled lazily. "Good morning."

He stifled a chuckle at her sleep-laden voice. "Good morning to you." He crossed to the bed and sat on the edge near her hip, then leaned down to start the day with an affectionate kiss. "It's early yet. Why don't you try to sleep a bit more since we don't have chores to tend to?"

Samantha twisted around a bit beneath the covers, snuggling against the pillows. "I don't know if I can. Once an early riser, always an early riser." And she smiled again contentedly.

"Well, then," Adam suggested, "why not take advantage of our private bath and start your day with a nice soak in the tub?"

Samantha's eyebrows raised, and she looked toward the door that led directly to the attached bathing room. "Mmm, that does sound nice." But she remained in her nestling spot. She held out a hand for Adam to hold, and they sat in quiet contentment for several minutes with Samantha under the covers, Adam perched beside her. Slowly her eyes slipped shut.

Adam said, "So are you getting up or not?" His voice was very soft.

Her eyes still closed, Samantha answered. "Not."

Adam smiled, placed her hand back beneath the sheets and tucked the covers up to her chin. He gave her a kiss on the forehead, then sat for a few minutes, gazing down at her sleeping form. When she began to lightly snore, he chuckled, rose, and disappeared into the bathroom to enjoy his own soak.

Samantha slept peacefully until the hour hand on the little clock on the bedside table pointed to eight. Adam was sitting in one of the velvet-covered chairs beside the windows, looking at a newspaper when she sat bolt upright, eyes wide and hair flying around her face. Adam put down the paper and laughed at her startled expression. "Well, hello again, sleepyhead. Are you awake for good this time?"

Samantha hunched her shoulders sheepishly. "It was perfectly lazy of me, but we are on a little vacation, aren't we?"

"Yes, we are, and being perfectly lazy is part of the plan." He held up his paper. "I've been out and about already, though, and I'm starting to get restless. Why don't you get your bath, and then we'll rustle up some breakfast."

Samantha swung herself out of the warm bed and headed to the bathroom. She called through the open door, "If we eat a late breakfast, we won't need lunch, and we'll save ourselves the expense of three meals out today."

Adam released an amused snort. Would she never let up? "Samantha, will you please stop worrying about money? We're set just fine."

The squeal of spigots being turned and the spatter of water hitting the claw-foot tub sounded through the now-closed door. He had to lean forward in his chair and strain to hear her say, "But, Adam, we'll have the cost of the doctor's exam, too, plus the train fares, and the hotel, and food. . . . I just don't want us to run short."

He chuckled indulgently. "Stop worrying. I've got things under control." But her focus on their finances pleased him. If she was concerned about money, she wasn't worrying about the doctor's verdict.

The water stopped, and the sounds of mild splashing and the occasional squeak of wet skin against slick porcelain carried into the room. Then her voice came again, subdued this time. "Adam?"

"Yes?"

"What do you think he'll say?"

Adam closed his fists around the paper. "I don't want to guess, honey. Let's just wait—and trust."

A long pause, and then her quiet response. "Yes, Adam."

But Adam had a hard time following his own advice. All during the morning as he and Samantha wandered the shops of Rochester, his thoughts ran ahead to the two o'clock appointment with Dr. Zimmerman. What would the doctor say?

Part of him hoped they had found something to explain why Samantha hadn't conceived a child yet. After all, if there was absolutely nothing wrong, then it would only frustrate her further, wondering why they hadn't been blessed with a child. But if there was something wrong, what if it couldn't be fixed? Finally he gave himself a mental kick, determined to put it out of his mind. As he'd told Samantha, the only thing they could do was wait and trust. And pray. A constant prayer hovered at the back of his mind.

⌒⌒

Samantha found herself silently praying as she and Adam moved from shop to shop. She would look at a fine piece of lace and comment on it, all the while thinking, *Please, oh please, God!* When she and Adam stopped to eat a late breakfast— what the young man who took their order called a brunch— one word echoed over and over in her mind with every bite, *Please, please, please, please* . . . So much depended on what Dr. Zimmerman would say, it was impossible to think of anything else.

She nearly sagged with relief when one-thirty rolled around and she could give up the pretense of being interested in their surroundings and return to the hospital. A solemn-faced nurse led them into Dr. Zimmerman's office. Samantha tried not to read anything into the woman's expression; she reminded herself that all the staff had looked that way yesterday, and she hadn't been examined yet. She sat in the same chair, crossed her ankles in the same way, rested her hands in her lap—right over left—and waited.

Adam couldn't seem to sit still. He twisted this way and then that way in his chair, propping an ankle over a knee, then putting it down and reversing the process. He placed his arm across the back of Samantha's chair, tapping with one finger against the wooden frame. Softly, between his teeth, he whistled as he tapped his finger and bobbed his foot. Samantha bore it as long as she could, but finally she could not bear it any longer "Adam, please! You're making me nervous!"

He gave a start, then smiled apologetically, dropped his foot, and removed his hand from her chair. "I guess I'm a little anxious."

She shook her head, raising one eyebrow. "A little? I'd hate to see you a lot anxious!"

Their shared chuckle relieved an edge of the tension in the room, but Samantha's pulse immediately sped up when the office door opened and Dr. Zimmerman entered. His gaze fell on her, and for a moment he paused. Then he shut the door and came across the room, hand extended.

Adam half rose with the handshake, then seated himself again as the doctor hitched up his pant legs and sat down across from them. Samantha pinned her gaze on the doctor's face as the big man leaned back in his chair, lacing his fingers and resting the heels of his hands against his stomach. Samantha's heart beat in her throat, and she held her breath, wondering what he was going to say.

Dr. Zimmerman cleared his throat. "Mrs. Klaassen, I have completed a study of your examination, and I believe I know the reason for your barrenness."

In unison, Samantha and Adam leaned forward. Samantha groped for Adam's hand, found it, and clung. Finally, she'd have her answers.

But Dr. Zimmerman surprised her by asking a question. "Are you familiar at all with the female reproductive system?"

Samantha's breath released in a whoosh. She looked at Adam, too startled to reply. Adam lifted one shoulder and stammered out, "Well, we know where babies come from—and how, if that's what you're asking." He sounded as confused as Samantha felt.

"It is." The doctor dropped his hands, then turned sideways in his chair and picked up a black and white drawing which he

angled toward Adam and Samantha. As he talked, he pointed to the picture to illustrate his explanation. "In order for a child to be conceived, an egg must travel down from a woman's ovaries through the Fallopian tubes to the uterus, where it is fertilized by the male's sperm.

"Now, I know you have already been told that certain days of the month are considered fertile days, while others are not, so I will not waste time discussing that. However, given the fact that the egg must move through the Fallopian tubes between the ovaries and uterus, I believe I can determine why Mrs. Klaassen has not been able to conceive."

Dread and hope warred within Samantha's heart. She doubled her grip on Adam's hand. Between her palms, his fingers trembled, communicating his own mix of emotions.

"Mrs. Klaassen, it appears you have scar tissue around the uterus. In all likelihood, it also involves the Fallopian tubes." The doctor leaned forward, his eyebrows coming down into a sharp **V**. "Have you ever suffered trauma of the abdomen?"

Samantha stammered, "I—I'm not sure what you mean."

"Have you ever fallen against something very hard, or been struck with something, here?" He placed a hand low on his own belly.

Unpleasant childhood memories surfaced, and Samantha grimaced. She couldn't bring herself to answer the question. She pressed her lips tightly and willed the ugly images filling her mind to disappear.

Adam replied, "When Samantha was a child, she was beaten . . . by her father."

The doctor's thick gray eyebrows came down in a stern scowl, and he looked sharply at Samantha. Something flickered in his eyes—sympathy tangled with fury. "I see." Great meaning underscored the simple reply. He spoke again, this time very gently. "May I ask—was this abuse a one-time situation, or did it occur with regularity?"

Adam turned his hand, twining his fingers through Samantha's. "It occurred regularly."

Dr. Zimmerman heaved a sigh. Scowling he shook his head briefly, and then he shifted his attention to Adam. Samantha sensed he didn't intend to exclude her, but to protect her, and her appreciation for the big man increased in those moments while he explained, in the kindest of tones, his findings.

"Mr. Klaassen, when your wife suffered trauma, there was apparently internal bruising that resulted in scar tissue, a thickening of the tissue of the Fallopian tubes. These tubes are quite narrow, you understand, and anything like this causes a closure of the opening. Because of this closure, the egg cannot come down from the ovaries to reach the uterus. Therefore it cannot be fertilized."

Samantha, listening, experienced a rising sense of dread. A question formed on her lips, but fear of the answer kept her from voicing it. Adam—ever attune to her—asked it in her stead. "Is there any way to open the Fallopian tubes again, once they've closed?"

The doctor pursed his lips and slowly shook his head—left, right, left. Then he looked at Samantha and said very softly, "I am sorry."

The words registered in Samantha's brain. She wanted to block them out, but she couldn't. Her ears were ringing—high and shrill—that should have cut off the sound of anything else, including those horrible words, "I *am sorry*." But instead they reverberated again and again until she wanted to scream.

Dr. Zimmerman stretched his hand toward Samantha. "I wish I could offer you more, Mrs, Klaassen. I realize a recognition of the problem solves nothing for you unless there is some resolution. But we are limited; we cannot perform miracles." He placed a big hand over Samantha's knee and gave a light, apologetic squeeze. "I wish I could."

Adam stood. "Thank you for your time, Dr. Zimmerman. At least now we know. I think—" His voice broke, and he cleared his throat twice before continuing. "I think now we can go on. The not knowing is sometimes worse than the knowing."

Samantha hung her head, tears stinging behind her eyelids. *Oh, no, the knowing is far worse. Now I have no hope. No hope at all . . .*

amantha?" Adam touched her shoulder. She gave no indication that she was being spoken to. Adam raised his voice a bit. "Samantha, honey, it's time to leave."

Samantha lifted her head, but with such effort—as if it weighed more than her muscles could support. And when at last her eyes met his, the lack of emotion in their depths stunned him. The blank stare was more frightening than the distress he had expected.

"Come, sweetheart, let's go now," Adam coaxed and took her hand. She rose as if pushing through a full flow of water. Adam's heart beat fearfully for her.

Dr. Zimmerman touched Adam's arm. "Perhaps I should order a sedative for your wife."

Had the situation not been so heartrending, Adam might have laughed. A *sedative*? For a woman who seemed incapable of functioning? Adam shook his head. "No, thank you, Dr. Zimmerman. I'm sure she'll be fine."

Dr. Zimmerman said once more, "I am sorry. I wish there was more . . ."

Adam nodded. "Thank you, doctor." He guided Samantha into the busy hallway, but she seemed oblivious to everything except some inner torment that had closed down her emotions. He told himself not to become overly alarmed. Surely it was shock, and it would wear off soon. In the meantime, he tried to downplay his own crushing disappointment. He must take care of Samantha first.

He kept up a steady stream of conversation in the hopes of restoring some sort of normalcy to the situation. "Well, we might as well go pack up our few things at the hotel and check the train schedules. I'm sure we'll be able to find one running yet today that will get us home. Would you rather walk to the hotel or find a carriage? It might be fun to take a carriage ride; we haven't done that yet. What do you prefer?"

Samantha walked woodenly beside him, putting one foot in front of the other but with no other indication of awareness. He waited, but she didn't reply. He tightened his grip on her arm and went on casually, "Yes, I think a carriage ride is just the thing. Let's stay here by the corner and flag one down."

In short order Adam waved over a carriage driver and told him their destination. He helped Samantha step into the sleigh-like carriage and sat down close beside her on the padded seat, placing an arm around her shoulders. He smiled into her empty eyes. "Now, isn't this nice?" And he tried to swallow the fear that rose within when she seemed to stare right past him.

～⊙

On her side of the carriage seat, Samantha felt as if it took every bit of strength she possessed just to breathe. She concentrated very hard—breathe in, release; breathe in, release. . . . Did she feel devastated? No, devastated was an understatement, far from capturing her grief. Sorrow this deep had no description.

The doctor had looked at her, had said in a kind, sincere tone, "I am sorry." With three simple words—words that had always meant healing and comfort in the past—he had destroyed her. A part of her wanted to reach out to Adam, to comfort him and receive his comfort. But to do that would be to acknowledge that the doctor's verdict was final. It would mean accepting this horrible nightmare as reality. And Samantha couldn't do it.

So she remained in her shell, shut off and reeling, waiting for the moment of awakening. *This is a dream*, she told herself while the world went on around her in blissful ignorance, *an awful dream that will soon end. Just wake up, Samantha. Wake up. . . .*

∽◯

Somewhere between the clinic and the hotel, Adam made a decision. They wouldn't go straight home. Looking at Samantha's white, emotionless face, he knew she wasn't ready to face the family and answer questions about the unsettling news Dr. Zimmerman had delivered. They would all react with sympathy and no small amount of tears, but an emotional display—however sincere and well-intentioned—wouldn't be what Samantha needed right now. And if he was honest with himself, he needed some time to digest this information before having to talk with everyone at home.

Instead, they would take a trip straight north to Minneapolis and spend a few days with his oldest brother Daniel and his family. Daniel was a lawyer, able to mask his feelings. His wife, Rose, was forthright and steady. There would be no blatant displays of sorrow from either of them, he was certain. They would be able to talk things out sensibly and begin to put it behind them. That was what they needed now—calm, rational conversation.

Adam left Samantha in the hotel room to organize their belongings while he walked to the telegraph office to send a wire to his parents. While dictating the brief message, tears gathered in the back of his throat. Telling the family back home made it all so . . . well, real.

He would never be a daddy. He would never pace the floors at night with a teething baby, warn an inquisitive toddler about the dangers of a hot stove, remind a lost-in-play son to feed the horses, or tease a blushing daughter about her host of beaux. All of his long-held dreams of parenthood were crumbling and being whisked away by the winds of reality.

It's not fair! Oh, dear God, it isn't fair!

"Let's see if we got this right." The thin, bespectacled man behind the desk held Adam's message at arm's length. "TO S. KLAASSEN STOP DOCTOR'S REPORT NOT GOOD STOP THERE CAN BE NO CHILDREN STOP DETAILS LATER STOP GOING TO MINNEAPOLIS FOR FEW DAYS STOP A.K."

The man's monotone recital gave Adam time to regain his composure. "Yes, that's correct, thank you." He dictated a second wire, this one to Daniel and Rose, telling them the unhappy news and alerting them to the impending arrival. He paid the required fees, and from there he headed to the railroad depot to determine train schedules. He purchased tickets for the next train to Minneapolis, which didn't leave until the following morning. It didn't register that they would need to spend one more night in the Rochester hotel until he was two blocks away from the train station. He hoped Sammy hadn't finished packing, or she'd just have to undo it all.

Thinking about Samantha immediately brought thoughts of what had been taken from them with Dr. Zimmerman's examination. Adam felt as if he'd been robbed of something priceless. And how much greater must be Samantha loss?

Samantha had never known the love of a mother—or a father, for that matter. The lack of parental caring had made her long even more fervently for a child to cuddle and nurture. She'd lost so much already in life. How could anyone expect her to blithely accept the fact that she would never bear children of her own?

It had never occurred to either of them that a family wouldn't be possible. They had planned for children as matter-of-factly as they had planned where to place their furniture or what they would have for the evening meal. In their conversations, it was always *when* we have children, never *if*. Having grown up in a large family, of course Adam had wanted his own boisterous brood someday. How disheartening to realize someday would never come.

Eagerness to be with his wife—to hold her, comfort her, and be comforted by her—welled in his soul, and he increased his pace. When he entered their hotel room, he found her sitting on the edge of the chenille-covered bed, the valise beside her, gaping open but still empty. He couldn't help but compare the empty travel bag to the equally empty expression on his wife's face. The sight of Samantha so obviously heartbroken and withdrawn nearly did him in. He understood completely—her dreams of motherhood were gone! It was too horrible to accept. Yet he realized it must be accepted or it would destroy them both. But how to help her understand that? Ah, that was the problem.

"Well, Sammy, it's a good thing you haven't packed up yet." He crossed the carpet and sat beside her. Although in the past he'd always found it easy to take her in his arms, for some reason his hands remained cupped over his knees. He swallowed. "It looks like we'll be here another night. And instead of going back to Mountain Lake tomorrow, I thought we might make a real vacation out of this little trip and go to Minneapolis instead."

Very slowly Samantha turned her head, but her gaze landed somewhere on the buttons of his shirt rather than meeting his eyes. "Minneapolis? But why?"

Adam forced a cheery tone. "We don't get to see Daniel and Rose much. We've traveled this far, why not go a little farther? I thought it might be nice." He paused, trying to read her closed expression. "Is that all right with you?"

Her head dropped, and a tired sigh passed her lips. "Yes, that's fine, Adam."

Encouraged by her brief response, the first words she'd spoken since they left the doctor's office, Adam's heart fluttered with hope. Maybe she was coming out of her shock enough to talk about Dr. Zimmerman's discovery. How he needed to discuss it. Placing a gentle hand on Samantha's arm, he said, "Sammy, honey, Dr. Zimmerman—"

Samantha leaped up as if fired from a cannon. She swung around, her eyes, steely and snapping, pinning him to his seat. She hissed, "I do not wish to speak of Dr. Zimmerman—not today, not tomorrow, not ever. This day does not exist in my life, Adam, do you hear me?"

He sat still, completely stunned by her vehemence. He had expected sorrow, even anger—but this defiance was a total surprise.

Through clenched teeth she demanded again, "Do you hear me?"

"Yes." Adam finally managed a choked whisper, too afraid to say anything else. Maybe he should have allowed the doctor to prescribe some sort of sedative.

Samantha's shoulders wilted. Gazing toward the open window, she said evenly, "Since we'll be here another night, I believe I'll relax a bit with a bath." She moved toward the bathroom, as stiff as a wind-up toy, entered, and turned to firmly lock the door.

Adam begged, *Please, God, let me be able to reach her. We need each other now. Help her to see that.* With Samantha behind the bathroom door, safely out of sight and hearing, Adam dropped his facade of strength, buried his face in his hands, and wept.

hen Samantha closed the bathroom door and turned the brass lock, she leaned against the solid wood door, her head back, her eyes closed. She knew why Adam wasn't taking her home right away. Humiliation gripped her. She was barren, unable to give Adam what he wanted most—a family. She was only half a woman, her ability to conceive and bear children snatched away from her. None of this was Adam's fault—all hers. Obviously Adam didn't want his parents, his family, to see his heartbreak and her shame. They couldn't go home.

Oh, Adam, I'm sorry. So, so sorry . . .

She pushed away from the door and numbly crossed to the tub, plugged the drain hole, and turned the brass faucets on high. But she didn't undress, just stood staring unseeingly at the spattering stream of water as she replayed the afternoon in her mind. The doctor had said there could be no babies. No babies because of scar tissue. Scar tissue because of trauma. Trauma because her father had been a drunk with a temper who had taken his frustrations out on his children.

Anger—an impassioned, fiery anger that burned white-hot—exploded through Samantha's whole being. Fists pressed to her trembling lips, she moaned out her fury. "Pa, you had no right! No right to do this to me—to Adam. You stole my childhood from me with your senseless, fearful rages, and now you've stolen my chance to regain that lost childhood with a child of my own. You took my dream—no, *our* dream!—away

from us! I don't deserve this. And Adam—Adam deserves children, a family. How could you do this to me—to Adam?"

She reached through the cloud of steam to stop the water
with a violent twist of the faucets. With shaking hands she
tugged at her garments with jerky, disjointed motions. She
threw the clothing into a jumbled pile in front of the bathroom
door. Her throat ached with the desire to cry, but her eyes remained dry. Crying might give release. And Samantha didn't
want release. She wanted to nurse this anger, hold it, savor it.
By focusing all of her energy into anger with her father, she
could fend off any other emotions.

She submerged herself in the tub until only her head was
above the water. Heat surrounded her—hot water and billowing
steam. And from deep within, the burning flame of anger at the
injustice of it all. The bath water grew tepid as minutes passed,
but Samantha's anger did not cool. Sorrow, disappointment,
even guilt for Adam's sadness, took a backseat to her fury at the
man who had robbed Samantha of her chance for motherhood.
It was all that could sustain her now.

⌒☉

The train ride from Rochester to Minneapolis was a silent
one. Oh, there were noises around them—the chatter of other
passengers, the clacking of wheels against rails, the whistling
of wind through a crack in the window. But between Samantha
and Adam not a word was spoken. Adam gazed quietly out the
window, watching the landscape whiz by, aware of Samantha
still and tense on the bench beside him. He longed to reach
out, put an arm around her in the old, familiar way. But he felt
rebuffed and unsure of Samantha's reaction to any overture of
comfort, so he remained separated and aching.

Somewhere behind them a baby fussed, and Samantha shot from the seat. "I need some air." She stalked to the door leading to a small landing outside of the car. Adam didn't offer to join her. If she wanted his company, she would ask. Although her silent presence had been difficult to bear, sitting here alone was even worse. He missed her. He missed how they used to be. But how to regain it?

Nearly half an hour later Samantha returned, her face white and pinched. She slid into the seat as the conductor passed through the car, announcing, "Next stop Minneapolis, folks. Minneapolis is the next stop."

Adam gathered his courage and eased his fingers along Samantha's arm. "Do you suppose Daniel and Rose will be waiting for us?"

Samantha shrank from his touch and shrugged.

Her withdrawal and the aloof, uncaring gesture angered him. He gritted his teeth and turned his attention outward again.

⁓⦵

Samantha's chest tightened. She was adding further pain to her husband's sorrow. This wasn't his fault. She shouldn't punish him. But what to say? She didn't want to see anyone and wanted to talk even less. So she sat in grief-filled silence, feeling guilty and small but unable to get herself to change it. She was as lonely here beside him as she'd been on that landing outside, clinging to the railing, shivering against the sharp wind generated by the speed of the train.

The train hissed to a halt at the busy station in Minneapolis. By the time they had gathered up their bags and jostled their way off through the sea of other travelers, Samantha's head was pounding. She yearned to lean into Adam's strength, but the tense set of his jaw kept her at bay.

"Adam! Sam!" A familiar voice rang over the chatter of the crowd. Adam's brother Daniel stood near the long sidewalk beside the big depot, waving a hand. Adam placed his palm on Samantha's back to guide her along, but the moment they reached Daniel, it slipped away. Samantha blinked back tears as Daniel leaned down to give her a brotherly kiss. "How was your trip? Did you enjoy the train ride?"

Samantha gulped and forced her lips into a tight smile. "It was fine."

Adam's mouth looked grim, but before he said anything, Daniel captured him in a one-armed hug. "My car is this way. Let's go." Daniel set a brisk pace, escorting Samantha along beside him with a hand under her arm. Adam trailed behind. Daniel kept up a steady stream of conversation that filled the uncomfortable silence between Adam and Samantha. They reached a black Model T, and Daniel turned to grab the carpet-bag from Adam and tossed it into the vehicle's rumble seat. "Well, here we go!"

"Samantha, we can all crowd into the front seat, I think, and give you a better view of the city. You've never been to Minneapolis before, have you?"

He didn't wait for an answer, just pressed on cheerfully as he twisted the key, pulled the throttle, and set the car in motion. "Rose has all sorts of plans for you while you're here—a shopping trip and lunch in town as well as joining her Junior Leaguers for tea. You won't lack for entertainment, that's certain! And, Adam—" He leaned forward to peer around Samantha—"I hope you'll spend a day at the office with me. Otherwise we won't see much of one another, I'm afraid. I've got several cases I'm juggling right now, and I can't afford to be away for long."

Samantha appreciated Daniel's attempt at normalcy even while she inwardly objected to it. Didn't he realize everything had changed? How could he blithely make plans as if the world still turned on its axis and all was well?

Adam's voice was hesitant as he asked Samantha, "Would you mind if I spent a day with Daniel?"

It would be good for him to get away from all the disappointment, the distance she'd created between them. "Not at all, Adam. I'm sure Rose and I can manage to occupy the time."

Daniel added enthusiastically, "And don't forget the girls—Christie and Katie are all excited about your visit. And wait until you see how Camelia has grown; you won't recognize her! She's walking already, has a mouthful of teeth which she'll cheerfully use on your fingers if you aren't watchful, and she's attempting to talk. I tell you, it's thrilling to see how those little ones take off!"

Daniel's exuberant pride in his children pierced Samantha to the depths of her soul. She pressed three fingers to her mouth, holding back a sob. Through her tears she saw Adam's hands clenched into fists.

Daniel emitted a strangled sound. "Argh. I wish I could bite off my tongue. I'm so sorry. I'm trying so hard not to say the wrong thing, I—"

Adam said, "It's all right, Daniel. You have every right to talk about your girls."

Although her aching throat kept her from speaking, Samantha offered a weak nod. If she had children, she'd never stop talking about them to others. But how long would it be before hearing others brag about their youngsters didn't break her heart beyond repair?

Daniel blew out a noisy breath and shot a quick, sad smile in their direction. "I'm glad you two came. Rose and I . . . we want to help you get through this. With prayer, and with to-getherness, we'll make it . . . our family will all put in our oars to pull you through."

Adam gave a firm nod, and Samantha forced a small ac-knowledgment of her own. But inwardly she trembled. How could they work together when she and Adam had lost even their ability to look one another in the eyes?

"Daniel? Are you asleep?"

Rose's soft voice cut through the fog, rousing Daniel. He rubbed a hand across his eyes and rolled over to face his wife. "No, honey, I'm awake. What's wrong?"

"I'm really worried about Sam."

In the dusky shadows, Daniel read the concern in his wife's face. He folded an arm beneath his head, and with his free hand he massaged Rose's shoulder. "I know. She's having a rough time of it, isn't she?"

"She's in agony." Rose's urgent whisper indicated her own heartache. "But she refuses to talk about it. I don't know how long she can keep all of those emotions locked up inside. She'll sit and hold little Cami, and you can feel her anguish. Yet she won't say a word." She captured Daniel's hand and drew it be-neath her chin. "Has Adam said anything?"

Daniel released a brief huff. "Adam has talked incessantly. Of course, the prospect of no children in his life is daunting. He's disappointed and heartbroken, but I think he could accept it. What he can't accept is Samantha's emotional withdrawal. He is more upset by her reaction to the situation than the situ-ation itself. As he put it, he can live without children, but he can't live without Sam."

"Do you suppose she blames Adam? Maybe that's why she's been standoffish toward him."

Daniel shook his head. "No, quite honestly, I think she blames herself. After all, it isn't a problem with Adam that's keeping them from having children."

Rose shook her head, her brow furrowing. "Then why treat Adam as if—"

"Because she feels guilty." Daniel gave Rose's hand a squeeze. "Think about it. Facing Adam, knowing what she's taken from him, is painful for her. So she pulls away. And in so doing hurts Adam more than the loss of children could."

Rose conceded, "That makes sense, I suppose. But she doesn't act as if she feels guilty. She acts as if she's angry."

Daniel thought about that for a moment. "Perhaps she's angry with herself."

"Perhaps . . . but I don't think so."

"Then what?"

A heavy sigh from Rose. "I don't know, Daniel. I feel so sorry for both of them. Adam and Samantha both are in deep pain, and I want to help them, but I don't know what to do. They almost make me feel guilty for having the girls."

"Now don't think that way," Daniel chided gently. "It won't help to feel badly about a blessing the Lord has chosen to give us."

"I know, and I do feel blessed, Daniel. But I also feel for Samantha. Now that I have our girls, I can't imagine life without them. I think I can understand, somewhat, what Samantha is facing. I just wish she'd talk about it. It's not healthy to keep all of those feelings inside."

"No, it's not." Daniel agreed, but he cautioned, "You can't make her talk about it until she's ready."

"So what do I do?"

Daniel pulled Rose into his embrace. She rested her head on his shoulder and snuggled, content within the comforting circle of his arms. "I don't know that you can do anything, honey, except be available should she choose to talk. And, of course, we can always pray for them." He paused for a moment, stroking Rose's hair, before saying quietly, "Yesterday Adam and I talked about how Mother always says God never closes a door without opening a window. She believes sometimes God allows unpleasant things to happen, knowing later a reward even better than what we had planned will come.

"Adam wants to believe there is a purpose for this. Of course, we can't know what the purpose is, but it's a matter of faith. If only Samantha would believe it, too."

Rose didn't reply, and Daniel lifted his head to look at her. Her eyes were closed, her face relaxed. Daniel chuckled softly at the irony of her waking him to talk, then falling asleep mid-conversation. Now fully awake, Daniel decided to make good use of the time. He closed his eyes and took his concerns for his brother and sister-in-law to the One who never sleeps.

cross the hall beneath an appliquéd quilt, Adam lay on his back, hands beneath his head, staring at the ceiling. Samantha was on her side facing away from him, hands curled beneath her chin. Adam shifted slightly, looking at the back of Samantha's head. Her hair was in wild disarray—evidence of the tossing and turning she'd done earlier. What would she do if he reached out and smoothed it down?

Probably stiffen up and shift away from me. Ever since Dr. Zimmerman's verdict, she'd been skittish and aloof. Although he ached to cradle her against his side, the way they'd slept before, he brought his arms downward and laced his fingers together across his stomach. His chest hurt. He longed for that closeness he'd had with Samantha. Affection had always come easily between the two of them. He missed it—the smiles, the touching, the sharing of small events and deeper feelings. The contentment. Would they ever get it back? Would the fact they would never have children take all of that away?

If only she'd talk to him, even if it meant screams and tears and accusations. He could take the anger he suspected she was harboring if she would just let it out. Her silent withdrawal tore him apart inside. He moved his head sideways on the pillow, staring at Samantha's still form beside him. Her stony silence was as impenetrable as a brick wall. He would not attempt to break down a brick wall unless well armed. And he was too weary, holding too much pain himself, to wield whatever that might require.

He rolled over, also presenting his back to his wife, and closed his eyes against hot tears of sorrow for his double loss.

～◌◞

The sun was inching its way above the horizon when Adam eased his way out of bed, taking care not to pull the covers off of his wife's sleeping form. He knew she hadn't been sleeping long; he remembered the sound of her crying into her pillow before he had finally drifted off only a few hours ago.

He padded quietly to the window, rubbing the back of his neck and lifting the curtains aside to peer outward. Sunrises had always been a symbol of promise to Adam. He looked back at Samantha, heart lifting with a small measure of hope. Maybe today held a promise of change.

The patter of little feet in the hallway captured his attention, and he crossed to the door. Katrina, still in her nightgown, was headed for the stairs. He smiled at the bobbing, multicolored twists of cloth that held her long hair in pin curls. "Hi, sweetie," he whispered, stepping into the hall.

Katrina's face broke into a huge grin, and she ran to him for a hug. "'Morning, Uncle Adam!"

He silenced her with a whispered, "Shh!" and lifted the six-year-old to settle on his hip as he cracked the door behind them and pointed at Samantha. "Auntie Sam is asleep. Let's not wake her."

Katrina nodded, covering pursed lips with one finger. When Adam closed the door again, she whispered, "Why is Auntie Sam still sleeping? It's time to get up."

Adam chuckled. "Well, just because the sun is rising doesn't mean people have to rise too, you know."

Katrina seemed to think about that for a moment before tipping her head and fixing Adam with a frown. "Is Auntie Sam tired from being sad?"

The child's question took him aback. "What—what makes you think she's sad?"

Katrina's face crinkled in thought. "Well, she isn't laughy like she used to be, and even when she smiles it's only in her mouth. Her eyes don't smile—like this." The little girl gave a beaming, gap-toothed smile that lit her whole face. Adam couldn't help returning it with one of his own. Then she sobered again and asked gravely, "Is she sad 'cause she can't have no babies?"

If Adam was startled before, he was dumbfounded now. "How did you know that, Katrina?"

She shrugged. "Heard Mama and Daddy talkin'. Is that why she's sad?"

Adam answered honestly, "Yes, Katie, it makes her very sad."

"And you too?"

Adam swallowed. "Yes, me too."

Katrina wrapped her arms around Adam's neck and pressed her cheek to his. "I'm sorry, Uncle Adam."

Katrina's sincerity made tears prick at the back of Adam's eyes. He hugged her tightly, reveling in the feel of the sturdy little body in his arms, the tickle of the coiled hair against his cheek, the sleep-tumbled smell of the child. *Oh, Lord, I've wanted this so much for myself!*

Katrina pulled back and took Adam's face in her stubby hands. "Uncle Adam, if Auntie Sam can't have babies, maybe I should come live with you and be your little girl."

Adam melted. "Oh, sweetie, that's awfully nice of you. And Auntie Sam and I would dearly love to have you for a little girl. But don't you think your mama and daddy would miss you?"

Katrina wrinkled her nose. "They'd still have Christie and Cami."

Adam smiled. "But they wouldn't have Katie anymore, and that just wouldn't be the same."

The child sighed, her warm breath caressing Adam's cheek. "You're right. I guess I better stay here." She rested her head against his shoulder briefly before straightening and adding, "But, Uncle Adam?"

"Yes, sweetie?"

"I'm gonna pray to Jesus that you get some little girls even if it don't be from Auntie Sam. Daddy says ever'body needs little girls around to keep life int—int—" She scratched her head, obviously trying to remember something. Then her face brightened and she finished, "Interesting. That's why he and Mama had three of 'em."

Adam pushed back the chuckle. She was so sweet and serious! "I suppose your Daddy is right."

Katrina nodded. "That's why he's a lawyer. He gots a good thinker."

Adam laughed aloud. "I'll remember that." And then it was as if a light turned on inside. Innocent Katrina had given Adam an idea. The desire to discuss it with Samantha nearly overwhelmed him. He set Katrina down, sending her toward the spindled staircase with a light pat on her backside. "Now you'd best catch up with your sisters and go get your breakfast."

Katrina scampered forward a few steps, then stopped, asking over her shoulder, "Aren't'cha comin' too?"

"In a bit," Adam said, his mind racing. "I need to talk to your Auntie Sam first."

"Oh. Well . . . see ya!" Katrina bounced around the corner out of sight.

Adam returned to the bedroom, his heart thumping. Katrina's comments had given him a sunrise-bright promise. He replayed her words in his mind—". . . get some little girls even if they don't come from Auntie Sam . . ." *Heavenly Father, could this be our answer? Oh, please let Samantha agree with me!*

But Samantha slept soundly, and he didn't have the heart to disturb her. He knew how badly she needed this rest. So he quietly dressed and went down to breakfast. Sitting between Katrina and Christina, he found himself caught up in a wonderful daydream of someday sitting between some little girls—or boys—who would call him Papa. He smiled and teased, snitched bits of hotcakes from the girls' plates and made them squeal.

"Uncle Adam, you're so funny," Christina told him, and he felt like the wittiest man in the world.

When the girls finished breakfast and headed to their rooms to dress for school, Adam leaned back in his chair, sipped his coffee, and sent his brother and sister-in-law a little smile.

Daniel observed, "You look like the fox that raided the henhouse."

"Yes." Rose peered at Adam over her china cup. "Not that it isn't wonderful to see you in good spirits, but would you mind letting us in on what has you so cheery this morning?"

"Nope," Adam said with a grin. "Oh, you'll hear about it soon enough. But not until I've talked to Sammy." He set the cup aside, then rested his elbows on the lace-covered tabletop. He grinned at Daniel and Rose above his joined hands. "You know, you've got a very bright little girl."

Rose corrected archly, "We've got three very bright little girls."

Adam conceded with a bow of his head. "Yes, you do. But I'm referring now to your middle daughter."

"Katie?" Rose's eyebrows rose in curiosity. "What does she have to do with your rather perky demeanor this morning?"

"You'll find out," Adam promised, a smile twitching at the edges of his lips, "just as soon as I talk to Samantha."

"Talk to me about what?" came a voice from the doorway.

Adam turned to see Samantha, her disheveled hair and the blue smudges beneath her eyes giving her a tired, old appearance that tore at his heart. How he wanted to remove the haunted expression from her face.

"A-Adam?" Her voice quavered. She took a hesitant step into the kitchen. "What do you want to talk to me about?"

Adam opened his mouth to share his idea, but he felt a wave of apprehension. Should he wait? After all, they'd only just been given the news. Maybe this was too soon. He sent up a quick prayer for guidance, but even before he voiced the "amen," Samantha caught hold of the doorframe and gaped at him, tears flooding her eyes.

"You're sending me away, aren't you?"

Chapter Nine

*A*dam had leaped out of his chair, and shock widened his eyes as he stared at her across the room. "Sending you away?"

Samantha blinked back her tears and forced herself not to recoil. She wouldn't blame him. And she would be strong, no matter what he told her. "I would understand, if you did. After all, I—"

Adam dashed to her and captured both of her hands, looking directly into her eyes. "I will never send you away."

"But—"

"You're my wife. I married you for richer, for poorer, remember? For better, for worse, in sickness and in health, till death parts us."

His voice rose with conviction, lighting a fire of remorse in the center of her soul. She didn't deserve a man like Adam.

He squeezed her hands and said in a ragged tone, "I love you. Nothing will change that."

She tipped her head, her tangled hair trailing across her shoulders. "Then what is it, Adam, you are wanting to tell me?"

Adam looked over his shoulder at his brother and sister-in-law. "Let's go up to our room. We can talk there."

Samantha allowed Adam to guide her up the stairs and into the guestroom. Relief that he still loved her made her knees weak, but worry about what he might say made her breath come in little spurts. She sank onto the foot of the bed and fixed her gaze on Adam. But instead of talking, he began pacing back and forth across the room, his brow furrowed. His unusual behavior increased her anxiety. "Whatever it is, just say it!"

He slowly turned to face her. Something flickered in his eyes. Uncertainty? Fear? Before she could determine the emotion, he moved over to her and dropped to one knee. Twining his fingers through hers, he drew in a breath. "Sammy, earlier this morning, Katrina—bless her heart!—said something that got me thinking. . . ." He paused.

Samantha wondered if her heart might pound its way from her chest while she waited for him to share his thoughts with her.

Sympathy glowed in Adam's eyes. He gave her hand a gentle squeeze. "Sammy, it tears me apart to say these words out loud, but they must be said."

Samantha's chest began to heave with her short, stuttered breaths. She tried to pull her hands away and rise, but he held tight.

"We cannot have children." Adam's voice, so tender, stabbed as painfully as if he'd plunged a knife into her breast. "We want children. We've dreamed of children. But there will not be any children—not by birth."

Samantha jerked her gaze away from his. "I know, Adam."

"Yes, we know," Adam agreed quietly. He cupped her chin and turned her to face him. "But we haven't accepted it, have we? Instead, we've avoided it. And, sweetheart, we can't avoid it any longer. We really must talk about it."

Samantha ducked her head and clenched her hands so tightly her fingernails dug into her flesh. "Talking about it won't change it. Talking about it only makes me feel bad. And I don't want to feel bad!"

"Neither do I," he countered evenly, "but I don't think pretending this problem doesn't exist will solve anything." His tone took on a pleading quality as he said, "Honey, you and I have always been able to talk things out. No matter what the problem was, we could share it with each other, and it always helped."

She brought her head up sharply. "But before we could always solve the problem by talking it out. This time, there is no solution, Adam!"

"But there is a solution. I've found the solution, thanks to Katrina."

Adam's wide, guileless eyes begged Samantha to listen, but she couldn't imagine how a six-year-old child could possibly solve a problem a highly educated medical doctor couldn't. She blinked once, slowly, and dared to ask, "What is it?"

A smile grew across his face. "Katie and I were talking this morning, and she said she was going to pray that even if you couldn't have any babies, we'd still be able to get some babies."

Samantha shook her head, impatience again rising. "Adam, I don't understand. . . ."

"We could . . . someday, when we're ready . . . adopt a baby."

Samantha felt like her insides were being squeezed, and the room seemed to reel around her. Adopt a baby? As if that could possibly be the same! How could he even suggest such a thing? After a week of silence—of avoidance and tension—he had the audacity to suggest taking in someone else's child? She hadn't even had time to come to terms with the fact that she was barren, and he was ready to set aside her long-held dreams of having a baby and just go to some orphanage and pick one out. How could he? "Oh, Adam . . ."

Adam tugged at her hands. "'Oh, Adam,' what?" His head tipped to the side. "We both want a baby, don't we? And if we can't have one, then—"

Samantha jerked her hands free and shot out of the chair, pushing past him to stand before the window. Her stomach ached with an emptiness nothing would ever fill. She wrapped her arms around her middle, wishing . . . oh, *wishing* . . . her arms might be crossed over a pregnant belly.

Adam came up behind her and gripped her shoulders. He spoke against her tousled hair. "Tell me what you're thinking, Sam dearest."

A harsh, dry laugh exploded from her mouth. She shook her head. "Oh, you really don't want to know what I'm thinking." She spun around and glowered at him. "How could you even suggest something like this? As if—as if it doesn't matter that I can't bear children. As if our baby can be replaced by some . . . some little foundling no one else wants!"

Adam stared at her. "I never meant to imply it doesn't matter. Of course it matters! It's horrible and unthinkable and beyond the scope of reason that you can't bear our children. It hurts me as deeply as it hurts you, believe me, Sammy."

"It *can't* hurt you as badly as it hurts me."

"Why not?"

"Because it isn't your fault!" She thumped her own chest. "It's my fault!" Then she clenched her hands before her and shook her head wildly. "No, it's not my fault. It's my father's fault! And because of what he did to me, you're being punished, too!"

Adam pulled Samantha into his arms. Although over the past week she'd yearned for his embrace, now she fought for freedom. Freedom from his kindness, which she didn't deserve. Freedom from the pressing truth of her inability to conceive. Freedom from the pain that held her captive. But Adam's arms, as strong as he'd always claimed his love for her was, held tight, and eventually she collapsed against his chest. Her silent tears soaked his shirt.

"Samantha . . ." Adam's voice drifted softly to her ears, tender yet sad. "You told me long ago that you'd forgiven your father. Forgiving him helped you heal. Please don't open those old wounds again."

Her face pressed to his shirtfront, she groaned. "I can't help it. How can I not revisit the wounds he inflicted now that . . . now that we know how terribly he hurt me?" She gulped out a sob. "It isn't fair that you can't have children because of what my father did to me. Can't you understand?"

He kissed the top of her head. "Sammy, honey, I do understand. But you need to understand something, too. You are not responsible for what your father did to you. I don't blame you, and neither should you."

Samantha shifted her face to the familiar curve of his shoulder, breathing in his unique scent. "I can't help but blame me. Because of my father, you can't have any children."

Adam's hand stroked through her hair, the touch so sweet and loving it made her heart ache anew. "We *can* have children—by adoption. Daniel is a lawyer. He could—"

"No!" She swung her arms outward, knocking his hands from her shoulders. She skittered sideways until she was out of reach.

Adam took two steps toward her, his hands held out in a gesture of entreaty. "Why not? It would be a way to have the family we dreamed of, Sammy. It would give a little one a chance—"

The moan from the very center of her fractured soul escaped, and both hands went to her mouth. How could she make him understand? And then a long-buried memory surfaced. Her body trembled as emotions from years ago collided with the tension of the day. On shaky legs, she returned to the bed and seated herself. With a pleading look for Adam to listen, she began to speak.

"When I was a little girl, I found a baby bird in the yard. It had fallen from its nest. I knew it would starve on its own, so I put it in a little basket and took care of it." Adam's brow was puckered, but he remained silent. Slowly, he approached the bed and sat beside her, his knee brushing against hers. With his brown eyes locked on her face, she continued her story. "For three days I took care of that little bird. I kept it warm, covering it with a piece of flannel Gran gave me. I dug worms for it and gave it drinks by dipping a cloth in water then holding the cloth above and letting drops of water fall into its mouth." A mirthless chuckle found its way out as she recalled, "I even sang lullabies to that stupid little bird."

Adam placed his hand over her knee and squeezed gently.

"On the fourth morning, I went to the basket, and the bird was dead. I was inconsolable. I had grown to love it. I had fed it and played with it and dreamed about the day I would see it grow strong enough to fly. I felt like a part of me had died too. . . ." Samantha put her hand over Adam's, needing contact. "Davey helped me bury it, then I just sat by the tiny grave for hours. I couldn't stop crying. My heart was broken.

"That afternoon, to cheer me up, Gran went to town and bought me a lollipop. It was as big as my pa's hand, with a coil of pink, green, and white stripes. It was a wonderful lollipop, and since Davey and I rarely got candy, it was a very special treat. I thanked Gran, then I took it outside and gave it to my brother. I couldn't eat it. There was no way that a lollipop—even a big, beautiful lollipop like that one—could make up for the loss of my baby bird. I appreciated what Gran was trying to do, but it wasn't enough."

Samantha looked at Adam, his image swimming through a mist of tears. "Don't you see? For me, adopting a baby would be like a lollipop after the promise of a bird in flight. I can't accept it. It would be a distant second best." Hot tears rolled down her cheeks as her heart begged for his forgiveness. "Please don't be angry with me. Please try to understand."

⌒◯

Adam lowered his head and squeezed Samantha's hand. "I understand, honey." And he did. All through her life, she'd been forced to accept whatever life threw at her—a drunken, abusive father instead of a caring, nurturing one; a grandmother who was unquestionably loving but was with her for only six short years and could never take the place of a mother; a childhood filled with hard work and mistreatment instead of lighthearted-ness and caring. Then she became an adult, gradually learned to accept Adam's love, and then dreamed of giving birth to her own child. A child by any other means was to her another lost dream, and it could never be a replacement for that dream.

Adam once again put his arms around his wife and pulled her close, resting his chin on the top of her head. She sat pas-sively within his embrace. Somehow he felt she was asking for understanding for more than her feelings on adoption; she needed understanding for the way she'd reacted since the day they'd visited the Mayo Clinic. Now that she'd shared her feel-ings with him, he could offer a more complete understanding and support. What a heavy burden of guilt and shame she'd carried so bravely on her own.

"I'm not angry with you, Samantha." He meant it. "I've never been angry, but I have been hurt." When Samantha tried to shift away, he cupped her cheeks and raised her face. "I've been hurt by your withdrawal from me. Sweetheart, I love you, and I've needed you desperately these past few days. We were handed a great disappointment! And by pulling away from me, you've only made things harder on me. And maybe on yourself, I think."

Tears left a silvery trail down her pale cheeks. She gripped his wrists. "I didn't want to hurt you. I love you, too. I'm just so full of pain, I haven't known what to do."

Adam swallowed as he looked into her red-rimmed eyes, so full of sorrow. Caressing her temples with his thumbs, he dared to share the deepest fear he'd carried over the past week. "Sammy, I told Daniel a few days ago that it would be difficult to give up my dream of having a family, but I could do it. What I could not give up is you." He paused, searching her face. "Am I to lose you, Samantha?"

A ragged sob burst from her throat. Her arms flew around his neck, and she buried her face against his shoulder. Her tears flowed, as did his. Despite their anguish, Adam couldn't deny his heart thrilled at holding her, comforting her, joining her in sorrow at what had been taken from them. He rubbed her back and felt her hands paint circles on his shoulders.

Their shared mourning was bringing them together again. *Thank You, Lord. Thank You.* . . .

In time she pulled back to wipe her eyes and finally answer his question. "No, Adam, you aren't losing me. And I'm so sorry I hurt you. I love you so much! I've been miserable thinking of how I've disappointed you. I couldn't face that thought."

Adam looped her tangled hair behind her ears, leaning in to deposit a kiss on her lips. "You didn't cause my disappointment, Sammy. Do you believe me?"

"I'm trying to." Samantha's shoulders slumped, and her voice dropped to a whisper. "I just ache so much inside . . . I feel as if my heart is crying."

Adam drew her against his chest and rocked her gently, but he had no words to comfort her after a confession like that.

t a light tap at the door, Adam reached into his back pocket for a handkerchief which he offered to Samantha. He waited until she had wiped her face before he went to the door and opened it. A plainly dressed young woman waited in the hallway, looking at him through a fringe of unevenly cut bangs. Her hands twisted nervously on the wooden handle of a feather duster.

"I'm sorry t-t-to disturb you, sir, b-b-but I do h-housekeeping f-f-for Mrs. Klaassen, and I'm to clean the upstairs, and I-I-I've done all the rooms but this one. C-c-could I c-c-come in and clean now?"

Adam glanced over his shoulder at Samantha, still on the edge of the bed in her nightwear. "Would you give my wife a few minutes, please?"

"Oh, yes, s-s-sir." The woman waved the feather duster to include Samantha. "I'll j-j-just go on downstairs and d-d-dust the parlor first."

Adam closed the door and returned to Samantha, taking her hands and offering a smile of encouragement. With her red-rimmed eyes, raw nose, and hair in disarray, she looked very young and vulnerable. Adam hoped he was doing the right thing. "Sweetheart," he said as kindly as one would speak to a frightened child, "I told Daniel I would spend some time with him at the office today. But after that visit, I would like to buy some train tickets and get us headed home. Would that be all right with you?"

Samantha looked down at their joined hands for a moment before nodding. "I want to go home, Adam."

He drew her in for a brief hug, then set her away from him and instructed gently, "Get dressed, then ask Rose's house-cleaner to help you pack our things. I'll see if I can't get us home by nightfall, all right?"

Samantha rose and moved to the dressing table in the corner. Adam watched her for a few minutes, wondering if he should leave her alone. When she noticed him, she sent him a quavery smile. "Go on and see Daniel. I'll be fine."

He blew her a kiss before leaving her to dress in privacy. He headed downstairs and found Rose in the butler's pantry, arranging fresh-cut daisies in a china vase. Cami sat nearby in her high chair, messily gumming a biscuit. He planted a kiss on the top of the baby's head—the only clean spot he could see—and told Rose, "I guess I'm going to pop in on Daniel a bit early. Samantha is dressing, and then I'm wondering if your maid could help with some packing."

"Packing?" Rose asked. "Are you planning to leave?"

Adam fingered the curl on the top of Cami's head. "Yes, our time here has been good for both of us, but we need to get back into our normal routine."

Rose placed the last flower in the vase and wiped her hands on a towel. "I suppose there is work to be done, and busy hands are good therapy."

"Thank you for letting us join your family for a while, Rose."

Rose chuckled and came at him, arms outstretched. "You know you're always welcome here, Adam. We were glad to have you."

Adam savored her hug, then stepped back. "Thank you. Would it be all right for the cleaning girl to help Samantha pack?"

"Perfectly all right." Rose used a rag to clean Cami's face. At her protests, Rose raised her voice to be heard over the baby's complaints. "Esther is usually finished by noon, but I'm sure she won't mind spending a few extra minutes to assist Sammy." She lifted the baby from the chair.

Adam headed for the front door, an arm around Rose's shoulders. "Well, then, I'll go say my good-byes to Daniel and stop by the train station before I come back for Sam. Don't hold lunch for me. I'll pick up a sandwich along the way."

"Would you like me to call a carriage?" she asked.

"Nope. It's pretty out. I'll walk." He gave Rose one more hug, tweaked Cami's nose and laughed when she swatted at him and burbled, then headed out the door.

❧

Samantha finished dressing, then opened the door to let the maid know she could come in. The woman, who introduced herself as Esther, nodded her agreement when Samantha asked for assistance in packing. She carried the clothing articles from the wardrobe and set them gingerly on the bed where Samantha folded them and placed them in the travel bag.

When the last items had been fetched, Samantha offered the other woman a small smile. "Thank you for your help."

Esther's gaze flitted in Samantha's direction as she nodded. "Y-you are welcome, ma'am. I'm—I'm glad to help you."

Samantha couldn't help but notice Esther's eyes, which were large and expressive, a deep brown that reminded Samantha of Adam's, and the only attractive feature in an otherwise plain face. Esther's brown hair had been pinned back in a severe bun, but over the course of the morning several lank strands had escaped around her narrow face. Her brown calico dress and tan apron, both of which were well worn and patched, only increased the woman's colorless appearance. The simple

clothing, the plain face, the stammering, and the begging eyes all seemed to indicate an unhappiness that tugged at Samantha's heartstrings.

But Samantha tried hard not to look at Esther too much. The pleading brown eyes pulled at her, but the woman's expanded belly—obviously pregnant—created a stab of pain in Samantha's chest. So she remained quiet.

"You—you have s-s—such pretty things," Esther offered shyly as she watched Samantha snap the closure on the carpet bag.

Samantha glanced sideways to see Esther fingering the frayed pocket of her apron. "Thank you," Samantha managed to say, unreasonably piqued by the pregnant belly that seemed to mock her. Then feeling small for being standoffish—it wasn't Esther's fault Samantha would never experience her own pregnancy—added more kindly, "I have lots of time to sew, so it isn't that expensive for me to have several dresses."

Seemingly encouraged by the friendly overture, Esther said, "I—I sew, too—for m-m-my children. But—but with working, I—I d-don't have time to—to sew for m-me."

Samantha's gaze dropped to the woman's stomach, then up to her eyes again. She couldn't determine how old Esther was. The woman gave the appearance of age with her severe hairstyle, plain clothing, and somber face. Her eyes, though, were unlined and held the intensity of youth, although there was a pleading undertone Samantha didn't understand. In all likelihood, Esther was younger than Samantha yet already had children to sew for, as well as another baby on the way. The thought rankled her.

Samantha turned away and swung the valise off the bed. She moved to the door and let the bag drop with a *thump*. Turning to the other woman, she said in a tight voice, "Yes, well, I'm

sure you'll have time to sew for yourself when your . . . children
. . . are older."

Esther's eyebrows crunched together. Head down and
hands twisting in her apron she scurried to the door like a
whipped pup. "If—if there's—there's n-nothing else, ma'am?"

Samantha's heart caught in her throat. She'd hurt the Esther's feelings. She must get these racing emotions under control and stop taking her frustrations out on everyone around
her. *Lord, help me, please!* By way of apology, she pulled a coin
from her little carry purse and offered it to Esther with a smile.
"You've done quite enough for me, Esther." She placed the coin
in Esther's thin hand. Esther opened her mouth to protest, but
Samantha shook her head. "No, this was not one of your usual
duties, and I appreciate your help . . . and your company. Please
keep it."

A look of uncertainty crossed Esther's face as she stared at
her closed fist. Then she raised her eyes and met Samantha's
gaze. She gave a small, hesitant nod. "All right, ma'am—and
th-th-thank you. Have a—have a g-good trip home."

Samantha closed the door behind Esther and leaned against
it, releasing a heavy sigh. Home sounded better all the time.

Adam settled into the wingback leather chair facing Daniel's
impressive mahogany desk. Pride swelled as he looked across
the desk at his brother busily scribbling on a notepad. Dressed
impeccably in a three-piece suit, precisely pressed white broad-
cloth shirt, and deep burgundy ascot, Daniel looked every bit
the picture of the successful lawyer. This wood-paneled office
was a far cry from the farm in Mountain Lake where they'd both
grown up. Daniel looked nothing like a farmer's son.

Daniel placed his pen in its holder and pushed the pad aside. His eyes narrowed thoughtfully as they met Adam's. "Your conversation with Samantha? It did not go very well."

Adam gave a rueful smile. Was it the lawyer's mind that made Daniel make statements rather than ask questions? "What makes you think that?"

"For starters, you're here early." Daniel glanced at the Moderator wall clock which read 10:15 before turning back to Adam. "You're alone, and you're looking rather serious."

Adam shrugged. "You're right. She and I . . . well . . ." He ran a tired hand across his face. Leaning forward, he rested his elbows on his knees and looked up at his brother. "I made a suggestion, but she didn't take to it."

"And the suggestion?"

"That we adopt a baby."

Daniel's chair squeaked as he shifted positions. "Ah."

Adam sat back with a wry grin. "She insisted on finding out what we had been talking about at breakfast, and I tried to break the possibility of adoption to her gently. But to her, it sounded like she'd be giving up her dreams."

"And she's not ready for that." Again, a blunt statement.

Adam fell back in the chair. "No, she's not. Not yet." He sighed. "To be honest, it's possible she never will be."

Daniel rested his forearms on the polished top of his desk. "Well, as you've realized, it is rather soon, Adam. Give her time. Don't give up."

Remembering the sad story about the baby bird, Adam grimaced. "Samantha wasn't raised like we were. She didn't have much—not in any sense. But I think what she missed the most was not having a mother."

Daniel frowned thoughtfully. "She had a grandmother who lived with her, didn't she?"

"Yes," Adam said, "and Gran was a loving influence. But she died when Samantha was so young. And we both know what kind of parental experience she had after that." Thoughts of Burt O'Brien brought a surge of righteous anger through Adam's chest. "Being a mother has always been so important to Samantha. She wanted to give her own child all the love she longed to receive as a child. Her heart is broken, knowing it cannot be."

Daniel leaned forward and rested his elbows on the desk. "I wish I could do something to make things easier for you." He chuckled and shook his head. "My job is helping people solve problems. But there's nothing in the law books that can do anything about this."

Adam gave his brother a small smile. "Actually, Daniel, you've been a lot of help. And my conversation with Sam this morning really did end on a slightly hopeful note. We both finally were able to talk about things that will help us move forward. Having you to talk to also has helped me a great deal. Thank you."

Daniel flipped his hand outward. "What are brothers for?"

Adam grinned briefly, then his brows came down. "Could you do one more thing for me?"

"What's that?"

"Dr. Zimmerman is an expert, and he told us there was no way to fix what's wrong inside of Samantha. But if you hear about any other doctors that might think otherwise—"

"I'll contact you right away, Adam, I promise." Daniel paused, his brow puckering. "But I need you to give me a promise, too."

Curious, Adam said, "To do what?"

Daniel assumed his lawyer's pose—hands crossed formally one over the other on the satiny desk top, shoulders back, face devoid of emotion. "Be realistic. Of course if there is some way for Samantha to bear children, you will want to pursue it. But for her sake—and yours—be very careful before spending time chasing after a dream. Some dreams just aren't meant to be fulfilled. I—" He blew out a breath. "This is tough, trying to separate the lawyer from the brother here." He ran his hand through his hair. "I don't want to see either of you get hurt any more than you have already been. Do you understand?"

Adam's chest expanded with gratefulness for family who cared. "I understand. And I'll be careful."

"Well, then . . ." Daniel cleared his throat.

Adam quickly said, "Samantha and I have spent enough time in Minneapolis. We need to get on home."

"Don't feel as though you have to run—"

"I don't, Daniel. But there's work waiting for me, and it's time for us to settle back in our old routine and . . . well, get on with things."

"Do you think Samantha is ready?"

Adam thought for a moment. "Yes. Our talk this morning helped. She got a few things out in the open, which she needed to do. Our visit here gave both of us time to gather our wits, but now . . . we need to go home."

Adam rose, and Daniel followed suit, reaching across the wide desk to clasp his brother's hand. "Adam, I'm glad you came."

"Thanks again, Daniel, for everything." Emotion caught Adam in its grip. He stepped around the desk to embrace Daniel, unashamed of the tears stinging his eyes. Adam gave his brother a few thumps on the back, and they pulled apart with Daniel keeping a firm grip on Adam's shoulder.

Daniel said, "I'm going to keep my ears open for word of any abandoned babies, Adam. Just in case."

Adam smiled but shook his head slowly. "Thanks, brother, but please . . . Samantha—" He broke off, looking downward. No matter how much he wanted a baby, he wouldn't force Samantha in that in direction. Daniel squeezed Adam's shoulder hard once, then let his hand drop. "All right."

Adam turned toward the door. He paused, a hand on the doorknob, and looked back. "Daniel, don't ever take your children for granted."

"I never have, Adam."

Adam nodded and gave a brief wave.

Chapter Eleven

*B*ack in her own home, Samantha soon busied herself with her fall routine. The familiar tasks offered a sense of normalcy she sorely needed right then. But then some little thing would remind her, and disappointment would once again overwhelm her, causing her to react to situations far differently from what would have been normal before the life-altering trip to Rochester.

She couldn't bear the hard, bitter edge that could emerge without warning. When she'd first arrived in Mountain Lake, hurting and wounded, she'd worn a mask of defiance to protect herself. The love of the Klaassens and their God had helped carve away the barriers of anger. But this new deep pain seemed to bring the old Samantha to the surface. She watched her family and friends—and Adam—step carefully around her, and she hated making them uncomfortable, yet she couldn't seem to control her emotions that could erupt without notice. She prayed often for God to forgive her anger and heal her heart, and she wondered why He didn't hurry and answer.

Adam's sister Josie stopped by in early September with six quart jars of strawberry preserves. She pulled the wooden crate containing the jars out of the wagon and said with a grin, "These aren't a gift. I need to trade you for a bushel of dried apples. I didn't get any done this year, and I'll need them for winter pies. Can we swap?"

Josie's little son, Simon, refused help and climbed down to stand beside his mother. Samantha scooped him up for a hug. "And would you miss having apple pies this winter, Simon?"

The boy nodded, aiming a thumb at his own chest. "I wike pie."

Samantha said, "Then I'd better trade with your mama." She led Simon into the house.

Josie followed, grousing good-naturedly, "Now that we've got that settled, where can I put these down? This box is heavy!"

Samantha pointed Josie to the kitchen sideboard. "Adam can carry it to the cellar later." She leaned down to Simon's level and asked brightly, "Do you like molasses cookies?"

Simon's eyes widened, and he looked up at his mother. "Tan I, Mama?"

Josie smiled. "Just one—" she raised one finger—"or you'll spoil your supper."

Simon trotted behind Samantha to the kitchen table where she fished a golden molasses cookie from a crock jar. Simon scrambled up on a chair and seated himself with his legs sticking out as straight as pokers. Samantha placed a cookie on a plate and set it in front of the little boy.

"What do you say, Simon?" Josie prompted.

Simon looked up at his aunt and asked innocently, "Tan Mama hab one too?"

Samantha and Josie exchanged amused looks, but Samantha felt her heart catch. Oh, to have a little one to look out for her in such a way! To cover her heartbreak, she reached for a second cookie. "Of course Mama can have one, Simon."

But Josie held up a hand and said laughingly, "No, thank you, Sammy! They look wonderful, but I really don't need it."

Samantha shrugged, put the cookie back, and replaced the lid. "Let's go sit and visit a bit then, while Simon has his treat."

"Lean over the table, Simon," Josie instructed from the doorway as the two women headed for the parlor. "We don't want to spread crumbs all over Auntie Sam's nice clean floor."

Samantha cupped a hand along the side of her mouth as she leaned toward Simon and whispered loudly, "Don't worry about a few crumbs, Simon. Auntie Sam can always sweep them up afterward."

Josie frowned but didn't comment. As she settled back in the tapestry settee in front of the parlor's bay window, she gestured toward the backyard. "I noticed the garden is bare. Have you finished all your canning?"

Samantha rocked in her chair. "Yes. I've been working like a dervish since . . . well, since we got back from Rochester." She tried a smile and confessed, "I'm trying to stay too busy to think." Josie smiled and nodded her understanding, and Samantha continued, "I still need to dig the potatoes, then finish turning the ground under."

"Why don't you let Adam do that?" Josie asked.

"Because he's busy with his own work," Samantha said. "Besides, the garden has always been mine. No matter what has . . . has taken place, there's no reason for him to mollycoddle me."

Josie opened her mouth to reply, but just then Simon entered the parlor with a face full of crumbs. Josie jumped up. "Simon! Come quick, let's get back to the kitchen before we spread cookie crumbs everywhere."

Samantha felt her hackles rise. There was no need to get so agitated over a few crumbs! If she had children, she would let them scatter crumbs everywhere in the house. She pushed herself out of the chair. "Let him be, Josie. Crumbs can always be cleaned up. There's no need to holler at him and hurt his feelings."

Josie pulled back. "I didn't holler at him, Sam. But he knows to stay at the table until he's been cleaned up."

"Maybe at your house," Samantha shot back, "but he doesn't have to here." She took hold of Simon's small hand.

"I want him to clean up before leaving the table."

"It isn't that important, Josie."

"It is to me."

"But it's ridiculous! There's no reason to be so particular."

Josie glanced at Simon and said evenly, "Let me clean him up now, Samantha."

Samantha looked down at the little boy standing between his aunt and his mother, looking from one to the other with a wide-eyed look of confusion on his face. She released his hand and sighed. "All right, Josie. Go ahead."

Josie walked Simon back to the kitchen, and Samantha sank down in her rocking chair. She covered her face with her hands, willing herself to calm. Shame washed over her. She tried so hard to curb her anger. Why did she so easily lose control?

When Josie returned to the parlor, Samantha apologized immediately for her behavior.

"It's forgotten, Sam." But when Simon would have gone to his aunt, Josie pulled him into her own lap instead. "I understand you're bound to be a bit . . . high-strung."

Samantha grimaced. *High-strung!* Well, perhaps Josie was right. Even so, defensiveness sharpened her tone. "I don't like feeling this way, Josie."

Josie sat in silence.

Samantha sighed again and rose from the rocker. "I'll go get your apples." She headed outside to the cellar door. But when she'd opened it, instead of going down, she stood at the head of the earthen steps, her head drooping low and her throat stinging. She spun when someone touched her on the shoulder.

Josie stood there, her eyes sad. "Samantha, I'm sorry I was impatient with you just now. I don't suppose any of us really understands what you're going through. We already have what you want, so we look at things differently." She took a step closer and put her hand on Samantha's arm. "But you must try to understand that parenting can't be shut off when we come to your house. You have to respect my position as Simon's mother and allow me to guide him, discipline him, even if you don't agree with me and would do things differently if he were yours."

This time it was Samantha who remained silent.

Josie lifted her arms, her eyes begging for Samantha to allow her to offer comfort. Samantha stood stiffly for a moment, then stepped into Josie's embrace. The two women clung for a long, hard minute. Against Samantha's hair Josie whispered, "I'll try to be more patient."

Samantha said raggedly, "And I'll try to get my emotions under control."

But how? If she only knew how . . . She pulled away and said, "I better get those apples."

~⊙

The winter-readiness duties that had given Samantha much pleasure before had become drudgery instead of delight. The last two weeks of September she dug up the mounds of potatoes and carried the gunny sacks full to the root cellar. Carrots, turnips, and onions were already there, as well as pumpkins, squash, ten-gallon crocks of sauerkraut, and row upon row of canned fruits and vegetables of every variety. All evidence of Samantha's industry.

The first day of October found her carrying a final batch of applesauce to the cellar where she placed the quart jars on the rough pine shelf next to the peaches and strawberry preserves. The poor shelving bowed beneath the weight of their bounty. The task completed, Samantha stood back, hands on hips, and surveyed her handiwork. In the past, it had given her a heady, satisfied feeling to see all the food ready for the long winter months. But now she caught herself muttering dismally, "At least there's something I can do like the other women."

She gave herself a little shake and said loudly to the rows of jars like so many obedient soldiers, "Enough! I have a good life here—a good home, a wonderful husband, and a family who loves me. I have many things to be thankful for, so I must stop being so melancholy!"

Deep down, Samantha indeed knew she was a very blessed woman. Having Adam and all of Adam's family to call her own was much more than she could have ever imagined as a little girl growing up on the wretched, impoverished side of Milwaukee. And her own brother, David, was the epitome of kindness and patience. He called regularly for chats on the newly installed telephone, always maintaining a measure of light-heartedness she knew was difficult for him when he saw her unhappiness. Of course it was impossible to avoid speaking of their children—they all had them! The subject of babies couldn't be ignored—Frank's wife, Anna, was only weeks away from delivery of their third baby, and all were concerned since she had lost the second, a boy, the year before—but when it was mentioned, it was mentioned briefly, ever mindful of Samantha and Adam's heartbreak.

Yes, in many ways she was fortunate, she reminded herself as she turned toward the cellar stairs. She watched her feet as she mounted the uneven steps. The brisk early fall breeze whizzed down, whirling her skirts around her ankles and sending shivers up her spine. She clutched her shawl more snugly around her shoulders as she emerged, then leaned down to lift the heavy wooden door and swing it closed. The tail of her shawl blew over her face, and she pushed it back, reaching for the door again.

"Here, Sammy, let me do that," came a deep voice, and Samantha straightened to find Adam's father, Si, hurrying toward her.

"Oh, thank you, Papa Klaassen," Samantha said as Si swung the door into place and secured the latch. "That door is troublesome in the best of times, but nearly impossible in this wind!"

Si turned up his collar and grinned at Samantha. "On days like these, a cup of hot coffee is a welcome thing."

"It just so happens I put a pot on to brew before I took that applesauce downstairs," she told him with a smile, "and I have a fresh applesauce cake to go with it."

"Sounds fine to me." Si followed Samantha through the back door into the toasty kitchen smelling of coffee, cinnamon, and apples. Si seated himself at the table in the center of the kitchen, and Samantha cut a sizable square from the applesauce cake and handed it to him on a plate before reaching for the coffee pot.

Si said, "*Dank*, my dear," and took up a forkful of the moist cake. "Mm!" He raised an eyebrow in pleasure.

Samantha settled herself across from him with her own cup of coffee. "Adam isn't back yet?" Adam had left early in the morning with Frank to take the first wagonloads of wheat to the railroad. He had been fretting about the lower wheat prices and whether he would receive enough for his wheat to meet their financial obligations. Si swallowed. "Nah, haven't seen the boys yet." He lifted his cup for a sip, then scowled at her over the rim. He shook a finger at her. "Now, none of that stewing, young lady. Adam knows things can be unpredictable in a farmer's life. It's part of relying on nature for your livelihood. We might not get the price we want this year, but that doesn't mean next year won't be better. Worrying won't change the prices, you know."

She nodded and lifted her cup.

Si took another bite of his cake, then said, "*Solang ein Brot im Kasten, brauchen wir nicht zu fasten.*"

Samantha nearly choked on her coffee. "What?"

Si grinned and looked pointedly at the loaves of bread cooling on racks near the stove. "I said, 'As long as bread is in the cupboard, we need not fast.' I'll start to worry when there isn't enough wheat harvested to provide our own loaves of bread, and I can't imagine that happening any time soon." He leaned back, the cake gone, and rested a forearm on the table.

His teasing apparently done, he said seriously, "We got more than a fair price for our wheat during the war, Sam. Any farmer with an ounce of sense—and that certainly includes Adam—put money aside for a rainy day. I know it's hard to take a lower price when you've put your hard work into it, but that's only fair play, when you balance it against the years when we got more."

"That makes sense," Samantha admitted, "and I suppose you're right." She thought about the storehouse of food in the cellar, letting complete satisfaction roll across her for the first time since she'd loaded the shelves. "We aren't going to starve no matter what the wheat may bring this year. But I know Adam's worried about the mortgage on our house. We've got that payment to make at the first of the year, and if he doesn't bring in much with his crop, then—"

"Then we'll work it out together," Simon put in gently. "That's what families do—help each other out." He pointed at her with his coffee cup and added, "And that brings me to the purpose of my visit."

"Oh?"

"Butchering time is just around the corner," Si said. "This year is Frank and Anna's turn to sponsor the butchering, but with Anna . . ." Si paused and scratched his head.

Samantha prompted quietly, "Anna being in a family way—"

"—being in a family way," Si repeated, "she really isn't up to the amount of work it takes. Would it be all right with you if we had the butchering here this year and at Frank's next year? I know it makes a mess of a kitchen, but the other ladies will be here to help."

Her heart twisted. Every other family had to contend with wee ones underfoot or worry about overtaxing an expectant mother. . . . She said, "That would be fine. I don't mind at all, and I'm sure Adam won't mind. There's plenty of room here . . . and no reason why I can't keep up with the work."

Si reached across the table to cup Samantha's cheek with a work-roughened hand. "Thank you, *liebchen*," he said with deep affection. "I'll let the others know about the change." He dropped his hand then, and Samantha busied herself cleaning up the table. Si rose. "I'd better head toward town. I'll see if I can round up your husband and send him home. Keep your chin up and don't fret. Everything will be fine."

Samantha suspected he was speaking of more than the price of wheat, so she said, "I'll be fine, Papa Klaassen. Don't you worry about me."

He grinned then reached out to pull her against his solid chest for a breath-stealing hug. "Take care, Daughter," he said and plopped his hat back on his head before heading out the back door.

Samantha waved as he strode toward the waiting wagon. She closed the door and turned to the empty kitchen. Her long sigh broke into the silence of the room. "I'll take care," she said aloud. "What else can I do?"

ince coming to Mountain Lake in 1917, Samantha had learned that hog butchering—sometimes
called *Schwienskjast*, meaning "pig's wedding"—was
an all-day occasion of hard work as well as much merriment.
Several days prior, Samantha prepared for the arrival of Adam's
extended family by baking—extra loaves of bread, countless
zwieback, a variety of pies, and two large cakes. She also carried
up several quart jars of her own canned vegetables to include
with the meals. It would take a great deal of food to satisfy the
appetites of the twenty-three people converging on Adam and
Samantha's farm place. And it would take every able-bodied
person a whole day to butcher the hogs that had been raised
solely to provide a winter's worth of pork and related items for
six families.

The group began arriving well before the sun was up. Frank
and Anna and little Laura Beth were the first, then Jake and
Liz with their twins and baby Amanda. Jake and Frank immediately joined Adam in the summer kitchen where he was stacking wood beneath three large cauldrons of water that would
be used to scald the carcasses. Liz and Anna and the children
joined Samantha in the warm house, fragrant with delightful
dishes to feed hungry troops.

Anna looked particularly bulky, one shawl around her shoulders and another over her head like an oversized babushka.
After hanging the shawls on the hooks by the back door, she
came at Samantha belly-first with hands outstretched. "Poor

Samantha," she said, "having all this work dumped on you! But I promise I'll make up for it. Next year it will be at our place no matter what."

Samantha smiled and squeezed Anna's hands. Her sister-in-law had always been a bit on the plump size, and her latest pregnancy only made her rounder. "I don't mind the extra work at all, Anna. And it only makes sense that you take it easy this year. We need to look out for this one." And Samantha dared to place her hand on Anna's extended belly. The mound was hard and warm under her palm, and beneath the layers of clothing she thought she felt a rolling push against her hand. Her eyes widened, and she pulled her hand back.

Anna clutched her belly with two hands and nodded at Samantha's inquiring look. "Yes, that was the baby. This one is going to be fun to keep up with if it's as active after it's born as it's been in here. Sometimes I think it never sleeps. Here, feel it again," and Anna reached for Samantha's hand so she could feel the kick.

"You feel that a lot?"

Anna nodded, heaving a sigh. "Yes, I do. Especially at night when I'm trying to sleep. And sometimes I wish . . ."

Samantha's heart twisted, and she bit down on her lower lip.

Anna clamped her mouth closed and lowered her head for a moment. When she looked up, she wore a bright smile. Rubbing her palms together, she said, "What can I do to help?"

"I want to help, too," Liz said, bouncing Amanda on one arm while the twins and Laura Beth played under her feet.

Samantha stared, transfixed, at the pleasant scene of Liz surrounded by children. But then she gave herself a little shake and turned Anna toward the kitchen table. "Neither of you need to do anything. Just sit and visit. I was able to get everything ready. Everyone will pick up a plate here"—she pointed to the breakfront cupboard, which held stacks of tin plates, silverware, and cotton napkins—"and serve themselves at the stove. Then they can sit wherever they can find a place! Breakfast will be a rather informal affair, and lunch will be catch-as-catch-can between other duties. But I promise we'll all be able to sit together for the evening meal."

Anna's gaze roved across the skillets of scrambled eggs, sausage, and fried potatoes waiting to be spooned onto a plate. "And *zwieback* to go with it all! You must not have gotten any more sleep last night than I did!"

Samantha laughed lightly, looking again at Liz who now crouched to play a finger game with Laura Beth while the twins and Amanda looked on. She said with a wobbly grin, "No, but it was all my own doing—no little person nudging me awake." Being able to tease Anna about her little sleep-stealer somehow lessened the hurt around her own heart. She breathed easier. I *can do this*.

A firm knock sent Samantha to the door. "Come on in," she greeted Si and Laura. Their three youngest—Becky, Teddy, and Sarah—trailed them inside.

Sarah beamed at Samantha. "Hurray! Butchering day!"

Teddy shot his sister a frown. "Since when have you gotten so excited about work?"

Sarah giggled. "I'm not excited about work. I'm excited to have the day off from school!"

Laura clicked her tongue on her teeth and shook her head, and Sarah shrugged sheepishly.

Josie and Stephen with little Simon came in before the door was closed, then Priscilla and David carrying a well-bundled baby Jenny along with Joey. The little boy galloped across the floor and greeted everyone boisterously, earning a mild reprimand from his father.

The kitchen had become crowded, so Samantha instructed, "When you've got your wraps removed and hung, just get a plate and start eating, then as soon as you older kids are done, bundle back up and head out of here to make room for the others!"

Everyone laughed and obeyed.

By seven o'clock the sun was up and Si's brother Hiram and wife Hulda bustled in. Hulda took over scrambling more eggs to feed the last arrivals. Breakfast was nearly finished by the time Arn arrived with his young fiancée, Martha Kornelson. He took some good-natured ribbing about stopping along the way to do a little spooning instead of getting right to work, and poor Martha blushed profusely at their warmhearted speculations.

"Better be careful," Arn warned Stephen, teasing right back, "or you'll find a pig's tail hanging from your backside!"

Arn's comment earned another round of merry laughter as they recalled times past when each of them had unsuspectingly worn a pig's tail. They played the joke on an unsuspecting recipient every year, and it never ceased to be a great source of amusement to all of them—especially the young boys.

Breakfast over, the real work began. Samantha marveled that such a large task could be completed in one day. Butchering had been done every year for as long as any of the Klaassen siblings could remember, so for the most part they pitched in without having to be told what to do.

Young Sarah was delegated to watch her nieces and nephews in one of the large, empty rooms upstairs. She pulled a face. "Why can't I be in on the real work? I'm old enough to help with the butchering."

Laura responded in her gentle way, "You are helping the most by keeping the little ones out from under foot and entertained."

"But Ma—" Sarah ceased her argument when Si gave her a warning glance. She sighed, turning to scoop baby Jenny from Priscilla's arms. "Come on then, everybody. Let's go find something to do." And she herded the crew of toddlers upstairs.

Samantha was glad she had the dishes to wash before going out to the barn. She always tried to stay far away from the pigpens until she was sure the hogs were dead. The high-pitched squeal when the hog was killed tormented her dreams for days afterward. Adam had assured her that it was over quickly, and the hog didn't suffer, but still she stayed away.

"I'll help with the dishes, Samantha," Arn's Martha offered shyly.

Samantha smiled at the girl. "That would be a blessing, Martha. There's quite a pile this morning."

"I don't mind." Martha rolled up her sleeves. "At home, there's ten of us kids, so I'm used to a pile of dishes."

Ten kids! Envy twined through Samantha's middle. She watched the younger woman covertly as they cleaned up together. Martha was tall and thin, with a rather long nose but a sweet mouth and sparkling green eyes. She was so bashful, she didn't say much, but she was certainly not afraid of work. Her thin arms had more strength than one would think possible. In no time at all the kitchen was clean and orderly, and the two women walked out to the barn to see what should be done next.

They passed the yard where two hogs hung side by side from an oak tree. A thick piece of wood inserted through the tendons of their back legs was attached to a rope-and-pulley rigging over a sturdy tree branch, holding the hogs at a height that made it easy for the men to reach them.

Martha blanched and turned her head away. "My, that's ugly."

Samantha confided, "The first time I saw where pork actually came from, I wasn't sure I could ever eat it again."

Martha giggled, covering her mouth with a slender hand. "I'm glad we just buy our meat from the butcher. I don't like seeing it like that."

"Then I guess it's a good thing Arn is planning to be a merchant rather than a farmer. You can continue to buy your meat at the butcher's shop."

Martha nodded in agreement and the women entered the barn. Laura sat in front of a large washtub, cleaning intestines. She looked up and greeted, "You two are a welcome sight. I can use some help here."

Samantha stifled her sigh. It had to be done, but such cleaning was a tedious and onerous task. First they had to be turned inside out and scrubbed thoroughly. Then they were turned back and the excess fat scraped away by pulling the intestines between two knitting needles held against one another. One had to be careful not to scrape away too much fat and poke holes in the intestine wall, thereby making them unusable. They were needed as sausage casings—the small intestines for red-meat sausage and the large intestines for liver sausage.

As Samantha took the clean intestines and began the scraping process, she commented, "I'd just as soon forget about the liver sausage."

Laura chuckled without looking up from the tub. "It's not as tasty as the others, in my opinion, but some would disagree with me." She laughed again, then went on to tell a funny story about her grandfather who had once eaten so much fresh liver sausage that he had ended up spending the night in the outhouse. Samantha, listening, was struck again how fortunate she was to be part of a family that had a history of memories—both humorous and pleasant—to share. She took careful note of the story so she'd be able to share it with her children someday. The thought brought a stab of pain. *Our own family,* she mourned once again.

Teddy carried in another container of entrails and plopped it next to Laura. He turned to Samantha. "Sam, could you come give Josie a hand? She's grinding meat for sausage and having a hard time keeping up."

"Where's Priscilla?" Laura asked. Samantha hid a smile, knowing Priscilla's penchant for avoiding work, especially this kind. She could imagine Priscilla even hiding in the outhouse.

Teddy said, "David's got her taking turns with Liz, stirring the lard cauldron."

One of the least desired tasks, Samantha thought, trying not to smile over Pris's bad luck. Not only was the smell unpleasant, one tended to be coated with a fine film of grease from the smoke by the end of the day. Laura grimaced. "She'll likely be in fine fettle this evening! Oh, well, it must be done by someone." She looked at Samantha and said, "Go ahead and help Josie, Sammy. Martha and I can handle this."

Samantha crossed the yard toward the house and waved to Adam who was scraping the bristles from the scalded hide of a large hog. He waved back with his knife and called out a warning. "Be on the lookout! Arn has three pigs' tails, and he's looking for victims!"

Arn indignantly looked up from cutting the skin from the lard. "Hey, it's not fair alerting people!"

Samantha laughed and called back, "I'll be careful! Maybe one of them will turn up on you, Arn!" She noted the butchering was well under way, everyone industriously working. Adam and Frank scraped bristles; Arn and Jake cut the lard into pieces for boiling; Si and Hiram sawed the carcasses of two hogs, separating the lean from the fatty meat; David and Stephen readied another hog for slaughter. She asked Teddy, "How many are already done?"

"Four—and it's only a little after nine. We're doing fine."

Samantha entered the house to find Josie on her knees in the back-porch area of the kitchen, cutting the lean meat into chunks small enough to fit through the hand-cranked grinder.

Josie released a relieved sigh when she spotted Samantha. "Oh, thank you for coming. I can't keep up. They're going so fast out there!"

"What do you want me to do?" Samantha sank down by Josie with her skirts in a pouf around her.

"I'll cut while you grind," Josie replied, her hands still busy. "When your arm gets tired, we can switch, all right?"

Samantha had ground enough meat to fill two gallon-sized crocks when they heard a loud burst of laughter from the yard. The two women grinned at each other and rushed to the back stoop to see what was going on. Hulda also left her post in the kitchen where she was mixing seasonings with ground meat. Hands on hips, she said, "What are those silly men up to now?"

David, laughing, was threatening Arn with a sturdy stick. "You rogue, you!" David waved the stick. "You just put that pig's tail right where it belongs—on your own hind end, Arn, my man!"

Arn hooted, "Ha-ha! You do make a skinny pig, David. Not much lard on you!" Everyone laughed. The fattest pigs were the most prized since they delivered larger quantities of all-important lard.

Priscilla called out, still stirring the lard cauldron, "You just hush your insults, Arnold Klaassen! I happen to like my meat—and my man—lean!"

They all roared. The joke gave them a welcome respite from the hard work and a second wind to get back to it. As they headed to their respective jobs, David tucked the pig's tail he had pulled off the seat of his overalls into his pocket and yelled, "You just wait, Arnold ! When you least expect it, I'll get even!"

Hulda closed the door on the antics, chuckling. "Those men, cutting up like boys. And I know a treat they would all like."

Josie grinned. "*Bubbat*?"

Hulda nodded, her expression smug.

Samantha turned eagerly. "Oh, yes, make a batch of *Bubbat*. Josie and I will get your other work done."

Hulda's blue eyes twinkled behind the round spectacles. "But you have all these nice loaves of bread here for our lunch."

Josie said, "They won't be wasted, will they, Sam? Go ahead, Tante Hulda, and make *Bubbat*."

Hulda joked, "But then everyone might sleep the afternoon away!" They all knew that *Bubbat*, a yeast bread seasoned with chunks of sausage, was almost a meal in itself, tasty and very filling.

"Then make it for our evening meal," Josie suggested. "It can be a surprise."

Hulda nodded. "All right." She scooped out a hefty dish of the ground pork. Hulda, with Becky's help, had taken the responsibility of preparing the noon meal. As Samantha intended, it was a catch-as-catch-can affair, with people coming and going as they could leave their tasks. After the little children were fed, Sarah put them all down for naps and then cheerfully relieved Priscilla and Liz of their lard stirring so they could come in and eat.

"Oh, I'm simply a mess!" Priscilla rolled her eyes. "I shouldn't even sit on anything!" She grabbed a tea towel from a small rack. "I'll sit on this so I don't spoil your chair." She bent to drape the towel across the seat of the chair. Liz pointed, burst out laughing, then clapped a hand over her mouth. Samantha,

Josie, and Hulda looked, too, and had to stifle their own laughter. Priscilla's gaze narrowed. "What's so funny?"

Josie and Samantha exchanged amused looks. Samantha said, straight-faced, "Oh, nothing really."

"Well, it must be something or you wouldn't be giggling like a gaggle of geese. And it isn't polite to giggle but not share the joke," Priscilla scolded.

"I'm sorry." Liz's voice quavered with amusement. She tapped her chin with one finger, assuming a thoughtful air. "I'm wondering if David likes his meat—and his woman—lean or fat."

Priscilla's lovely blue eyes widened as she stared at the others. Then she bounced from her chair and turned circles, trying to see her own rear end. Josie and Samantha howled with laughter. "There's one back there, isn't there?" Priscilla pulled the back of her skirt to the side with two hands, craning her neck to see the back of her dress. "Someone's put a pig's tail on me, right?"

"Yes!" Josie managed between giggles.

Priscilla pointed her backside at Josie. "Well, get it off!"

Still chortling, Josie did as she was bid.

Priscilla snatched it from Josie's hand. "Give me that vile thing. I've got a score to settle." They all laughed again as she marched out the door, her head held high.

The afternoon passed much as the morning had, with efficient routine. When the little ones awoke from naps, Teddy took a couple of clean pig bladders, blew them up, and tied them with a string. Under Anna's watchful eye, the children spent a pleasant time kicking the bladder balloons around the yard. While they had their fun, Arn continued to pursue his own—Si, Hiram, and Stephen each had the dubious honor of wearing a pig's tail at some point during the day, but Arn always escaped retaliation. He took great pleasure in taunting the others about his ability to elude them.

By seven o'clock that evening, all six hogs had been butchered. The hams, chops, roasts, and sausage to be kept by Adam and Samantha were already hanging in the smokehouse or soaking in a salt barrel. The others had loaded their wrapped portions in wagon beds to be preserved in their own smokehouses or cellars. The head cheese had been mixed and would be divided up the following day, after it had a chance to jell. The lard was divided and poured into crocks, and the leftover bits of meat from the spareribs, which had been boiled in the lard, were scooped from the bottom of the cauldron. The bits of meat, called cracklings, were very rich, and were saved for special occasions—such as the end of a successful day of butchering.

"Oh, goodie!" Sarah exclaimed as Laura placed the bowlful of cracklings on the makeshift table. Si and Frank had set up sawhorses and planks in the barn so everyone could sit together. "We're going to have a feast!"

The women filled the table's top with bowls and platters containing roast chicken, fresh sausage, boiled potatoes and gravy, canned green beans seasoned with onion, and stewed tomatoes. Hulda's *Bubbat* loaves, two huge applesauce cakes, and several pies completed the meal. Si thanked the Lord for a fruitful day, and everyone ate until their bellies ached.

Priscilla looked rather smug while the others chattered away during the meal. David looked a question at her from time to time, but she just gave a secret smile and refused to comment. Across the table, Anna took a bite of cake and called to Samantha, "Sammy, this applesauce cake is wonderful! It's better than any I've ever had. Could I get your recipe?"

Before Samantha could answer, Arn teased, "Anna, you don't need any applesauce cake. Your tummy's so big now, you can't sit up to the table!"

Anna threw a chicken bone at him, missing him by a mile. She turned back to Samantha. "Could I have the recipe, Sammy?"

Samantha nodded. "Yes, but not today. My hands are worn out from cranking that silly grinder. I don't think I have enough energy left to write it down."

When the serving platters were empty, Arn leaned back, rested his hands on his full midsection. "Martha, are you ready to head back to town?" he asked.

Martha looked around the table uncertainly. "Maybe I should stay and help Samantha clean things up before I go home."

Anna said, "Josie and I are going to stay and help with the cleanup, Martha. You've more than earned your keep—go on home."

"If you're sure . . ." Martha hesitated.

Arn cut in, "Aw, come on, Marty. You'll have plenty of time to clean up after these mess-makers when we're married." He stood and took her by the hand to urge her from her chair. "Come on, let me run you home before your folks wonder what I did with you."

Martha blushed. "All right, Arn. But at least let's carry our own dishes to the kitchen."

"Yes, ma'am." Arn stood at attention with a mock salute.

Martha's mouth dropped open in surprise, and then she started laughing. Arn looked startled, and Martha continued to laugh, a hand over her mouth. She pointed at something behind Arn.

"What is it?" Arn asked, frowning as he turned to see what she was referring to.

Everyone joined Martha in gales of laughter. The children danced around excitedly, and one of Liz's twins, Andy, burst out, "Uncle Arn's a piggy!" The other children took up the cry, repeating in a singsong manner, "Uncle Arn's a piggy. Uncle Arn's a piggy!"

Arn himself had been fooled! He yanked the tail from his backside and looked around in disgust. "All right, David, you said you'd get even. When did you get me?"

David held up his hands, palms outward. "I'd love to take the credit, Arn, but it was not I."

Arn glared. "Well, then, who put it there?"

Priscilla stood, proud as a peacock, and raised her hand, even waving it a little. "I did," she sang out.

David placed an arm around his beaming wife and crowed, "Oh-ho, Arn! The king is dead; long live the queen!" Everyone cheered as Arn made a face, then gallantly bowed before Priscilla, presenting her the pig's tail on his open palms the way one might bestow a crown of jewels. Priscilla took it with a pretty curtsy.

"Well, family," Si announced when the hilarity calmed, "we've put in a productive day, but now it's time for rest. Everyone grab an armload of dishes and head for the house. We'll get Samantha's kitchen in order and all head for home."

With the family all inside, the kitchen was so crowded that Samantha suggested, "Why don't you all leave the cleanup to Adam and me and get on home? You've all got children to get to bed and meat to put away. Adam and I can do this ourselves."

Laura asked, "Are you sure, Sam? We don't mind helping."

Samantha shook her head in mock exasperation. "It will take twice as long with all of you underfoot!" She made shooing motions with her hands. "Please, just run along and let me take care of my own kitchen."

Laura crossed to give Samantha a hug. "If you're certain . . ."

Samantha repeated, "Adam will help me. Please—you may go."

Hugs, thank-yous, good-byes, and more jokes were exchanged as everyone bundled up for their rides home. When Adam finally closed the door on the last of them, he turned and gave his wife a smile, shaking his head. "Alone again."

Samantha nodded. Her mind followed the others who were far from alone, all with little ones bouncing in the wagons from leftover excitement. It had been a day filled with family, and now it was quiet—too quiet. An all-too-familiar wave of envy washed over her. She sighed.

Adam stepped up behind her and gave her shoulder a loving squeeze. "This is nice, isn't it? Just us."

Samantha turned and looked into his deep brown eyes. Tears pricked. Having Adam for her husband, having his family to call her own, was such a blessing. Lord, *please let me see what I have as enough.* She leaned into his embrace, wrapped her arms around his torso, and held tight. He rested his lips on the top of her head and rocked her for several seconds. In his arms— his strong, warm, secure arms—Samantha experienced a sweet whisper of peace. *Thank You, Lord.* . . .

Renewed, Samantha pulled back and smiled. "Come on, my man, let's get this mess cleaned up."

Chapter Thirteen

The next morning, Samantha felt Adam nudge her awake. She opened her eyes, squinting into the early-morning darkness. "Yeah, what?" she asked in a sleep-thick voice.

"Good morning." He scooped her close, and she snuggled her head against his shoulder. He smoothed down her hair and gave her a kiss.

She received his kiss willingly, then protested, "I wasn't ready to wake up yet."

Adam chuckled. "I know you're tired. You put in a hard day's work yesterday. I just woke you to tell you I'm going to ride over to Pa's and help him today. He's got some fence down, and it will probably take most of the day. Don't expect me for lunch. Go ahead and sleep till noon if you want to."

Samantha scrunched her face up. "You woke me up to tell me to sleep till noon?"

"Does sound kind of foolish," he admitted. "But if I'd just left a note, I couldn't kiss you." He delivered another kiss on her forehead, then gently pushed her back into her warm cocoon. He tucked the blankets around her and gave her one more kiss before padding to the hallway. "Brrr, it's cold this morning!" she heard him complain.

By the time Adam had washed and dressed for the day, Samantha had drifted to sleep again with only her nose sticking out from beneath the pile of quilts. The next thing she knew, she felt herself startle awake. She brought up a hand to rub her nose. When she saw Adam's face only inches from her own, she groaned. "You woke me up again."

Adam swallowed his chuckle. "I'm sorry. I only meant to give you one more kiss for good measure."

"Well, you've done it. Good-bye, Adam." She rolled over and pulled the quilts high.

~~⌒~~

Snug under the covers, Samantha heard Adam's boots as he tiptoed down the stairs. She sighed at the rattle of the stove lids as he stoked the fire, and then pulled her pillow over her head. But it wasn't enough to muffle the squeak and snap of the screen door as he headed outside. Every sound was an intrusion on the possibility of more sleep. Huffing her aggravation, she muttered to the room, "Who can sleep with all this racket?"

She threw back the covers, shivering as the cool air reached her body, and she raced for the water closet. She performed her morning necessities, then headed back to the bedroom with her arms wrapped around herself. She dressed as quickly as she could, brushed her hair into a neat twist, and quickly tidied the bedroom before going down to the warm comfort of the kitchen.

Usually it was late October before she and Adam closed off the parlor, dining room, and unused bedrooms to make it easier to heat the common rooms of the house. As Samantha got the coffee perking, she wondered if they should close things off earlier this year; it seemed colder sooner. Would it be easier to see a closed door, knowing there was nothing—and no one— behind it? She wasn't sure.

She looked around at the spotless kitchen, then wandered through the other rooms on the first floor, needlessly adjusting crocheted antimacassars and swiping a finger across dust-free picture frames. Nothing required her attention. Her thoughts flitted back to the empty rooms upstairs. If only there were children in the house, her day would be full. She returned to the kitchen and poured herself a cup of coffee, seating herself at the kitchen table. It was hard to imagine all the joyful commotion filling the same room just yesterday.

"I need something to do today," she said aloud. It seemed she spoke to empty rooms a lot these days, just for the sound of a human voice. She sipped her coffee, her eyes idly roaming the neat room until they focused on the upturned crockery bowl covering a leftover wedge of applesauce cake. *Yes, that's right, Anna requested the recipe.*

Samantha went over to the backdoor and peered out. The gray morning assured her of a cold walk, but she would have someone to talk to for a good part of the day. The decision made, she quickly wrote her recipe on a square of brown paper, bundled up, and set out at a good pace for Frank and Anna's farmhouse.

The distance would have required only fifteen minutes on horseback, but she chose to walk, stretching out the time. The air was crisp, but when the sun broke through the clouds, it took on a crystal brightness that warmed her from within. Her feet crunched against the hard dirt, startling two gophers into a skittering escape. She laughed aloud as the tiny striped animals ran frantically to their burrow, disappearing into the mound of dirt.

Her eyes squinted against the sun, slanting through leafless branches above her head, and birds peeked down at her as she passed, tipping their heads curiously and their bright eyes shining. Samantha paused once and waved a friendly finger at a pair of brown finches. The birds swooped away into the skies with her laughter following them. Her happy chuckles disturbed a red squirrel, and it scolded from high in the tree.

"What a cheerful world You created, God," she heard herself say, and she realized her heart felt light. By the time she reached the front porch of Frank and Anna's sturdy house, she was whistling between her teeth and had set aside her earlier dismal feelings. She skipped up the two wooden steps and rapped her knuckles against the door. She leaned sideways to peek through the lace-covered window. When no one answered, she frowned and knocked again, harder this time, looking toward the barn for any sign of activity.

After several minutes, the door finally swung inward with little Laura Beth holding onto the brass knob with two hands. She peered at Samantha from between her elbows. The little girl was dressed, but her hair was uncombed, and her red-rimmed eyes told Samantha the child had been crying. Samantha's heart thumped in sudden fear. She crouched down to her niece and greeted gently, "Hi, honey. Where's Mama?"

Laura Beth threw herself at Samantha, pressing a tear-stained cheek against her aunt's dress front. "Mama's to bed. She won't get up. I been really scared."

Samantha took Laura Beth's hand. "Let's go see Mama." The little girl led her eagerly to Frank and Anna's bedroom. When Samantha saw Anna lying in the bed with her white face holding an expression of pain, Sam rushed to the edge of the bed and placed a shaky hand on Anna's cheek.

Anna's eyes fluttered open. "Oh, Sammy . . ." She struggled to smile. "Thank heaven you're here. I've been praying someone would come. . . ."

"Anna, what is it? It isn't time yet . . . ?" Samantha smoothed Anna's hair from her face.

Anna groaned, suddenly wrapping her hands around her extended middle and curling into a ball. She broke out in a sweat, and the muscles in her neck stood taut. Samantha's muscles tightened in response to Anna's discomfort. After what seemed like forever, Anna relaxed, flattening herself in the bed again. "The baby's coming, Sam."

"But it's too early!"

Anna managed a weak laugh. "I don't think the baby knows that. It's coming now."

"Where's Frank?"

"Turning under stubble in the north fields—oooh!"

Samantha stood helplessly by as Anna held her breath through another contraction. How horrible, seeing Anna in such agony and not able to help. Although close by when several of her nieces and nephews had entered the world, Samantha had never been directly involved with the birth process. And she sure didn't want to be this time!

When Anna had fallen back against the bed, Samantha placed a trembling hand on her shoulder. "Anna, I'm going to the barn. I'll saddle a horse and ride for Doctor Newton or Mother Klaassen. You need one of them with you now."

Anna reached up and grasped Samantha's hand. "No, Sammy, please don't leave me! The baby is coming, and there isn't time for you to go after anyone. We'll have to deliver it ourselves."

Samantha's heart leaped into her throat. "But I—I can't, Anna! What if—?" She remembered Frank and Anna's tiny baby boy who had been buried a little over a year ago.

Anna repeated, "We have to, Sammy. There isn't time for anything else! Please! Don't leave me!" And she coiled again as another spasm struck.

Samantha spun and spotted Laura Beth leaning against the doorframe, a finger in her mouth, her brown eyes wide and fearful. Samantha ran to Laura Beth, knelt, and took the child by the shoulders. "Laura Beth, do you know the way to Grandma Klaassen's house?"

The little girl nodded.

Samantha wondered at the wisdom of sending a not-quite-four-year-old child on such an errand, but what other choice did they have? She couldn't leave Anna alone. She hurried back to the bed. "Anna, I'm going out to the barn to saddle a horse. I'll only be gone a few minutes. Will you be all right?"

Anna shook her head and moaned, "No, Sammy, don't leave me now. . . ."

Samantha didn't have time to explain. "I'll be right back," she reassured Anna as confidently as she could. Grabbing a little coat by the door and a scarf, she took Laura Beth by the hand and flew out the back door to the barn where she saddled Rocky, the calmest of the horses. Her fingers were shaking and clumsy, and she prayed as she tightened cinches—*Oh, Lord, please let everything be okay with Anna and the baby! And get little Laura Beth to her grandma safely!* It seemed to take ages before she'd managed to cinch the saddle securely in place, but at last she lifted Laura Beth, now wrapped in coat and scarf, onto the horse's back. Laura Beth clutched the saddle horn with both small hands.

"Now, listen, sweetie—" Urgency underscored her tone— "you ride straight to Grandma's house and tell Grandma your mama needs her. Can you do that?"

Laura Beth looked down at Samantha with wide, serious eyes. She nodded slowly. "Yes, Auntie Sam, I've rode lots of times with Daddy. I can get Grandma." Her face puckered up in worry. "What's wrong with Mama?"

"Mama will be fine, honey." Samantha reached up to pull the scarf tighter around Laura Beth's cherubic face, inwardly praying she was telling the truth. "And after Grandma comes, you'll get to meet your new baby brother or sister."

Laura Beth brightened. "I want a sister."

Samantha said, "That would be nice. But now go get Grandma, Laura Beth. Mama needs Grandma's help, okay?"

The little girl nodded again. Samantha made sure the reins were wrapped around the saddle horn, then led Rocky out of the barn, turning him in the direction of the big farm. "Hang on tight," Samantha instructed, and when Laura Beth had crouched over the horse's neck, Samantha brought her hand down sharply against Rocky's flank. The horse took off at a trot. Samantha watched long enough to make sure Laura Beth would hold her seat, then raced back to the house.

Chapter Fourteen

*A*nna was moaning, rolling side to side in the bed. Samantha sat down on the edge of the rumpled quilts and smoothed Anna's damp hair from her face. "Anna, I'm here."

"My water broke. I've made a mess of the bed."

"No matter." Samantha forced her voice to be calm despite her inner quaking. "We can clean up the bed. Where are the sheets?"

Anna pointed weakly to a large chest against the wall, and Samantha fetched a clean set of linens. She helped Anna roll to one side of the bed and pulled the sheets free on the empty half, then shifted Anna to the bare mattress and removed the sheets completely. She remade the bed the same way, moving Anna back and forth gently.

"I'll ruin—the mattress—if there's not something—under me," Anna panted as the pains came fast and hard. With each one, a trickle of wetness seeped from Anna's body.

Samantha dashed to the kitchen, snatched up a pile of newspaper, and came back to place layers of paper on the bed, then covered them with a cotton sheet. As Anna sank back on the pallet of paper, it crinkled beneath her, and Samantha asked, "Is it uncomfortable?"

Anna shook her head with a winced smile. "It's nothing—compared to this." She held her belly with both hands. Her back arched and she clenched her teeth. "Here comes another one!"

Samantha clasped Anna's tummy too, rubbing lightly with her open palms. Beneath her hands, muscles contracted, then relaxed as Anna's body fought to bring forth the child. Samantha ran her hands comfortingly over the hard mound of flesh until she felt the muscles calm. She looked at Anna. Her eyes were closed, her lips parted, and she was breathing shallowly. "Anna, are you all right?"

Weakly, Anna nodded. "It isn't going to be long now. I can tell—the pressure. . . . We need to be ready, Sam."

Samantha's heart pounded against her ribcage. "What do I do?"

"Get some . . . scissors . . . and clean towels. And some string. You'll find everything you need . . . in the kitchen. Put some water on to boil. . . . We'll need to . . . get the baby warm . . . right away." Anna lurched upright and clutched Samantha's dress front with more strength than Samantha would have thought possible. She ordered harshly, "The baby comes first, Sam! Don't be worrying over me—just take care of the baby, you hear?"

Samantha promised fervently, "I will, Anna. I'll take care of the baby."

Anna fell back on the mattress, limp. While she was relaxed, Samantha ran to the kitchen and gathered the things Anna had listed. She set two big pots of water on the stove to boil, then placed clean towels, scissors, and string in a basket. Once the pots were getting warm to the touch, she scooped up the basket and raced back to the bedroom. She rounded the corner, and came up short at the sight. Anna's hands were above her head, wrapped around the iron rails of the headboard so tightly Samantha expected the bars to be bent. Her head was thrown back, her face twisted in a terrible expression. Samantha dropped her bundle and ran to Anna.

"I-i-it's c-c-coming!" Anna cried out.

And when Samantha looked, she gasped. A cap of dark hair! "Oh, Lord in heaven, help me!" Samantha prayed aloud as she positioned herself between Anna's knees, her hands ready to cup the tiny head when it emerged.

Anna panted heavily, giving instructions, "When . . . the head comes . . . you have to . . . clear its mouth. With your fingers." Anna arched again with the next pushing contraction, her hips leaving the mattress. She made a strange grunting sound, and suddenly Samantha was holding the baby's head. It seemed as if the baby would be strangled, and Samantha thought her heart would jump from her chest, it pounded so hard. She prayed constantly—*Let the baby be all right. Let Anna be all right*—as she opened the baby's mouth and scooped with two fingers inside.

With the next push, the shoulders came free, and Samantha cradled the little head in her hands until suddenly the whole body wiggled through, and Samantha was holding a tiny, perfect baby girl with spindly arms and legs that sprawled in every direction. Samantha breathed open-mouthed in short, hard spurts. *Oh, Lord, a girl! It's a girl!* "It's a girl, Anna!" she rejoiced, unable to take her eyes off of the red, wrinkled baby in her hands.

Anna panted and shook. "T-tie the c-cord, Sam. Then we h-have to m-make sure she's b-b-breathing."

Samantha's chest clutched. She placed the unmoving baby on the mattress and brought the basket to the bed. She snipped two pieces of string, tying off the ropelike umbilical cord twice—once close to the baby's round tummy, and again two inches further out.

"C-cut the cord, Sam."

Samantha shakily obeyed. A snip, and the baby girl was on her own. She picked up the infant. The swollen eyes remained closed, the little mouth puckered, as she lay limp in Samantha's hands. Samantha held her by the back of the head and her bottom and willed fearfully, "Breathe, baby. C'mon—breathe!"

Her mind raced—what should she do? She looked to Anna for help, but poor Anna was lying back with her eyes closed, quivering from the shock of the birth. There'd be no help from that direction. Samantha scrambled to recall the ways she'd heard doctors used to make a baby cry—a sharp slap or a dash of cold water? How could she do something so harsh to some-one this small and helpless? But somehow she had to scare the baby into taking a breath.

With sudden inspiration, she took a firm grip on the tiny in-fant, then swooped the little body through the air, ending with a jerk. The baby's tiny arms flew outward, her back arched, and she opened her mouth, sucking in a great gulp of air. With the release of the breath, she began to cry in a pitiful, mewling fashion. Samantha burst out with a half laugh, half sob. "Anna, she's breathing! And listen! She's crying!"

Anna's eyes opened and she smiled weakly. "It's l-like m-m-music." Both women listened to the baby for a moment, then Anna said, "Wr-rap her up, Sam. Keep her w-w-warm." Anna shivered so hard she could hardly talk. "Th-then w-we need t-to d-d-deliver the af-afterbirth."

Samantha wrapped the baby securely in two thick towels, then laid her carefully on the bed beside her mother. The tiny girl continued to cry in soft, hiccupping sounds as Samantha saw to Anna's needs. Afterward, she covered Anna with a heavy blanket. "I'll give the baby a bath, then I'll be back. Is there any-thing I need to know about that?" But Anna's eyes were closed, and she did not respond.

Samantha picked up the infant once more and carried her to the kitchen. She poured some of the boiling water into a basin, adding cool water until the temperature felt perfect against her inner wrist. She found some gentle hand soap, more dry towels, and placed the baby gently into the water, keeping a hand behind the small head to steady her.

Washing a newborn proved to be even more of a challenge than she'd thought. There were so many little crannies to clean, and the baby was completely uncooperative, coiling up like a morning glory blossom at sunset and complaining through the whole event. Samantha found herself chuckling softly as she pulled out a little arm and washed all the creases, then watched it fold back. "There's no need to take on so," Samantha cooed as she rinsed away the soap with warm water. The baby continued to sob in soft, raspy sounds that lifted her little chest jerkily. Samantha went on in a kind, soothing tone, "You sure know how to let a person know you're disgruntled! I imagine your parents are going to have their hands full with you."

Samantha couldn't stop smiling. How wonderful it felt to be running her hands over the silky newborn skin, listening to the sympathy-inducing cry, trying to calm and reassure the little one. She'd never performed a more satisfying task. When the baby was clean and dry, diapered and dressed in a soft flannel gown that tied closed at the bottom with a ribbon, Samantha held her snugly in the crook of her arm. The little girl had finally stopped fussing and seemed to look back at Samantha with wide, crossed eyes of darkest blue. Joy coursed through Samantha's chest. She touched a downy lock of hair on the baby's slightly misshapen head. "You're a precious thing. You and I are going to be good friends, little one."

With slow steps she returned to the bedroom, reluctant to take the infant back to her mother. But Anna slept, her mouth hanging slack from exhaustion. She roused, though, when Samantha placed the tiny bundle against her side. Anna touched the baby's cheek, and the little girl turned her face, her lips open and seeking. Anna laughed softly. "Hungry already? You're going to be like your daddy, I can tell."

Samantha watched Anna open her gown and place the baby against her breast. At once the infant found what she wanted and began sucking softly, one tiny hand slipping from the blanket to lie curled against Anna's neck. Something welled within Samantha's own breast at the sight, and tears stung her eyes. "I'll leave you two to get acquainted." Samantha gathered up the soiled bedding and headed for the door.

"Sam?"

Samantha half turned, looking toward the bed but not directly at Anna. "Yes?"

"Thank you. I can't tell you how grateful I am that you came, that you were here."

Samantha shifted her gaze until her eyes met Anna's squarely. A smile trembled on the corners of her lips. "I am, too, Anna. I feel like—" She paused, searching for words to describe all of the emotions that boiled inside of her. At last she finished, "I feel as though I've been part of a miracle."

Anna smiled, too—a soft, expression of understanding. "You have been."

Samantha left, closing the door quietly behind her. She placed the pile of sheets in a basket on the service porch and straightened the kitchen. As she put away the last pan, she heard the rattle of a wagon entering the yard, and she ran outside. Adam was driving the team with his mother on the seat beside him holding Laura Beth. The three looked at Samantha expectantly, but she couldn't speak. Not yet. She stood beside the wagon with satisfaction rolling through her.

Adam tipped his head, his brows pulling together. "What exactly has gone on here? You look as if . . . well, as if you just got nominated for president."

"Better than that." She lifted Laura Beth from her grandma's lap. "You got your wish, sweetie. If you go in to Mama, you'll get to meet your new baby sister."

Laura Beth's eyes flew wide. She wiggled free of Samantha's grasp and ran to the house, her little braids flopping.

Laura hovered half off the wagon seat gaping at Samantha and speechless for the first time in Samantha's memory. "You mean—the baby—did you—?"

Samantha laughed. "Yes, I did! And she's a beauty."

Laura fell back on the seat, a hand fluttering near her chest. Then she broke into a wide smile, hopped down, and trotted to the house, her skirts held high.

Adam stared at Samantha, then eased himself down and stepped toward her as if his boots were made of concrete blocks. "I sent Pa after the doctor and Frank. We figured the baby was coming, and he'd want to be here. But you . . .? Already?"

Taking Adam's hand, she said, "Would you like to come inside and meet our new niece?"

Adam nodded, but he didn't move. His voice filled with awe, he said, "Did you really deliver the baby, Sammy?"

Samantha threw back her head with laughter that captured all the joy and relief she was feeling. "Yes, Adam, I delivered her. And it was . . ." More feelings rushed over her and words escaped her. All she could do was smile—a beaming smile of wonder.

"Oh Sam . . ."

Samantha threw herself against her husband, wrapping her arms around him and laughing against his neck. "Adam, I delivered her, and gave her a bath, and talked to her until she stopped crying, but it was so wonderful to hear her cry for the first time! Oh, she's just so tiny and so perfect!"

Adam held her close, running a hand up and down her back, his cheek warm against her hair. After several minutes, he tugged at a loose strand of hair and whispered, "I'd like to go see this tiny, perfect baby my amazing wife just helped bring into the world."

Samantha laughed again, giving Adam one last squeeze, then caught his hand, and they ran together into the house, laughing some more as their feet pounded the hard-packed earth.

dam curved his arm around his wife's waist and escorted her to the bedroom where his mother perched on the edge of the bed, gazing with delight at the baby nestled in the bend of Anna's arm. Little Laura Beth knelt beside Anna's hip. "Oh, Mama, she's a little dolly!" Laura Beth exclaimed. "I want to play with her."

"No, sweetie, not a dolly," Anna corrected gently. "You can't play with her yet, but it won't be long before she'll be a good playmate for you."

Laura Beth hugged her mother's neck then said matter-of-factly, "I want a cookie."

The grown-ups laughed, and Adam gave Samantha's waist a squeeze. "What about you? Do you need a reward, too? After all, you had quite a morning."

Samantha moved to the bed and placed a hand on Anna's arm. "Anna did all the work. I just happened to be here."

Anna shook her head. "There's no need for modesty, Sam. Delivering a baby is certainly no small feat."

"But it's still easier than having one, I think," Samantha said.

"Perhaps," Anna sighed. "I'm worn out. It all happened so fast!"

Adam considered leaving the woman alone with this "female" discussion, but before he could make a move, a door slammed open and Frank's voice carried through the house, "Anna! Anna, where are you?"

Adam stepped into the kitchen doorway. "She's in the bedroom, Frank, and stop yelling. You'll wake the baby."

His brother's jaw dropped. "The baby!" Adam stepped back as Frank charged into the bedroom. Frank sank onto his knees next to the bed and took Anna's hand. Dr. Newton hurried in on Frank's heels.

Samantha eased past Adam and took Laura Beth with her for the cookie, but Adam couldn't pull himself away from watching the little scene and his brother's reaction. Frank grasped the edge of the blanket and pulled it down, then stared in wonder at his offspring. His work-toughened finger looked huge in comparison to the tiny baby. "What kind of baby is it?" he whispered.

"A girl." Anna seemed to search Frank's face. "Are you disappointed?"

Disappointed? Adam knew Frank had hoped for a son, but how could anyone be disappointed in something so small and perfect?

Frank's gaze went from the baby to Anna, and he stroked her cheek. "Never." He gave her a lingering kiss. At their shared moment of bliss, something rose inside Adam. Could it be jealousy? After all he'd said to Samantha? He gripped his fists and willed the feeling to pass.

Dr. Newton cleared his throat. "Papa, if you'd move out of the way, I'd like to get a look at that baby myself."

Laura chuckled and stood to step away. Frank moved aside but hovered near as the doctor examined the little girl, making her cry again. The cry was more like a kitten's complaint, and Adam discovered tears stinging his eyes. Such a beautiful, heart-melting sound. A sound he'd wasn't likely to hear in his own home. . . .

"Well," the doctor declared, "she's a little small—probably not much more than five pounds. But she seems healthy in every way."

"Thank goodness for that," Anna murmured.

"Now all of you can move along while I check Anna over," the doctor ordered. "Except for you, Mrs. Klaassen."

Frank leaned down for one more kiss and a whispered "I love you" before he caught Adam's elbow and the two left the room. Adam and Frank joined Samantha and Laura Beth in the kitchen. Adam sank into a kitchen chair, and Samantha sank on to his lap. He wrapped his arms around her, and she leaned against him, resting her forehead against his. She was still sitting thus when Dr. Newton entered the kitchen and stopped before her with his hands akimbo. "Well, young woman, what have you got to say for yourself?"

Samantha stood, her eyes wide. "W-what do you mean?"

The doctor pointed a finger at her. "Anna tells me you helped deliver that little one in there. Now, I'll let you get by with that this time, but don't go making a habit of it. You'll put me out of business!"

Samantha laughed in obvious relief and held up her hands in a mock show of surrender. "I promise, Dr. Newton. Once was enough!"

Dr. Newton put a hand on Frank's shoulder. "Congratulations, Frank."

"Thank you, Doc." Frank shook the man's hand and headed right back to the bedroom.

The doctor leaned down and shook Laura Beth's small hand. "Congratulations to you, too, Laura Beth. You're a big sister now."

Laura Beth nodded solemnly, her mouth encircled with cookie crumbs.

"Congratulations to all of you." Dr. Newton's gaze encompassed everyone in the room. "But now I think I'll get back to town. I'm not needed here any longer."

Adam offered to walk him out, and both men stepped out-side, ambling toward the buggy. Before stepping up into the conveyance, the doctor turned to Adam. "I'm wondering how Samantha is doing, Adam."

The two men looked at each other, and the doctor scratched his chin. "I'm wondering how she's doing since her visit to Rochester."

Adam lifted a shoulder, then said, "She is probably doing as well as can be expected. Things that didn't used to bother her, though, can upset her these days."

Dr. Newton nodded, his spectacles reflecting the sun. "It may be worse for a while. Her involvement in that baby girl's birth . . . well, she seems awfully happy right now, but I'm sure when the joy of the moment wears off, this experience will heighten her awareness of what she's lost."

Adam looked back toward the house, remembering his wife's beaming smile as she met him in the yard. He also re-called the mixed emotions rumbling through his own chest when he'd witnessed Frank's joy. Yes, they both might struggle for a while.

"Just be watchful," the doctor advised. "She may need a bit of extra care and attention right now."

Adam turned back to the doctor. "Thanks, Dr. Newton. I'll keep that in mind."

Dr. Newton placed a hand on Adam's shoulder, his brows arched high. "And how are you with all of this?"

Adam appreciated the opportunity to admit he'd lost something too. "It's been tough. I'd always planned on a big family, you know."

"Well, give it time," the doctor advised. "And don't keep all those feelings inside. Talk to each other. It will do you both good."

Adam nodded. "Yes, it took us a while, but we're learning how to talk about this difficult subject."

Adam watched Doc's buggy until it turned on to the road, then he moved back toward the house. How would Samantha feel when the euphoria of the day wore off? He prayed this experience would remain a joyful memory for her.

Samantha seemed far from despondent when Adam found her in Frank and Anna's bedroom. She was circling Laura Beth on her lap with one arm, her other hand clasping Anna's. As Adam entered the room, Sam looked up with a smile that lit her whole face. "Oh, Adam, guess what they've named the baby!" She didn't wait. "Kate Samantha! I have a little namesake now too!"

Adam remembered the pride he'd felt when his sister Liz had announced that one of their twin boys would be Adam James—A.J. for short. He smiled his thanks to Frank and Anna for honoring Samantha in such a way. "Kate Samantha, huh?" Adam said, placing his hands on Sam's shoulders. "She looks a little bit like you, too," he remarked.

Samantha smiled upward. "Really?" And how do you figure that—?"

"Yep." Adam pointed. "Look—her hair is standing on end just like yours does when you get up in the morning."

"Oh, Adam!" She laughed along with everyone else.

"It's a beautiful name, Anna and Frank," Adam said seriously. "And I hope your little Kate Samantha grows up to be as beautiful as this Samantha." He gave his wife a kiss, and Samantha's cheeks turned rosy.

∼♁

On the way home, Adam sent Samantha occasional sidelong glances. So far she was smiling and humming softly as they jounced along on the wagon seat. Maybe this day would signal the turning point, returning Sam back to her cheerful, peaceful self.

Beside him, Samantha shivered.

"Cold?"

She hugged herself. "A little."

"Well, come here." He lifted an arm, and she slid over. They rode in silence for several minutes, Adam holding her close.

Samantha tipped her head up toward him with a wistful expression. "Adam?"

"Yes?"

"After today I don't think I'll ever be the same."

"What do you mean?"

Samantha pursed her lips. "I helped bring a new life into the world. Honestly, when I saw that baby—that perfect little person—slip into my hands, I felt like I was holding a little piece of heaven. I was—I can't describe it. I was so *full*. . . ." She stopped and shook her head. "I don't know how to say it."

Adam tightened his hold around her waist.

She looked at him, longing in her eyes. "Do you think that's how Anna feels now? So full she can't describe it?"

Adam was uncertain how to answer. "Honey, I don't know. I can't begin to imagine how Anna is feeling right now. But I can tell you how I feel." He gave Samantha a smile. "I am so proud of you. What you did today took so much courage and spunk. I remember when Liz had the twins—just being in the house, knowing what was happening, was enough to scare the pants off of me! But you—you actually delivered a baby." He kissed the end of her nose. "You amaze me."

Samantha ducked her head and picked at the fringe on her shawl. "It went so fast, there wasn't time to be afraid. And afterwards, all I could think was—" She lifted her head, and her eyes were bright with tears. "All I could think was how lucky Anna was, in spite of the pain of the delivery. To create a new life . . ." She broke off, biting on her lower lip. Tears spilled down her cheeks.

His heart turned over. "Sammy—"

"I'm not feeling sorry for myself, Adam. Truly I'm not." She drew in a shuddering breath and whisked the tears away with her fingertips. "I'm grateful to have been there. It was a gift— something I will never forget. And I think little Kate Samantha will always be extra special to me because I was there when she was born." She straightened her shoulders. "If we hurry home, I'll have time to sweep out the upstairs bedrooms and the parlor, and close them up for the winter months."

Adam looked at her, startled. "Already? But it's only early October."

Samantha shrugged. "But it's cold. And it won't be getting warmer for a while. There's no point in heating rooms that aren't being used. It's time."

Adam watched as she turned her face forward, looking determined. He knew better than to argue with her. Samantha was closing doors—both literally and figuratively. And maybe, he conceded, it was time.

Chapter Sixteen

*I*t turned out Adam had to admit that winter had arrived early this year. He stood at the kitchen window, a cup of hot, black coffee in his hand, watching a flurry of snowflakes whirl past the frosted pane. Though he usually put off such chores until November, he'd already weatherized the henhouse with bales of hay and brought the livestock into the corral close to the barn so they could sleep inside nights.

Samantha's insistence on closing off the unused rooms of the house early proved to be wise. It took a heap of coal in the cellar furnace to warm the large kitchen and their own upstairs bedroom—keeping a flame going to make the other rooms bearable would have been an all-day task.

October had slipped by so quickly, he wondered where it had gone. The annual postharvest celebration had taken place as usual, but for the first time in his memory, he hadn't attended. Samantha had complained of a headache, but he suspected it was more heartache that had kept her home. She didn't say much, but he knew it was still difficult for her to be in places where mothers cradled infants, bragging back and forth about Susie's new tooth or Jimmy's first steps. He understood, and he didn't push her. Two steps forward and one step back was still getting her further along in her emotional healing than he could have hoped for.

In his mind, the idea of adoption still ran strong. A call to Daniel, and a baby no doubt could be theirs, and she would be in the circle of mothers who proudly showed off their offspring.

But whenever he was brave enough to hint at it, she would simply nod and change the subject.

Whenever they were together with any of Adam's siblings or her brother, Samantha was her laughing, smiling self, spending most of her time with the youngest family members. All of the children loved their Auntie Sam! And she loved them back, willingly playing games or telling stories or singing their silly songs with them. She never tired of it and was happiest surrounded by the little ones. Adam had come to memorize those scenes, drawing on them during the hours that would at times follow the visits—when she would sit in her rocker with tears of silent sorrow drying on her cheeks.

He now turned from the window and crossed to the stove. Holding his cooling cup between his palms, he stared at the flicker of fire between cracks in the stove lid and considered the upcoming Thanksgiving holiday. The family would all come together at his parents' home. There would be children underfoot, babies crying, and much chaos. He relished it—he'd grown up with it and eagerly awaited the reunion times when all of his brothers and sisters were under the same roof once more. He knew Samantha would go most willingly, would enjoy her time with them, but what about afterward? Would the memories of the happiness between parents and children once again rub salt into the wound in her heart?

He thought back to the day that little Kate Samantha had been born. Samantha had been over the moon, proud to have played a part in the baby's entrance into the world. The elation had carried her for several days, giving Adam hope that the depression was behind them, that she had finally been willing to accept their circumstances and seek happiness in other areas.

But the reality that the same joy Anna had would not be hers had come crashing down around her. That day had seen the start of new cycles of highs and lows that wore terribly on both hers and Adam's emotions.

It hurt him, seeing her in pain, but when would it end? Couldn't God give them the inner healing they needed? He wiped the back of his hand across his eyes and sloshed another half cup of coffee into his mug. A creaking on the stairs caught his attention, and he turned to see Samantha standing on the lowest riser, her hand draped across the railing. Her robe hung open—mute evidence of her listless state.

He put down his coffee cup and crossed to her. "Honey, it's too cold to come down like this," he scolded gently, pulling the robe closed and tying the belt. "You'll catch your death."

Her gaze dropped to her bare toes curled over the edge of the step. "I'm sorry. I didn't think."

Determined to bring her out of her melancholy, he rubbed noses with her and teased, "Well, that's obvious. You've lived through enough Minnesota winters to know you don't run around barefoot with your robe flapping." He lifted her into his arms, moving over to the rocker that always sat in the corner of the kitchen during the winter months. She sat in his lap, her legs across one arm of the chair, his arm providing support for her back. He captured one of her hands and turned his face to kiss her knuckles.

"Ah," he sighed, setting the chair into motion, "this is cozy. We haven't shared the rocking chair much since we moved out of the dugout. Remember how many evenings we spent like this?"

Samantha gave a small smile in response, nodding slightly.

Adam chuckled. "Lots of times my legs went to sleep, and I had a hard time walking to bed after you got off my lap."

She sat up and looked at him, a spark of interest in her eyes. "Really? You never said anything."

Adam tightened his grasp and admitted, "Because I was afraid if you knew, you'd never sit with me again. But it was worth it." He buried his face in her tousled hair, and she leaned against him, sighing deeply. The wind whistled outside, rattling window panes, but the kitchen was warm and smelled of fragrant coffee.

Suddenly she sat forward again. "Adam, can you stay home with me today?"

He feigned shock. "Why, Mrs. Klaassen, are you propositioning me?"

A small smile quivered on her lips. "Don't be silly." She shook her head at him. "Just because I'm sitting on your lap and asking you to stay at home with me doesn't mean I'm, well, propositioning you."

Adam pretended to be crestfallen. "Oh."

Samantha gave his chest a little push with the heel of her hand. "It gets lonely here, you know, all day by myself. . . ."

Her winsome confession tore at Adam's heart. If only . . . But there was just Samantha and Adam. It would have to be enough. Today, he decided, there was nothing more pressing than proving to her the two of them could be enough. "All right, Sammy." He lifted a strand of her hair and used it to tickle her chin. "I'll stay home with you today. But I'm not going to sit here and hold you all the time. My legs are already asleep!"

"Oh, you!" she exclaimed indignantly, swinging her legs down and lifting her arm over his head in one smooth motion. "Are you saying I'm too heavy?"

He laughed as she stood to her feet. "Go get some socks on," he ordered, aiming a playful swat at her rear, "and put on some chorin' clothes. We'll see to the animals, then we'll fritter the rest of the day away, just us."

She reached the stairs in four skips, but she paused with one foot on the first riser and looked at him over her shoulder. "Thank you, Adam."

He smiled and nodded. "This was an easy request for a yes. Now go."

She turned and ran lightly up the stairs. He gazed after her as she disappeared around the turn. She'd see—they could be happy, just the two of them. He'd prove it to her.

〜⟲

The day turned out to be nothing particularly special—just a together day that was memorable in its simplicity. Samantha accompanied Adam to the barn. While he milked Bessie, she played with the new batch of barn kittens, laughing at their antics. She insisted on leaving a sardine can of milk for them. When the kittens stood in a circle around the can with their tails sticking straight up over their little backs and the biggest of the group with one paw in the milk, she sent Adam a smile that came straight from her heart. And he winked back, his jaw pressed against the cow's flank, content.

They walked hand in hand to the chicken coop, gave the fowl fresh water and feed, and gathered the eggs. A good-natured contest on who could find the most eggs—the hens never laid them in the roosting boxes, but in the oddest places—sent them scrambling and laughing all over the coop. The loser, Adam, paid the winner, Samantha, a kiss of forfeit that was as much a reward as a penalty.

Back inside, they warmed up with steaming coffee, fried eggs still warm from the coop, and ate Samantha's homemade bread, which Adam toasted. After breakfast, Samantha took a soak in the tub, and Adam generously offered to wash her back.

She grinned and teased, "Now who's propositioning whom?" Adam threw back his head and laughed, delighted to see the sparkle in her eyes.

When Samantha was dressed, they opened the parlor, lit a fire in the fireplace, and spent a pleasant hour curled together on the sofa in front of a snapping flame, reading the paper aloud to each other. Adam, in a burst of silliness, intentionally twisted words around to make the more boring news items interesting. Samantha laughed until she held her stomach and finally begged, "Adam, stop! I can't take anymore!"

Adam tugged her over beneath his chin. "All right, I'll be good."

A bit of husband-and-wife spooning followed that took up the better part of another hour. By then the fire had died down, and a chill crept around them. Reluctantly, they scooped out the coals and closed the parlor up again, heading to the kitchen to chop vegetables for a pot of chicken soup.

"Thanks, but I can do this," Samantha said when brown scraps from potatoes Adam peeled littered her once-clean floor.

"Uh-uh." He shook his head, whacking the knife down again. "You asked me to spend the day with you, so with you I will be." He dropped a handful of cubed potatoes into the large pot on the stove, sending splashes of the broth over the edge.

Samantha squealed and jumped back. "Adam, be careful!" Grabbing a rag, she went after the mess.

Adam deliberately exaggerated indignity in his tone. "I'm only trying to help."

"Well, I already had my bath," she retorted, dropping the rag into the sink. He caught her around the middle from behind, and she shrieked as he spun her around and captured her against his chest. "Adam, I need to put the carrots in." But she made no attempt to free herself.

"The carrots can wait." He grinned down at her, lost in the delicate color of her eyes. Samantha tipped her head sideways, releasing an airy sigh. Adam asked, "Happy?"

Samantha nodded slowly, a warm light deepening her eyes to the color of a cardinal's wing. "Very much so."

"Me, too." Adam rocked her side to side—left, right, left again—before adding, "I'm also hungry. Let's go ahead and get those carrots in the pot." Tomatoes, cabbage, onions, garlic, and chicken pieces followed the carrots. Soon the kitchen was aromatic with the scent of the stew. Adam lifted the lid every few minutes, sticking his nose over the pot. "How long till this is done? My stomach is growling."

Samantha laughed. "You and your appetite. It won't be long now."

"How long?" he pressed.

Samantha peeked in the pot, spooned out a carrot slice and bit through it. "Another twenty minutes," she guessed.

"Twenty minutes! Twenty minutes?" Adam held his stomach and stumbled around the kitchen in a dramatic display. "A man could starve in twenty minutes!"

Samantha snatched up a slice of bread. "Then here you go—eat if you must!" She threw the bread across the kitchen, striking him on the forehead in a flurry of crumbs. He grabbed at it and mock-fumbled it for several seconds before he finally triumphantly clutched it above his head. Samantha doubled over in laughter.

"You little *Spitzmaus!*" He thumped the slice down on the table and came after her.

She let out a squeal. "Adam, no!" They played cat-and-mouse around the kitchen table, with Adam rumbling, "I'm gonna get you," and Samantha begging for mercy. At last he lunged, catching her around the waist and swinging her off the floor.

She clutched his neck, laughing in his ear. "I'm sorry, I'm sorry!" she giggled.

"Sure you are, now that I've got you." Adam grinned wickedly into her upturned face.

"So what are you going to do with me now that you've captured me, Adam dear?"

"I think . . . maybe . . . this . . ." And very slowly he lowered his face, watching until her eyes slid closed in readiness for his kiss. But instead he nipped her lightly on the end of her nose.

"Hey!" She struggled to get out of his arms.

Adam caught her again in a hug of happiness. "That was for throwing food at me, my little spitfire." This time when he lowered his head, the kiss was loving and long. The soup was left to simmer for quite some time after the vegetables were done.

༄

After a nice supper in the warm kitchen and tidying up together, Adam ran out to the barn for final chores while Samantha got two more loaves of bread ready to rise overnight and bake in the morning. Later in their room, Adam leaned across Samantha and turned the key on the bedside lamp, plunging the room into darkness. He flopped on to his pillow, his hand roaming in search of hers. She met it, holding tight, and he released a lengthy *ahhhh* of pleasure.

Samantha gazed at the outline of his face in the faint moonlight. Even with shadows across his face, she could see that his expression was relaxed, his lips uptilted. "It was a good day, Adam." She grazed the underside of his arm with her fingertips. "Thank you for it."

"Thank *you* for it," Adam replied, placing their clasped hands on his chest. He tugged a bit, and she rolled sideways, curling against his side. He chuckled. "Being with you sure beats clean-ing barns!"

"I'm not sure I like that comparison, Mr. Adam Klaassen!" They laughed together, then she asked, "Is that what you were planning to get done today? Maybe I shouldn't have asked—"

"I could have done it today," he put in quickly, "But, then, I can do it tomorrow. It wasn't a life-and-death matter that the barn get a shoveling out today."

Samantha scooted a bit closer and nestled against his shoulder. "Well, then, I'm sure glad you agreed."

They lay in quiet contentment for several minutes, warm and drowsy. Just as she was drifting off, Adam nudged her shoulder. "Sam?"

"Hmm?"

"Today . . . all the horsing around we did . . . You enjoyed it, didn't you?"

She took in a deep breath, sweet memories of their day flooding her mind. "Of course I did, Adam. It was a wonderful day—all of it."

"I was just thinking—" His voice held a hesitance that sent a prickle along Samantha's scalp. "If . . . if there were . . . others . . . in the house, we wouldn't have been able to have a day like today. Sometimes it's kind of nice, having you all to myself."

Samantha's heart constricted. She recognized his inten-tion, and tears of gratefulness built behind her eyelids. He was so good to her! *Oh, my sweet Adam, you try so hard to make me believe I can be everything to you when I know how much you too want a family. Your heart hurts too, yet you only worry about me. And I can make things so difficult for you. . . .*

She didn't know how to change what was in her heart, or even if she ever could let go. But she knew what she could do. She could let Adam know how much he meant to her.

She stretched her arm across his chest and hugged him tight. "I like having you to myself, too. You're the best thing that's ever come into my world, outside of God's forgiveness. I love you." She felt his lips against her hair, and she closed her eyes, savoring the secure, loved feeling his touch evoked.

"But, Adam?"

"Yes, Sam?"

"It still makes me sad sometimes."

Adam gathered her close and kissed the top of her head again. "I know, sweetheart. I know. Me too."

She blinked away tears and kissed the underside of his jaw. "But I promise—no crying tonight. I won't spoil our wonderful day with sadness." She could give him that small gift, at least.

He whispered, "Thank you, darlin'."

dam was carrying a stack of dishes to the dry sink in his parents' home, and he paused to bend down attentively to his nephew and niece. A.J. coaxed his little sister. "Tell Uncle Adam, Amanda, tell him what's a turkey say?"

Amanda, just past two years old, stared into Adam's face and puckered up to blow bubbles.

"Ew!" Andy, A.J.'s six-year-old twin, wrinkled his nose. "That's really icky!"

"She knows how to make a turkey sound," A.J. assured Adam. "She's just being stubborn." He scooped Amanda off the floor, holding her tight against his chest. "C'mon, Andy, let's go teach her somethin' else."

The two boys trotted around the corner with Amanda bobbing against her brother's shoulder.

Liz called, "Careful with her on the stairs, boys."

"Yes, Ma!" they chorused.

Pa had gotten up to pour himself another cup of coffee and chuckled. "Liz, it looks like Amanda is going to be as much of a show-off as her mother."

"Now, Pa," Liz retorted, "the only show-off in this family is Arn, and you know it."

Arn's fiancée, Martha, turned from the sink and nodded emphatically. "Oh, he sure is. I know he wouldn't be too shy to tell everyone what a turkey says."

Arn rose from the table, snitching the last two pickled beets from a relish plate on his way, and strutted toward Martha with his thumbs in his armpits, waving his elbows up and down and gobbling merrily. She flapped a hand at him, embarrassed, as he pranced around her in bent-knee fashion, bobbing his head, and emitted a distant imitation of a turkey's call.

From the parlor where the daughters and daughters-in-law had banished her for a much-needed break after all the Thanksgiving preparations, Ma called out, "Pluck that ol' tom, and we'll serve him for supper!"

Everyone roared with laughter. Even Arn dropped his pose to slap his knees and chortle.

"Yep, the family show-off, that's Arn." Adam chuckled. He plopped his load onto the sink and headed for the table to gather more, side-stepping around others helping with the cleanup. The kitchen of his childhood home was filled with Klaassen offspring, big and small. He found it noisy, crowded . . . and wonderful.

Ma charged through the kitchen doorway, waving her arms. "All right, I've sat long enough. You all clear out now so I can organize the mess. When everything is stacked and ready for washing, I'll recruit your help—a few at a time."

Adam and the others were unwilling to abandon Ma to the task, but she turned firm and shooed them out. Adam trailed Samantha and the others to the parlor. Just as he and Samantha sank onto the settee together, a crash sounded from overhead, followed by a frightened wail.

"Uh-oh." Josie looked upward, and she and Liz hurried for the stairs.

Samantha ran after them, holding out a hand. "Oh, please, let me go. You two take a little break from rescuing."

Liz and Josie glanced at her and at each other, then Liz nodded. "All right, go ahead, Sam—and thanks."

Josie walked into the kitchen, but Liz marched across the parlor and plunked herself down next to Adam. "So, baby brother," she demanded in her typically straightforward fashion, "how is it going with our Samantha these days?"

Adam chuckled. "I suppose it would be pointless to tell you to mind your own business?"

"Yes, it would be."

"How 'bout I plead the Fifth Amendment?"

After a punch on his shoulder, Liz prodded gently, "I wouldn't ask if I didn't care."

Adam gave his sister a one-armed hug. "I know, but I don't know what to say. Some days are very good, and some days . . . Well, some days aren't so good. I think she's arrived at a measure of reluctant acceptance, but I'm not sure she'll ever find real peace."

Liz's brown eyes were as soft as velvet as her gaze settled on Adam's face. "I worry about you. Everyone is concerned about Samantha—and I am, too!—but you lost something, too, and you are the one who must bear the brunt of things. How are you doing with all of this?"

Adam chewed the inside of his cheek for several seconds before replying, "It's tough, certainly. Especially on days like this when we're all together. I see all of you with your kids, and I think, I wish that's what Sam and I had. But then I think of Uncle Hiram and Aunt Hulda, how they never had children of their own and managed to be happy about it. I love your kids and all the other little ones running around here, and I think I can find my happiness in being Uncle Adam, if that's how things turn out."

"Can you really?" Liz's question came softly.

His voice was equally soft as he parried, "Do I have a choice?"

Liz glanced around at the hubbub of activity before squeezing his knee. "Adam, I know you'd like to adopt a baby—"

Adam shook his head. "Don't say it, Liz. Samantha and I have discussed it, and she is adamantly opposed to such an idea. I will not force her to my way of thinking."

"But, Adam, surely—"

"Liz, no!" Adam faced his sister squarely. "I understand your concern, and I appreciate it. I know you and everyone else see adoption as the perfect solution to our problem. But Sammy doesn't share the view, and she's the one who must feel comfortable with it." Liz dropped her gaze, and her lips quivered. He gentled his tone. "It wouldn't be fair to bring home a baby that would not be accepted as truly ours, would it?"

Liz raised her head. "Of course not. I'd never wish such a life on a child." She sighed. "I'm sorry I was pushy. I just want you to be able to be a papa. You'd make such a wonderful father."

"I appreciate your vote of confidence, Liz. But I've come to realize there likely won't be any little ones calling me Papa. I can live with that—as long as I've got lots of little ones calling me Uncle Adam and looking up to me."

Small Laura Beth skipped into the parlor and captured Adam's hand. "Uncle Adam, we wanna play hide-an'-seek, but we need a counter. Andy was bein' it, but he keeps cheatin'. Would'ja come count?"

"Do you think you can trust me?"

Laura Beth nodded hard enough to make her curls bounce. "Uh-huh. And you can count to a hunnert!"

Adam winked at Liz. "That's good enough for me." He allowed Laura Beth to tug him toward the stairs. But as he rounded its bend toward the hide-and-seek game, he heard his sister say, "Adam, I hope you're being honest with me—and yourself. I hope being Uncle Adam truly is enough."

Before the family returned to their respective homes that Thanksgiving evening, Si gathered everyone around the table once more to carry out a Klaassen tradition—the official giving of thanks. Samantha eagerly joined the others, basking the happiness of the family day.

They joined hands, and Si smiled down the two lengths of the table. "Thanksgiving Day is a time for counting blessings. I count each and every member of this family as a special blessing, and I know we all have much to be thankful for. Let's share our reasons for thankfulness with one another." He looked to the other end of the table, at Laura. "Mother, you start."

Laura didn't need encouragement. "I'm thankful all of my children and grandchildren are able and willing to come home for Thanksgiving dinner. It's wonderful to have all of you here again."

Martha, on Laura's left, said, "I'm thankful to be included as a member of this family. I have truly come to love all of you."

Arn squeezed Martha's hand and said, serious for once, "I'm thankful that by this time next year Martha and I will be joined as husband and wife." To Martha's great embarrassment, but also a blush of pleasure, he kissed her right there in front of everyone.

All eyes turned to Teddy, next in line. Bashful but forthright, he surprised everyone by joshing, "I'm thankful Arn's getting married so I'll have a room to myself." His comment earned a round of chuckles before Sarah piped up, "I'm thankful for four days off from school."

Becky, eyebrows raise, directed her comments toward her younger sister. "I'm thankful for the school here in Mountain Lake, and that I'll be graduating next spring. My teachers have given me a wonderful base of knowledge and prepared me well for what lies ahead."

Sarah rolled her eyes, earning a meaningful glance from her father, before young Katrina said, "I'm thankful I'm getting my pern-a-ment teeth in so I can eat corn on the cob next spring."

Samantha, watching and listening to them all, experienced a swell of longing. With several deep breaths, she managed to calm her tumbling emotions.

Daniel smiled down at Katrina. "I'm thankful those teeth are strong and healthy, and that we all share good health and happiness."

On Daniel's left, Rose cuddled little Camelia. "I'm deeply grateful for the three little girls who call me Mama and the man who calls me honey."

Christina looked up at her mother. "I'm thankful for you, Mama." She leaned forward to peer around at Daniel. "And you, too, Papa." Rose placed her arm around Christina and gave her a squeeze.

They'd reached the head of the table and Si, who beamed around at the many faces. "So many thankful hearts around this table! I'm thankful for your positive spirits."

Frank, next, placed an arm around Anna and smiled down at the infant she held. "I think everyone knows what I'm thankful for this year—a new little daughter, who is healthy and strong. And the one who was there to help her be born." The family all looked at Samantha, and she smiled and ducked her head.

Anna nodded. "Our little Kate Samantha is as much a blessing as Laura Beth. And I'm extra thankful for the telephone Frank just had installed in the kitchen so I won't have to send one of my daughters for help if I'm ever in trouble again!" Knowing how forcefully Frank had opposed the ring-ing box, calling it an intrusion and a nuisance even though everyone else in the community was getting them, Samantha swallowed her smile. Anna's emergency had proved the necessity of such a modern contraption, especially out in their rural setting.

Laura Beth bounced in her seat. "I'm fankful for Auntie Sam helping Mama an' Katie, an' I'm fankful for my baby sister."

Adam nudged Samantha lightly on the shoulder and grinned at her. She smiled in return, then turned her attention to the twins, who were next. Andy and A.J. looked at each other blankly, and simultaneously scratched their heads. They both turned to Liz. Andy said, "I dunno know what to say, Ma."

Liz prompted, "What are you happy about today, son?"

The twins both broke into matching smiles and shouted in unison, "Gran'ma's pun'kin pie!"

Hearty laughter circled the table, and Samantha marveled that such small boys could consume so much pie—they'd each eaten three pieces after a full meal.

Jake shook his head in amusement at the look-alike pair seated between himself and his wife. Turning back to the others at the table, he added, "I'm thankful for the bounty of harvests the past few years, that I'm able to provide for the needs of my family."

Josie's husband, Stephen, went next. "I'm too am thankful for the farmers' bounty since your crops keep my mill in operation. Your successful harvest makes my business successful." He looked over Simon's head to Josie, who wore a soft, secret smile. He looked a question to her, and she gave a small nod. Stephen leaned down to whisper in little Simon's ear. Samantha pulled in a breath to steady herself.

Simon grinned up at his parents, pulled at a corner of his mouth shyly, then announced in his sweet voice, "Me an' Mama an' Papa are glad 'cause I'm gonna be a big bruvver."

After silence for just a few seconds, Laura jumped up and dashed to Josie, hugging her daughter from behind and whispering something in her ear. Daniel, Frank, and Adam rose to reach across the table and shake Stephen's hand. Becky and Martha exclaimed and offered their congratulations. Teddy scooped young Simon out of his chair and tickled him soundly while Sarah laughed. Si proclaimed they would need a bigger table next year. Anna and Rose immediately volunteered to make one, and the laughter that followed their mock offer was deafening.

Every Klaassen family member rejoiced with Josie and Stephen. From Si down to Amanda, they all smiled and cheered and clapped with happiness. Congratulations and questions about when the baby would come and whether Josie wanted a girl this time filled the room.

While the celebration resounded around her, Samantha kept a smile firmly in place as she rose with a final peek over her shoulder to be certain she was unnoticed, and slipped upstairs.

Chapter Eighteen

*S*amantha escaped to Adam's old room at the top of the landing. She sat on the faded patchwork quilt covering the feather mattress and bowed forward, hiding her face in her hands. Oh, how she wanted to celebrate. To add her congratulations to those being offered by everyone else in the family. But how could she ever form the words? She was sure it couldn't happen . . . not until her heart had healed.

Why, Lord? Why did they have to share this today, when I'd been enjoying myself and basking in the love of family? Why, once again, did something have to remind me of what I so dearly want?

Footsteps sounded in the hallway, and Samantha looked up, expecting to see Adam. But Laura entered the room. At her mother-in-law's tender expression tears overflowed, and she held her arms out in a silent bid for reassurance. Laura immediately sat beside her and wrapped her arms around Samantha's frame.

The older woman's dress held the aromas of their Thanksgiving meal—homey, comforting scents that spoke of family, of joy, of God. Samantha breathed deeply, seeking those pleasant memories from the many meals eaten around the Klaassen table. "Oh, Mother Klaassen, I'm so ashamed . . ." Samantha turned her face into Laura's shoulder. "I want to be happy. I love Josie, and I am happy for her, but—"

"But you're envious." Laura patted Samantha's back, her voice holding no recrimination, yet the disagreeable word stung.

Samantha pulled free and wiped her eyes. "I know it's truly awful."

"Nonsense, Samantha. It's honest. And no one can fault you for your feelings."

Samantha peered over at Laura. "You don't think it's wrong for me to feel bad for myself when I should feel joy for Josie?"

Her mother-in-law's gentle smile soothed like a balm. "I don't think there are wrong feelings, Sammy—only bad reactions to feelings."

Samantha's brow furrowed. "I don't understand."

Laura took Samantha's hand. "A person can't always control her feelings. Emotions are a part of us, and feelings of joy or sorrow or worry or envy are normal. It's foolish to think we won't have those different feelings from time to time. God gave us emotions, and we shouldn't deny them. But what we do with those feelings . . . ah, that's where we need to have control."

Samantha dropped her gaze to her lap. "So I shouldn't have run out like I did."

Laura tugged at Samantha's hand. "I'm not faulting you, Samantha. And I understand your wish that it would be you and Adam making such an announcement. But running upstairs and hiding won't help anything, *ne leefste*."

Tears again welled in Samantha's eyes at the endearment. How could Laura call her "dearest" when she behaved so . . . well, so selfishly? "But it's very hard! How do I get past these feelings of . . . of inadequacy? Every time I see a baby, or see Adam with one of his nieces or nephews, I feel as though I've let him down."

"Adam doesn't blame you. Nobody blames you, Samantha."

Sometimes Samantha wished at least Adam would. Perhaps it would give her reason for her anger, and thereby ease her guilt. "I know. He's wonderful to me—you all are—but I blame me. I feel so guilty that we can't have children."

Laura cupped Samantha's face in her hands and spoke softly, sweetly. "E*n leefste*, I think what hurts Adam even more than the loss of children is your withdrawals from him. He wants your happiness so desperately. And he can't really be happy—or accepting—if you are not."

Samantha did appreciate Laura's honesty—the woman spoke to her the way a mother might to a beloved but mistaken child. The kindly worded reprimand, though, settled into her heart like a stone. She couldn't have children, and she couldn't even mourn that fact without upsetting those she loved.

"Sammy, come with me, please," Laura said, standing and holding out her hand. "I want to show you something."

Puzzled, Samantha followed Laura down the hallway to her mother-in-law's bedroom. Laura knelt beside the bed, reached beneath it and withdrew a large leather album. "Come, sit." Laura seated herself on the edge of the bed and patted the spot next to her.

Samantha joined her, and Laura pushed the album across her lap until the spine pressed against Samantha's hip. When Laura flipped the book open to the first page, a faded photograph lay across Samantha's knees. Laura reached in front of Samantha to tap the picture with her finger. "This is Si and me, on our wedding day." She laughed. "My, I was such a nervous bride! Si and I didn't know each other very well, you see. In those days, very little contact was allowed between unmarried boys and girls, so although we believed we liked each other, we really were almost strangers."

Samantha looked at Laura in surprise. She would have never guessed that the couple who shared such a close and loving relationship had felt like strangers on their wedding day. Laura turned the page, revealing a picture of a chubby baby in a long white gown. "Daniel was born only ten months into our marriage." Laura stroked the picture lovingly, smiling down at the image. "Si was so excited when Daniel was born—his firstborn, and a son at that! He told me over and over how proud he was of me. And he said our family would be perfect if I was to have a daughter next."

Samantha's heart constricted. Why would Laura be doing this? She knew how much Samantha wanted exactly this. . . .

Laura shifted the book slightly and pointed to the photograph on the next page. "Only a little over a year later, Hannah came to us."

Hannah? Samantha's gaze quickly moved from the album to Laura's face. Who was Hannah?

"We had her such a short time—only four brief months before she went back to heaven."

Samantha looked again at the picture. The baby girl seemed tiny and wan even in the black and white photograph. Although the infant was propped in a rocking chair, weakness showed in the slump of her body, her head angled toward her shoulder. She lacked the sparkle in the image of her brother Daniel. Samantha swallowed the lump of sorrow forming in her throat. "What—what happened to her?"

Laura sighed, her gaze locked on the picture. "The poor little mite was weak from the start. She didn't nurse easily, and oh, how she cried and cried. . . . The doctors couldn't tell us much. They called it a failure to thrive. It was very hard—for both of us—when Hannah died."

Samantha examined Laura's profile. Tears glittered in her eyes, her throat convulsed, and her lips pressed into a firm, quivering line. Hannah must have been gone for over twenty-five years, yet Laura still missed her. Samantha took her mother-in-law's hand. "I'm sorry, Mother. I didn't know."

Laura gave Samantha a small smile. "We don't talk about our Hannah much—it hurts yet, you see. At the time a great part of that hurt was remembering Si's joyful proclamation after Daniel's birth how a little girl would make our family perfect. I felt as if I had let him down by bringing a sickly child into the world. It was a very . . . a very difficult time."

Samantha didn't know what to say, so she sat silent, staring down at the picture of the weak baby girl named Hannah whose parting had left a permanent void in Laura's heart. After several minutes, Laura lifted the page and carefully turned the page of Hannah's picture. On the next page was a little boy of perhaps four, holding a rosy-cheeked baby in his lap. Samantha recognized the older child immediately as Daniel, and she pointed. "This must be Frank, then."

"Yes. This is Frank when he was almost six months old. He came along two years after we lost Hannah. He was a roly-poly baby with a headful of dark curls and the biggest, brightest eyes—a beautiful, healthy baby." Laura took in a deep breath. "And, Samantha, I am sorry to tell you that I was so angry he was a boy I refused to name him."

Samantha mouth fell open in amazement. Laura, the perfect, loving mother, would not even give him a name? "I don't believe you!"

"Oh, yes." Laura met Samantha's gaze. "I was furious. I had specifically told the Lord I wanted a baby girl to replace the one I had lost, and here He went and gave me another son. I already had a son. I didn't want another son—I wanted a daughter. Si finally picked Frank's name on his own. We certainly couldn't give him the only name I had selected—Elizabeth Laurene. So Si named him Franklin for a favorite uncle of his. I think it was his way of telling me he wasn't at all disappointed that this baby was a boy. But it took me weeks to accept Frank."

Samantha sat in stunned silence, unable to believe the Laura she knew would behave in such a way.

Laura went on, "Looking back, I know how wrong I was. My feelings were honest. I was terribly disappointed that I hadn't gotten a replacement for the baby daughter I had lost. And that disappointment by itself wasn't wrong. But the way I handled it all certainly was. It was hurtful to Si, and hurtful to Daniel who was thrilled with his baby brother and couldn't understand his mama's angry tears, and it was especially hurtful to Frank who was so small and innocent and only wanted to be loved. Sometimes I think he developed a temper just to demand the attention I refused to give him for the first months of his life."

Samantha looked at Laura, surprised again. "You think a tiny baby could sense it?"

"Babies aren't stupid, Samantha." Laura shook her head, her face crunched in a rueful frown. "Frank cried more than any of his brothers and sisters, and as a small child was much more demanding. He got frustrated easily when things didn't go the way he wanted. I'm sure he sensed my resentment. And of course, none of it was his fault."

Samantha put her arm around Laura's shoulders. "Frank knows you love him, Mother."

Laura patted Samantha's knee. "Yes, I'm sure he knows that by now. But I had to put to rest my feelings of anger and guilt before I could love Frank for himself. I had to learn to put aside my resentment about Hannah's death before I could even realize how much I loved this new gift from God to our family."

Samantha considered what Laura had shared. In a way, it was similar to her own situation. She of course hadn't given birth to a child, but in a way she had lost one—she had lost the dream of bearing her own baby. And that resentment burned inside of her, tempering her reactions to everything around her.

Laura went on to the next page, this one of a curly haired baby with bright eyes and a laughing smile. "By the time

Liz—my little Elizabeth Laurene—arrived, I had come to realize that another baby would never replace Hannah in my heart, and I was ready to love another little boy, if that was how God chose to bless us. Of course, I was thrilled to have a daughter, as was Si.

"But another little girl didn't make up for the loss of Hannah. The emptiness I felt at her leaving me will always be a part of me, but it ceased to overpower the joy I felt at the arrival of each of my other children. One child can never replace another, but you can find a new and different happiness that is just as special in its own way." Laura paused, smiling softly into Samantha's eyes. "Do you understand, Sammy?"

Samantha blinked slowly, absorbing the words. "I think so." But how would Samantha find a replacement for the children she longed to have? She wasn't like Laura, who'd gone on to deliver eight healthy children after losing Hannah. Samantha's happiness and contentment would have to be found in something other than her own children. Perhaps that contentment was waiting downstairs in the forms of the nieces and nephews she loved so much. And Adam, of course. Always there was Adam, who gave her more joy than she could ever have imagined.

Samantha threw her arms around Laura. "Mother, thank you for telling me about Hannah. I'm so sorry you had to lose her, and I know it still hurts to think of her."

Laura squeezed Samantha close. "The pain lessens, Samantha, with the passing of time. Your pain will lessen, too, I promise you."

Samantha rose, squaring her shoulders resolutely. "I think I should go downstairs and tell Josie how happy I am for her."

Laura reached out to clasp Samantha's hand. "That's a very good idea. I'm proud of you."

Samantha proved her mother-in-law's pride by giving Josie a congratulatory hug and the sincerest wishes for a healthy, beautiful baby. "Would you like me to deliver the baby?" she asked to another chorus of family laughter.

Chapter Nineteen

By the first of the new year, 1924, Samantha felt as though she'd recovered her old contentment. Although there were still times her empty arms brought a pinch of sorrow, she'd set aside those previous hours of despondency and gained control over the unpredictable emotional swings. Christmas with the family had been a joyful occasion, and to her great relief no tears had followed. The nightly prayers with Adam, asking God to fill her so abundantly no emptiness could remain, had accomplished their goal. Peace settled once more over her little world.

At Adam's request, she began accompanying him to the barn while he performed the morning chores. She loved the hand-in-hand walk with her husband through sparkling drifts of snow, followed by together time in the warm barn. She fed the horses their buckets of oats while Adam milked the cow, and they exchanged the chitchat of the comfortably married that started their day in the most pleasant way.

On one morning in early January, Samantha carried her tea-towel embroidery to the barn and sat with Adam while he rubbed saddle soap into a leather saddle thrown across a sawhorse. Midway through her stitching—the image of a gray cat busily scrubbing clothes at a washtub—Adam stopped and slapped his forehead. "Oh, Sam, I just remembered something." He reached into his jacket pocket and withdrew an envelope, and he held it out to Samantha. She didn't often get mail and took it eagerly.

"When did this come? Oh, it's from Rose!" she exclaimed without waiting for his answer. Rose's letters were usually full of amusing anecdotes about the girls or interesting news items from the city.

"It came yesterday." Adam sheepishly rubbed a finger under his nose. "I forgot to give it to you."

She shot him a saucy look. "Well, then that means I'll just read it to myself, and you'll *maybe* get to read it later." She laughed at his scowl, then relented. "Will you open it for me please?"

Adam used his pocketknife to slit the envelope and handed it back to Samantha. She unfolded the peach-tinted pages, sank onto a pile of hay, and began to read aloud.

Dearest Adam and Sammy,

Things here are as hectic as usual! Christmas break is over, and the two older girls are back in school, so my days are quieter. But little Cami is managing quite nicely to fill my time. She's decided to be my kitchen helper—at least, her opinion of helping. Actually, she's quite a hindrance. Yesterday she dumped five pounds of flour in the sink, then tried to wash it down. Needless to say, it set up like cement! We had to have a man come out and open up the drain pipes. Oh, I scolded, and Cami howled and cried and said she was sorry, and despite all the trouble she's still my little helper. I simply haven't got the heart to send her away.

Samantha laughed, imagining the scene. Adam laughed, too, then said, "It's so good to see you enjoying Cami's antics." She understood his meaning, and she sent up a prayer of gratitude. He headed for the little tack room at the back of the barn, scaring a barn cat from one of the stalls. It scampered to

Samantha and preened itself against her knee. She absently scratched its ears as she read on to herself.

> We had something far less amusing happen, also. I'm sure you'll remember Esther, the young woman who came to the house to clean for us—you met her when you were here last August. She and her husband, Henry, were killed in a tragic automobile accident two weeks ago. It was a used vehicle but a brand-new purchase, their very first ride, and apparently they blew out a tire. Henry lost control of the auto and it rolled. The only blessing is that they were killed instantly and didn't suffer. But they leave behind four children—two girls and two boys, the youngest one only three months old. Since there are no other relatives, the children have been taken to the Foundling Home until homes can be located for them.
>
> Daniel says he is certain the baby and the littlest boy who is not quite two will be adopted quickly. People are always willing to take in infants. But my heart aches for the older two. They are already well past the age of "baby" and will probably spend the rest of their childhood in dreary institutions. It saddens me to think of the four being separated—they've already lost their parents, and now they'll likely lose one another.
>
> You might remember these little ones in your prayers, as we are doing.

Samantha dropped the letter to her lap and stared up at the barn ceiling. Why had Rose thought to write about such an unsettling event? Samantha remembered Esther—a plain-featured young woman with limp brown hair but with the largest, most expressive eyes. She'd seemed to seek approval, and Samantha recalled wondering what the poor woman was lacking in life to give her that little-girl-lost look.

Adam returned to the saddle cleaning, a fresh rag in his hand. "Sammy? Bad news?" he asked, looking at her with concern.

Samantha gave a start. "What?" She gathered her thoughts. "Oh—yes, I'm afraid it is."

"Is it Rose or the girls—?"

"No—no, nothing like that. It's about her cleaning lady, Esther. She was killed." Samantha briefly told Adam about the accident, then said, "They leave four children. Rose says they're at the Foundling Home, and Daniel thinks they'll find homes easily." Her recital wasn't quite accurate, but for some reason it was too difficult to go into more.

"How tragic." Adam shook his head, his expression solemn. "We'll have to remember them in our prayers."

"Yes, Rose asked us to." She gently pushed the cat from its purring coil at her feet and scooped up her embroidery hoop and thread. "I think I'll go get our lunch started. Anything in particular you'd like?"

"No, whatever you fix is fine, honey." Adam crossed the hay-strewn floor to plant a quick peck on her cheek. "Don't let the letter trouble you, Sammy."

Samantha managed a small smile, reaching up to curl one arm around his neck for a hug. "I'll holler when lunch is ready." The cat followed Samantha to the house, quick-stepping it over the cold snow. Although she rarely allowed the barn cats inside, she held the back door open. "Come on in. I'd appreciate the company."

She pressed her palm against the pocket which held Rose's letter. Four children—two girls, two boys. One baby, one toddler, and two past the baby age, but all needful of a mother's loving care . . . Rose had asked them to pray for the children, and Samantha certainly would, but she found herself more than curious. What were their names? How old was the first one? Old enough to be a surrogate parent to the younger ones? How were they getting along at the Foundling Home? She wished she had more information about them.

Pulling out the letter, she scanned it again, going on to read the second page as well. There was no more mention of Esther and Henry's orphaned children. Samantha hugged the letter to her breast. *Poor little ones* . . . Children shouldn't have to suffer such loss. She imagined the two youngest, especially, not knowing where the familiar faces of their parents had disappeared to . . . would they be coming back . . .?

The cat arched its back and leaned against her leg with a low-toned mew. Samantha slipped the letter back into her pocket and scooped the purring creature into her arms. It lifted its head, bumping affectionately against Samantha's chin. Samantha stroked its silken fur, murmuring, "Yes, kitty, I know. Everybody needs a little love now and then . . . I hope those children all find someone to love them." Her heart lurched. She gave the cat a final sweep from head to tail before setting it on the floor. "I've got work to do, kitty." She turned her attention to lunch preparations.

Over the next several days, as she performed her duties, she found herself patting her pocket and encountering the square of paper containing the news of the tragedy. Each time she whispered a prayer for the children whose names she didn't know, that they might find a loving home.

"You did *what?*" Daniel hadn't intended to be brusque, but based on the defensive lift in his wife's chin, he was sure he had failed.

"I simply wrote to Adam and Samantha and told them about Esther's children." She flicked a glance toward the staircase. "And kindly do not holler at me. You'll wake the girls."

Drawing in a breath to chase away the angry words forming on his tongue, he settled for a simple query. "Why?"

Rose raised one brow. "Why do you think?"

Daniel dropped his stern, hands-on-hips pose and lifted his gaze to the ceiling. "Rose, you shouldn't have done that."

"Why not?" Rose flung out her hands and sat forward on the sofa. "On one side you have a wonderful couple who are childless and who would make wonderful parents. On the other you have four children who need parents. What could be more perfect?"

Daniel crossed the carpet and sat beside his wife, resting an arm across the back of the sofa. "Darling, I realize you meant well, but you know how Samantha feels about adoption. She wants her own children, not someone else's. By telling her about these children, you've no doubt roused her sympathies, but at the same time you'll have given her a reason to feel guilty. Don't you see that?"

Rose set her lips in a firm line.

"Besides that," Daniel went on, "a couple from Minneapolis have already petitioned the court to take custody of the baby girl and little Will."

Dismay bloomed across Rose's face. "Just the two youngest ones? What about Henry, Jr., and Lucy?"

Daniel sighed. "I understand completely how you feel, my dear. But taking in *four* children . . . The couple interested in baby Ellen Marie and Will already have three older children of their own. At first all they wanted was the baby, so I'm thankful they changed their minds about William. At least two of them will be able to stay together."

"None of them should be separated, Daniel," Rose insisted.

Daniel agreed, but he also knew the realities of the situation. "Insisting that they be adopted together may not be in the best interests of the children. They could wait for years until a family willing to take in four at once is found, and the longer they wait, the more unlikely it becomes that *any* of them will be adopted."

"But—"

"As difficult and unfair as it seems," Daniel said with a shake of his head, "the best thing to do is let Ellen Marie and Will go with this family—they are a good family and will provide well for the children. And we'll continue to hope and pray that young Henry and Lucy will find suitable homes in the not-too-distant future."

Rose folded her arms over her chest. "I still think Adam and Samantha—"

"We can't always arrange things the way we want." Daniel placed a hand on his wife's knee and squeezed gently. "We have to make the best of the situation. Please—no more mention of this. It's hard enough for me to be involved in the adoption of these children, and if I'm feeling censure from you about the decision it only is more difficult. I'm asking you to support me in this."

Rose stared off to the side for a moment. Then she sighed and leaned against Daniel's shoulder. "If you believe this is for the best, yes—I'll support you. But don't ask me to like it."

Daniel chuckled softly and dropped a quick kiss on her temple. "I suppose that would be asking too much of a matchmaker like you."

"Don't tease, Daniel," Rose said, but she didn't move from her nestling spot. "And I still think my matchmaking would be better for those children than anything you lawyers and judges could concoct."

Daniel wrapped his arms around Rose, his cheek against her forehead. Although he wouldn't admit it, in his heart he believed his wife was right.

he telephone hanging in the kitchen jangled merrily early on the morning of January 23. Samantha lifted the ear piece. "Hello!"

"Hello, yourself," came her brother's voice. "Happy birthday, Sam!"

"Thank you, Davey."

"Listen to this." Some odd fumbling noises filled her ear before Joey's childish voice began to sing off-key. "Happy birfday to you . . ." By the time Joey had finished the song, Samantha was holding her cheeks to keep from laughing into the receiver.

"Thank you, sweetheart. That was a wonderful present."

Joey said, "Dere's more present, Auntie Sam. Mama got a cake an'—"

David's voice cut in, "Joey, let Papa talk now."

"'Bye-'bye," Joey said, and then David's voice came through again. "Samantha, we'd like you and Adam to come over this evening for a little birthday celebration. Will that fit into your plans?"

Samantha warmed at his desire to celebrate her arrival into the world. "You don't need to go to any trouble for me, David."

"I missed too many of your birthdays when you were a child." His voice sounded tender with yearning. "Let me indulge you a little bit now, huh?"

Samantha smiled, cradling the earpiece two-handed against her cheek. "All right. We'd love to accept your invitation. Thank you."

"Great! Be here by six o'clock, sharp, for a birthday dinner."

"Yes, sir!" She replaced the earpiece and stood smiling at the instrument for several seconds, anticipating the evening with her brother. Then she ran to the base of the stairs and called, "Adam!"

"Huh?" His voice sounded faint, carrying all the way from the bathroom at the end of hall.

"David just called. He invited us to their place for the evening meal. All right?"

"Fine, but what's the occasion?"

"What's the—?" Samantha stared upward in disbelief. Adam had forgotten her birthday! She stomped up the stairs, one hand banging against the handrail, the other curled into a fist. She barged through the bathroom doorway. "What do you mean, what's the occasion? You know quite well what today is!"

Adam turned from the sink, his freshly shaved face looking completely innocent. "Well, sure, Sam. It's Thursday, the twenty-third day of January, and it's—" His arms snaked out, catching her in a hug that literally took her breath away. "It's your birthday!"

She laughed into his clean-smelling neck, holding on for dear life as he swung her in a circle. "You big tease, I thought you'd forgotten."

"Forget about the birthday of my favorite girl? Absolutely not." He set her back on the floor. "And I have something for you."

"You do?"

"Uh-huh, and you're gonna like it." He tipped up her face and very slowly he lowered his head until their lips touched once, twice, then again.

"Is that all I get?" she asked guilelessly.

Adam gave a brief huff of laughter then offered a mock scowl. "Shame on you. That kiss should be enough for anyone."

He shook a finger under her nose. "Better behave or you might end up getting something besides birthday kisses that isn't nearly as nice."

Samantha smirked. "You'd have to catch me first." She spun and dashed down the hallway to the stairs, laughing at him over her shoulder.

"Just wait till I get my hands on you!"

She reached the bottom of the stairs. "I can wait!"

His laughter followed her into the kitchen, and Samantha giggled as she pulled out a skillet to fry pancakes. Her happy, flushed face reflected back at her from the kitchen window. She looked lighthearted, relaxed, the way a twenty-three-year-old— no, a twenty-four-year-old—wife should look.

Thank You, Lord, for healing. The prayer winged from her contented heart. She blew her reflection a kiss then set to work preparing Adam's breakfast.

❧

"Absolutely not, Samantha." Priscilla put her hands on Samantha's shoulders and eased her back down onto the chair at the head of the table. "You are a guest, and it's your birthday. You will not be doing any kitchen duties tonight!"

Samantha gestured weakly to the array of dishes scattered across the lace-covered dining room table. "But—"

David held up a hand to silence her. "No arguments, baby sister." He grinned, arching one sardonic brow. "The boss has spoken."

Priscilla stuck her tongue out at her husband and shook her head.

David laughed at her and went on. "Besides, Pris is right; you shouldn't do kitchen chores on your birthday."

"I certainly won't do any on mine!" Priscilla shot over her shoulder as she began stacking dishes. "I'll get these out of the way for now and wash them later. Go settle yourselves in the parlor. I'll be out in a few minutes."

Samantha looked at Adam who shrugged and bobbed his head toward the parlor. "Shall we?" Samantha rose and Adam escorted her to the sitting room.

Joey scrambled down from his chair and dashed to the stack of wooden blocks he'd left in the corner. The three grown-ups settled into overstuffed furniture to enjoy a little after-dinner discussion. In a few minutes the clanging from the kitchen ceased, and Priscilla joined them, carrying baby Jenny who had been roused from her sleep, thanks to her mother's energetic plate stacking.

Samantha moved to the rocking chair and held out her arms. "Oh, let me hold her." Priscilla deposited the baby into Samantha's waiting arms, then seated herself nearby. "Hi, Jenny," Samantha greeted the bright-eyed infant. Little Jenny cooed at her aunt.

Joey galloped over to peek at his baby sister. "Whooo, Jenny," he prompted, and Jenny beamed at him, imitating, "Oooo." The grown-ups laughed, and Samantha started the rocker in motion. Joey returned to his block tower, and Priscilla reached beside the chair and brought up a snarl of pink yarn and two knitting needles.

"Not that again," David said with a wry smirk.

"You're the one who suggested I learn to knit rather than buy all of Jenny's items, so don't start belly-aching." Priscilla shot him a tart look.

David chuckled and gestured toward his wife. "I made one comment about the high cost of ready-made clothes, and she took it to mean she should never own another store-bought garment."

"Now, David . . ." Priscilla's tone held a mild warning.

Samantha exchanged an amused glance with Adam. No matter how irritated David and Priscilla pretended to be with each other, their sparring was never taken seriously by either party or their audience.

"I think it looks nice," Samantha said. "Is it a blanket?"

David snorted, and Priscilla wrinkled her nose at him. Her expression brightened when she turned to Samantha. "No, it's the start of a sweater." Typical of Priscilla, Samantha could spot no pattern—just pick up the needles and yarn and begin.

"Oh. I didn't realize you knew how to make sweaters."

"She doesn't." David shook his head indulgently. "But I have no doubt that by the time she's finished wrestling with that boulder of yarn, there will be a sweater in its stead. Once Priscilla sets her mind to something, there's no dissuading her."

Priscilla flipped a thick strand of hair over her shoulder. "That's right, so just sit over there and let me knit, Mr. O'Brien."

"Yes, Mrs. O'Brien," David conceded, hands up and palms outward.

The conversation moved from Priscilla's knitting abilities to the wonderful dinner, to mild complaints about full bellies, to various other topics. Eventually the conversational ball bounced back to Christmas, and Adam commented, "I missed having Daniel and Rose home for the holiday."

"That's right . . ." Priscilla held up the slightly off-square of pink yarn and examined it. Her survey complete, she began twisting the long needles once more. "I had forgotten they didn't make it home for Christmas this year. Have you heard from them since?"

Adam nodded. "Yes, Rose writes frequently. We got a letter from her about a week ago."

Samantha felt her chest squeeze as she remembered Rose's most recent communication. She put a kiss on little Jenny's forehead, praying someone might be doing the same for Esther's orphaned baby.

"Everything all right in Minneapolis?" David asked.

Adam glanced at Samantha and said, "Yes, just fine with Daniel and his family. Rose did share some rather unhappy news, though, concerning a woman who helped Rose with cleaning chores." Briefly, he explained to David and Priscilla about the accident and the children who were now orphans.

"That's sad," David said. He blew out a long breath. "Even after all these years, I still miss my mother. Poor kids . . ."

Something deep within Samantha twined around David's solemn words.

Priscilla's needles clacked an off-beat pattern. "So what's to be done about it?"

Samantha swallowed a sigh. "We're praying they'll find loving homes."

Priscilla looked over the top of her knitting. "Oh. I thought maybe you considered doing more."

Samantha lowered her gaze to Jenny's sleeping face. Her heart pounded fiercely in a rush of apprehension she didn't understand. "Such as . . .?"

"Such as giving them a home." Priscilla nonchalantly lifted one shoulder as if she hadn't just suggested Samantha and Adam turn their whole lives upside down by bringing home four unknown children.

"We couldn't do that." Samantha finally forced the words past her tight throat.

"Why not?" The square of knitted yarn bounced on the needles. "It seems to me that if anyone would understand a motherless child's needs, it would be you. After all, you were a motherless child."

David's jaw dropped. "Priscilla! That was extremely . . . well, it was insensitive!"

Joey looked up from his block building, his dark eyes wide and wary.

Priscilla's hands stilled, and she shot her husband a defensive look. "Well, gracious, David, you needn't shout at me. You've scared Joey." A brief glance at Joey confirmed it, and David reached a hand out to the little boy. Joey trotted across the rug and snuggled against his father's broad chest.

Priscilla's chin angled high. "I wasn't trying to hurt anyone's feelings. I was simply stating my opinion."

"Well, perhaps your opinion isn't warranted, Pris." David looked from his wife to his sister, his expression changing from stern to apologetic.

Defiance flared in Samantha's chest. "David could understand the needs of a motherless child, too. Why don't you consider adopting them if you feel so strongly about it?"

Priscilla didn't deliberate for more than a moment before saying, "David and I have Joey and Jenny already. But you and Adam—"

"Priscilla!" David rose from his seat with Joey in his arms. But the sight of the towering, red-faced David wasn't enough to silence the assertive Priscilla.

Her knitting needles clacked furiously. As her hands flew, she said without a hint of an apology in her tone, "I'm sorry if I've offended you, Sammy. That certainly wasn't my intention." David received another scathing look before she turned back to Samantha and continued in a much less abrasive tone. "I know sometimes I don't say things the right way, but all I meant was that if anyone could give an orphaned child the patience and understanding he or she would require, I think it would be you." Then she shrugged and added, "Or David, too, I suppose." To Samantha again, very kindly, "I believe you could empathize with such a child, where others would simply sympathize. There is a difference, you know."

"Yes . . ." Samantha considered Priscilla's final comment. "I suppose there is."

Priscilla held her work at arm's length. A satisfied smile broke across her face. "There! That should be large enough for the back of a sweater for Jenny, don't you think so, Sammy?"

Samantha looked at the twelve-inch square of knitted pink yarn, then down at the baby who slept contentedly in her arms. "It looks big enough. After all, there isn't much to Jenny yet, is there?"

Priscilla laughed, tied off the end of the yarn, and began removing the knitted piece from the needles. "No, there's not much to her now, but she'll grow in a hip and a hurry!" Priscilla dropped the handful of yarn, needles, and knitted square into the bag beside her chair, then boosted herself up. She reached for her daughter. "I'll take her to bed now. Thanks for rocking her, Sam."

Samantha stood and passed the slumbering infant to her mother's arms, one hand stroking the cap of black curls a last time. Her fingers lingered on the baby's soft hair. "Thank you for letting me rock her. I enjoyed it."

Priscilla stood for a moment with Jenny in her arms, her sharp gaze centered on Samantha. Samantha, watching the play of emotions on Priscilla's face, braced herself. Sassy, assertive Priscilla was preparing to offer more unsolicited advice.

"Samantha," Priscilla announced, "you just said you enjoy rocking Jenny, and I know you do. You enjoy every minute you spend with any of your nieces and nephews, and they all love you to pieces. But, at the risk of being accused of insensitivity"—she sneaked a peek at David, who glared silently at his wife—"I have to say . . . they aren't yours."

Samantha bit down on her lower lip.

David, his mouth set in a firm line, put Joey on the floor and headed for his wife. Priscilla increased the volume as he advanced. "They aren't yours, but you love them just the same. I fail to see how that can be any different than a child you would adopt."

David slipped his hand beneath Priscilla's elbow. "Pris . . ."

Priscilla jerked her arm from his grasp, and at the abrupt movement, Jenny stirred and began to howl. Without a moment's hesitation, Priscilla plopped the baby back into Samantha's arms, and she automatically began rocking and crooning to the wailing infant. Priscilla crossed her arms and grinned in satisfaction. "See?" She flipped a palm toward Samantha and cocked a saucy eyebrow at her disgruntled husband. "You put a baby in her arms, and it becomes hers."

David's arm slipped around Priscilla's shoulder, and the two of them gazed down at Samantha while she calmed the fussing baby. With hiccupping noises, little Jenny ceased her wails and nestled into Samantha's shoulder. Samantha tipped her cheek against the baby's soft curls and sighed. Such a delight she'd found in comforting this little one.

Priscilla now turned her attention on Adam. "I think you should go to Minneapolis as soon as possible and bring those children back here before someone walks off with that baby. Someone will, you know. And Samantha should have the pleasure of rocking a baby that nobody will remove from her arms."

As if on cue, Jenny's eyelids slipped closed, and Priscilla picked her up once more and headed for the hallway. Samantha looked after the two and wrapped her now-empty arms across her stomach. When Priscilla turned the corner, disappearing from view, Samantha turned to discover both David and Adam examining her with serious expressions.

She forced a feeble laugh. "David, despite your best efforts, Priscilla is still sassy."

David sighed. "Yes, she is. I'm sorry, Sammy."

Samantha's cheek twitched. Laughter threatened. She swallowed to hold it back. "Don't apologize. Pris just says what she thinks." She shook her head, muttering to herself. "She's also right."

"What do you mean?" Adam asked quickly.

Samantha crossed to Adam, taking his hands. "Adam, you married a real dummy."

He angled his head. "Well, then, what does that make me?"

Samantha raised up on tiptoe and delivered a light kiss on his lips. "That makes you a real sweetheart, for putting up with this dummy." Before Adam could reply, she released his hands and darted away, suggesting over her shoulder, "But sometimes, sweetheart, you might try putting your foot down."

Adam flicked David a dry look. "I imagine that would do me about as much good as it does you."

Samantha grinned. "Ha-ha." She finished up behind the rocking chair and clasped the high back with both hands, giving it a push that set it into motion. "Adam, I have spent the last five years wasting a perfectly good rocking chair sitting in it all by myself. Priscilla is right—if you put a baby in my arms, it does become mine. I don't know why it's taken me so long to come to my senses, but . . ." She lifted her shoulders in a shrug, then held her hands high, smiling sweetly.

Awareness dawned on Adam's face. He moved toward her. "Sam, do you mean . . .?"

"Yes, Adam, I do mean . . . Let's call Daniel right away and start adoption procedures."

Adam paused, his body looking tense. "There are four of them, Sam."

Samantha felt her chin quiver. "I know there are four of them, and I want to bring every one of them home to live with us." Her gaze flitted briefly to David then back to Adam before she finished quietly, "Brothers and sisters should never be separated, Adam."

Adam rocked in place, as if his boots had been nailed to the floor. "Are you sure, Sammy? Are you absolutely, positively, without any doubts sure this is what you—what we should do?"

Samantha skittered around the chair and clasped Adam's hands, needing at this moment to be physically connected with him. "Adam, at Thanksgiving your mother showed me pictures of a sister you never got to meet. Among other things, she told me that losing Hannah left an empty spot in her heart that was never filled, but that it didn't keep her from loving the rest of her children.

"I know I've stubbornly clung to the idea of having our own children, and I suppose a part of me will always regret that I couldn't birth your babies. But you and I have love we need to share with a child, and in Minneapolis there are four children who have lost their mother and father. Surely they need us as much as we need them. So . . . yes, I'm positively, absolutely, without any doubts sure this is what's right." By the time she'd finished, she was smiling through happy tears, and Adam's face was lit with his own beaming smile.

"Oh, Sam!" Adam scooped Samantha right off the floor with his hug.

Squealing, she clung to his neck. "Adam, put me down! You can't just go around picking up expectant mothers!"

Adam roared his laughter and squeezed her hard enough to leave her breathless before lowering her to the floor. Completely forgetting about their audience, they shared a joyous kiss. When they separated, David came over and wrapped his arms around both of them "What a birthday present." His voice shook slightly. "A family. A ready-made family."

Samantha tipped her forehead lightly against Adam's lips. She heard him murmur, his tone awed, "A family, Sam." She smiled to herself. A family! At that moment, it seemed that nothing could go wrong.

Chapter Twenty-One

*A*dam, I wish you'd called two weeks ago with this."

Adam's hand tightened around the telephone earpiece. He had put a call through to Daniel immediately upon their return home from the birthday dinner. He'd expected an enthusiastic response, but his brother's regret-filled tone created a sense of dread. "Why? What's the matter?"

Samantha tugged at his sleeve. "What's wrong?"

Adam held up a hand to her before asking, "Is there a problem, Daniel?"

Daniel's voice crackled through the line. "A local couple, Dr. and Mrs. Vanderhaven, have petitioned the court to adopt the two youngest children. They are a well-established family with three older children. Their hearing is on the docket for tomorrow afternoon, and it looks quite promising that they'll be granted custody."

"So soon?" Adam was unable to hide his dismay.

"What is it, Adam?" Samantha, brow furrowed, fidgeted in place. "What's wrong?"

Adam shifted the mouthpiece to address her. "Another couple has expressed interest in adopting two of the children."

Samantha's eyes flew wide. "They can't separate them! Let me talk to Daniel." She pushed in front of him, grasping the earpiece so they could press their heads together and share it. "This is Sam. Can't you stop the adoption from taking place? Since it would separate—?"

"It's not that simple, Samantha." Daniel's voice held patience but firmness. "The children are wards of the state, and a wealthy family like the Vanderhavens would provide a fine home for the children."

"But not for all of them!" Samantha argued. "Only two of them! And it isn't right that they be separated."

A sigh carried all the way from Minneapolis. "I agree, Sam, but judges try to do what they feel is best. And a home with the Vanderhavens would certainly be preferable to remaining in the Foundling Home."

"I don't see how separating those children can be the best thing, no matter how rich the people are who pull them apart!" Samantha thrust the telephone earpiece back into Adam's hand and stalked a few feet away, facing the wall and hugging herself.

Adam spoke quietly into the telephone "Is there any way you could postpone the hearing? Maybe if the judge knew there was someone willing to take all of the children . . ."

"I can't make any promises," Daniel said, "but I will try. How soon can you and Sam get here?"

"We can pack tonight, and if the train schedules are running right, be there by tomorrow afternoon—evening at the latest. Do you think you could postpone the hearing one day?" On the other end there was silence. Samantha crept close again, her expression beseeching. Adam added, "Daniel, it's just one day. Surely it's not too much to ask."

"Judge Simmons is handling this case, Adam, and although he's much less . . . well, dignified . . . than many I've worked with, he's a stickler for following schedules. . . ."

Samantha put her face to the receiver again and begged. "Daniel, please?"

Daniel's huff of breath carried clearly through the line. "I'll see what I can do. You two get here as fast as you can."

Adam and Samantha shared a successful smile. Adam said, "Thanks, big brother. One more thing—would you be willing to represent Samantha and me at the hearing? Assuming there is a hearing on our behalf."

"I'd be honored." Adam envisioned Daniel's smile as he added, "I'll even give you my family rates."

Adam managed a brief laugh. "Sounds fair. As soon as our travel plans are set, we'll give you a call and—"

"Don't waste time and money calling," Daniel put in. "Just get on a train and get here. Take a cab directly to the office if you arrive before six, to the house otherwise. And, Adam? Just in case I can't stop the proceedings, would you and Sam consider adopting the older two? A girl and a boy? It will be tough to find a home for them at their ages."

"I'd rather wait and see what happens before I commit to anything."

"That sounds fair. I'll keep an eye out for you."

"All right, then. We'll see you soon. Good-bye." Adam placed the earpiece back in the hook and held his arms out to Samantha. She came at once, locking her arms around Adam's torso.

"Can he stop the adoption?"

"He's going to try."

Samantha buried her head against Adam's shirt front. "Oh, Adam, he's just got to! If we can't bring those children home . . ."

"Now, Sammy," Adam chided gently, "think positively."

"I can't help it! After what it's taken to get me to want them, I can't stand the thought of losing them now. And I just believe in my heart that those children need to be together. Here."

Adam rubbed his hands up and down her spine "I agree with you, and so does Daniel. You probably heard he's going to represent us in court, and I have every confidence he'll do whatever he can to sway the judge in our favor."

"Oh, I hope so," she murmured fervently.

Adam caught her shoulders and gently set her aside. "Now, Miss Birthday Girl, march yourself upstairs and pack your bags. Tomorrow we're going after our children."

Samantha nodded, dashed the sheen of tears from her eyes with the back of a hand, and offered her husband a brave smile. "That's right—*our* children." She ran lightly up the stairs.

~⊙

Adam hurried through the nighttime chores and headed upstairs to their bedroom. He stopped in the doorway, evidence of Samantha's preparations all over the room. The wardrobe yawned open, and a partially packed bag stood open by the bed. But Samantha was nowhere in sight.

"Sam?"

"In here," came her voice from the small room adjoining theirs. The door stood half open, and Adam crossed to it and stepped through. Samantha stood in the middle of the room, her chin in her hand.

"What are you doing?" he asked, certain he already knew.

"Planning." She turned a slow circle, tapping her lips with her forefinger. At last she dropped her arms and faced Adam. "I've got the room all arranged. The cradle here," she said, stepping to the corner farthest from the doors and gesturing with both hands, "since the noise from our room and the hallway will be least disruptive , and—" she moved briskly to the corner beside the door that led to their bedroom—"I'll put a rocker here. If we can afford a small dresser, it should go here." She pointed to another wall. "With a small lamp sitting on top of it. What do you think?"

Adam smiled and shook his head with admiration and love. In the dim light filtering through their bedroom doorway, she looked very young. He remembered Daniel's question about whether or not they would consider adopting only the older two children. Had Daniel asked because he knew that would more than likely be what was offered to them? In case she hadn't heard that part of the conversation, he should tell her what Daniel had said. But the look of innocent belief on Samantha's face—the expression that indicated her baby would soon be sleeping soundly in a cradle in the corner of the room planned as a nursery—stilled the words.

He stepped behind her and wrapped his arms around her waist. "I think not only should our baby have a dresser with a lamp, our baby should also have a rug on the floor and a wooden toy box filled with toys in that corner." He pointed as Samantha's gaze followed the direction of his finger. "And curtains on the window, and a bookshelf full of storybooks and—"

"Adam, Adam, Adam . . ." Samantha chuckled softly. "You're going to spoil the child if you fill this room with all of that."

"Nah, isn't going to happen," Adam insisted.

"I never thought you would be an indulgent parent," Samantha said, tipping her head and smiling up at him.

Adam raised his brows. "And I never thought you'd be so strict."

"Strict? Me?"

"Yes, strict. Denying our baby a rug and toy box full of toys and storybooks—"

"Adam." Samantha placed a finger on his lip, her expression serious. "Can we afford to do what we're doing? I know the crops didn't bring as much last year, and—"

"We're not wealthy people, Sam. Not like the Vanderhavens in Minneapolis. But we have the means to provide for four children."

"Are you sure?"

"I'm sure. Although we got less than in years past for last season's crop, we have sufficient resources to meet our obligations and with savings left over in the bank." His heart swelled in gratitude for the Lord's provision. "The children may not have dozens of toys or matching furniture or bookshelves overflowing with storybooks, but their needs will always be met. And they'll be showered with love."

Standing in the middle of an empty, echoing room, Adam could imagine it all—the dresser with its lamp and doll, the full bookshelf and toy box . . . all of it. And a sweet baby that would lift its arms to Samantha in eagerness to be held. He hoped the baby's first word would be "Mama."

Samantha relaxed against him, sighing contentedly. As if reading his thoughts, she said, "That sounds perfect." Then she straightened. "Adam, what happens when we bring them home? We don't have beds or clothes or anything ready—"

"One step at a time, Sammy." Adam rocked her back and forth. "First we see the judge, then we get the children, then we fill the house with beds and clothes and toys and all the other things that children need."

Samantha smiled and sheepishly said, "All right, Mr. Adam Klaassen, my wise husband."

"Now, how about you and I get some sleep so we'll be ready to head to Minneapolis first thing in the morning and bring home our children?" He pressed his nose to hers, smiling into her eyes.

Adam watched her enter their bedroom, noted the confident angle of her chin, and smiled to himself. He closed his eyes. Lord, I *believe what we're doing in trying to keep those children together is right. If this is a window You've opened for us, I just ask that You help us climb on through it. And if it's not . . .* He stopped, opening his eyes to stare at the doorway where Samantha had disappeared only moments ago. He couldn't bear to complete that final thought. There could be no more broken dreams for his Samantha. *Please, Lord . . .*

Chapter Twenty-Two

*S*amantha sat quietly on the padded bench seat of the passenger car while the landscape whizzed by the frosted window. They had risen early to finish necessary chores and arrange with family to take care of their animals for a few days. Simon took them in to town to catch the eight o'clock train. The gentle rolling motion of the huge locomotive had lulled a tired Adam into slumber. His head hung toward his shoulder, swaying with the train's rhythmic rock. Glancing at him, Samantha was mildly amused. He didn't look at all comfortable.

She turned her gaze to the snow-covered countryside. On another day she would have marveled at the sight of the sun reflecting off glittering snow, turning icy trees into a crystal forest. Another time she no doubt would have gasped in delight at the brilliant red flash of a cardinal contrasting beautifully against the background of pure white. But not today. Not now.

Though her gaze was directed outward, she was lost in thoughts of the last time she and Adam had traveled by train— the trip to Rochester and Dr. Zimmerman, remembering the sorrow of that time. But she pushed it all away because now here she was again, riding the rails on the way to a dream. The same dream, really, but pursued by an alternate means.

What would happen at the end of this ride? She wanted to believe that even as she and Adam made their journey, Daniel was convincing the judge to withhold granting adoption of the two littlest orphans to the wealthy Minneapolis family, the Vanderhavens. She wanted to believe that the judge would see the wisdom of allowing the children to stay together. She wanted to believe that her long-held dream of hearing a child call her Mama would soon come true.

But as much as she wanted to believe—as much as her heart clamored hopefully in her chest—she was afraid.

After all, she and Adam were much younger—and much less financially secure—than the other couple. How could their inexperience hope to compare to a man and wife who were already successfully parenting three children? How could their simple farmhouse and limited acreage, shared with two other families, possibly stand up against the untold wealth of the Vanderhavens? When viewed from a purely intellectual standpoint, the Vanderhavens were by far the more logical choice, she had to admit, even if it meant separating the children.

But, Samantha continued the argument with herself, why only look at it from the intellectual side? When viewed with the heart, she and Adam could offer just as much—maybe even more!—than the Vanderhavens. After all, they were willing to assume responsibility for all four children, which would mean no separation. And certainly they were capable of loving the children just as much as the other couple. There would be no competition with birth children for love and affection. They would have a wonderful country life, fresh air and animals, and . . .

Adam's head bobbed forward and awoke with a jerk. He straightened himself in the seat, and looked around blearily for a moment before he seemed to realize where he was. He lifted his elbows in a stretch, twisting his neck back and forth to remove the kinks. Only when his arms were lowered—one on the back of the seat, one on the armrest—did he look at Samantha and give her a reassuring smile. "Quit worrying."

Oh, how well he knew her. . . . But she feigned surprise. "What makes you think I'm worrying?"

He grinned and reached out one blunt finger to stroke a line across her forehead. "These furrow marks. When you frown like that, it makes you look old."

"I wish I were older." Maybe she'd be better able to compete with the older and more experienced Vanderhavens.

"You can always get older but you can't get younger, so don't go wishing your life away." Adam slipped his arm down around her shoulders and pulled her securely against his side.

"Oh, I'm not." She turned sideways in the seat to face him. When her back came in contact with the cold window, she shifted forward a bit. "I was thinking that when it comes to impressing the judge with our ability to be good parents, a few more years wouldn't exactly hurt us any."

Adam grinned and examined her with raised eyebrows. "Hmm. No gray hairs yet, and I think you still have all your teeth. Oh, well." He tapped the end of her nose. "Just keep frowning like that, sweetie—makes a few wrinkles, and you'll look like a granny in no time."

"Oh, you," she sniffed in mock impatience, settling against his side with her head on his shoulder. Worrying never changed anything, she told herself. And, as Mother Klaassen once told her, worrying says to God He isn't trusted to meet one's needs. Determinedly, Samantha pushed her negative thoughts away. But she offered a fervent prayer. *Lord, please let that judge see more than a young wheat farmer and his wife when he looks at us. Let him see our hearts . . . .*

∽⌒

When they reached Minneapolis that evening and disembarked, Adam hailed a carriage and gave the driver directions to Daniel and Rose's home. Adam was at once eager and hesitant to talk to Daniel. *Lord, calm my jangled nerves. Samantha's too*, he added with a sidelong glance at his wife.

The driver angled the carriage into the brick-paved driveway leading to Daniel's large stone house, and Samantha's fingers clamped down hard on Adam's. He gave her hand a reassuring pat and helped her down from the carriage. After swinging their bag from behind the seat, he dug fare from his pocket, added a dime for a tip, and handed it to the driver with a polite, "Thank you, sir."

The driver simply nodded and left. Adam and Samantha stood in front of the house, holding hands. Samantha seemed planted in place, so Adam tugged at her hand. "Come on, sweetheart."

She gave him a wide-eyed look. The apprehension in her face matched his stuttering pulse. But he managed to smile. He tugged again, and this time Samantha's feet moved toward the door. His finger against the door buzzer brought instant welcome by Daniel's wife and daughters. Christina, Katrina, and Camelia all clamored to be hugged. Rose called over her shoulder, "Daniel, it's Adam and Sam—they're here!"

Daniel appeared from his small office behind the staircase, a smile creasing his face and his hand extended in greeting. "Adam, Samantha, you look exhausted! Come in, come in! Girls, step back so we can shut the door." Daniel scooped up Cami and reached past the other two girls to swing the door closed.

Rose herded the older two toward the staircase. "You two were on your way to your rooms to get ready for bed. Now go on up."

"Oh, Mama," both girls protested at once, "we want to see Uncle Adam and Auntie Sam! Please? Can't we stay up?"

Daniel compromised with, "Go on up, get into your nighties, and then you may come back down and visit for a bit before bed."

"Remember to put away your clothes and wash your faces," Rose reminded them.

They gave their father one last pleading look which he chose to ignore, then they reluctantly plodded upstairs. Rose took Cami from Daniel's arms. "I'll get this little pun'kin tucked in and then I'll be right back. Adam and Samantha, make yourselves at home." She, too, headed upstairs.

With the girls gone, the house was suddenly silent, and the three remaining adults stood in a small circle, looking at one another. Finally Daniel broke into a smile and gestured toward the parlor. "Well, come on in and sit down. Can I get you something to eat or drink?"

"No, thank you," Samantha replied, following him. "We had some sandwiches on the train, and I'm never very hungry after being bumped around all day."

"I know what you mean," Daniel agreed. He sat in a side chair, and Adam and Samantha settled themselves on the settee in the parlor's bay window. "It's good to see you."

Adam leaned forward, resting his elbows on his knees and looking hard at his brother. "It's good to see you, too, Daniel, but the suspense is killing both of us. Did you talk to the judge?"

"I did."

"And—?" Adam prompted. Samantha sat up as well, her eyes wide and apprehensive.

"And he postponed the hearing until tomorrow afternoon."

Samantha collapsed against the seat's tufted back. Adam took her hand. "Then there's a chance."

Daniel took in a deep breath. "There's a chance."

"A good chance?" Samantha pressed.

Daniel linked his fingers. "There's no way of knowing how things will turn out, Sam, but I visited with Judge Simmons personally. I told him about you two, and your home, your farm, the rest of the Klaassen family nearby, and how you were willing to adopt all four children so they could stay together. Of course, he wants to talk to both prospective couples before making a decision, but I got the impression he was keen on keeping the children together."

"Oh, Adam . . ." Samantha clung hard to Adam's hand.

Adam smiled at her, reading the deep message beneath her simple utterance. This was real, they were hearing correctly, and by tomorrow—tomorrow!—their dream could very well come true. He laughed aloud to express his happiness. "See, Sammy? I told you things would work out. Didn't I tell you?"

Daniel cleared his throat. "Listen, you two. I don't want to throw cold water on your excitement, but let's try to not get carried away too soon. As I've said, the Vanderhavens are a very well-known and well-respected family in this town. The judge may not want to separate the children, but there's no guarantee he won't, based on the history of the other family and their ability to provide very well for the children. I will do everything in my power to get a decision in your favor, but I want you to be aware that there are no guarantees at this point. Do you understand?"

Samantha's bright smile faded, and her fingers dug into Adam's hand. Despite her obvious distress, Adam experienced a wave of peace that could only have been given by God. He faced his brother and spoke with conviction.

"Daniel, when we were here last, a doctor told us we would never have children. We were heartsick, but we had to accept it because it was something that couldn't be changed. But this time it's different. This time our dream can come true. Our desire to love and nurture children can be fulfilled, and I refuse to dash cold water on that flame of hope." He glanced at his wife, bolstered by her straight shoulders and the lift of her chin.

Admiration glowed in her eyes as she watched him. He continued. "Samantha and I both believe taking these children—all of them—into our home is the right thing to do for them, particularly with what they already have suffered, and we aren't going to let anyone—including the well-respected Vanderhavens—stand in our way. We have right on our side."

Daniel shook his head, a crooked smile lifting one side of his mouth. "You've certainly inherited the Klaassen determination, little brother."

"Yes, I have." Adam pointed at him. "And so have you. With us in this together—and with God going before us—we can't fail."

Chapter Twenty-Three

*S*amantha stood before the free-standing mirror in the corner of the same guestroom she and Adam had shared during their last visit with Daniel and Rose. She was focused intently on her reflection, having twisted her waist-length russet hair high and tight in a neat figure-eight at the back of her head. Although she had combed the sides back severely, the weight of the coil tugged it all downward, and a few strands struggled out from the pins. She'd fashioned this style for the court appearance, attempting to capture the essence of maturity. But the wispy tendrils of hair spiraling around her ears ruined the effect.

She surveyed her tidy ivory shirtwaist with its neat row of tucks and its simple string tie in a tiny bow at the back and the deeply pleated navy and brown watch-plaid skirt. The toes of her highly polished high-top shoes showed primly beneath the edge of the ankle-length skirt. Although her most mature-looking outfit, she shook her head at the school-girl reflection staring back at her. Young. Painfully young.

She spun on her heel and marched to her satchel, pawing through it until she located the watch pin David and Priscilla had given her for her birthday. She loved the gold filigree in the shape of a bow with its retractable watch hanging pendant-like beneath the bow. At least she possessed one pretty, very adult-looking piece of jewelry. She pinned it carefully just below her left shoulder, then hurried back to the mirror for another look.

Hands on hips, she frowned at her image. It would take more than a watch to make her look as mature as Mrs. Vanderhaven!

Unbidden, another image intruded—the shy, unprepossessing young woman who had helped Samantha pack all those months ago. Her eyes closed as she silently vowed to do everything she could for that woman's children, to keep them together and give them a secure, loving home. *Please, Lord,* she whispered once again.

The door creaked open, and there was Adam in his double-breasted suit of brown tweed, the crisp white cambric shirt she'd ironed once again this morning, and the deep brown and tan striped tie. He looked wonderful. *And so mature,* she noted with satisfaction. Her heart caught at the strength in his wide shoulders, the even, bold features. With his farmer's crow's feet from squinting into the sun, the smile lines from laughing and joking all the time, he looked every year of . . . of twenty-seven, his age. Samantha sighed.

"Are you about ready to go, Sammy?" He reached into his pocket for a handful of change, bouncing it idly in his palm.

"Do you think I should put my hair in a French twist?"

Adam was counting the coins, shifting them around with one finger. "Your hair is fine, honey."

"Adam! You didn't even look at my hair!"

Adam lifted his head, his eyebrows high. "Sorry, Sam, of course—I'd already seen it. I think it looks nice. Really nice."

She flapped a hand at him, then went seeking hairpins. "Oh, it looks nice, all right. It looks just wonderful—for a twenty-four-year-old. I need something more mature."

Adam pocketed the coins and stepped quickly to her side, pulling her hands away from her hairdo. "Samantha, you *are* a twenty-four-year-old woman, and that's surely no crime—at least that I'm aware of."

He tried to coax a smile from her, but she pursed her lips. This was not a time for teasing.

Adam fixed her with a steady look, gripping her shoulders. "You are a beautiful, bright, giving young woman, and I won't let you to pretend to be anything other than what you are for anyone." He brushed her cheek, adding, "Even for a judge."

Her frustrations melted at his support, though she still felt uncertainty. "But, Adam—"

"The Vanderhavens are no doubt older and richer, but that does not make them better," Adam insisted. "Actually, younger might be a lot better—we've got the energy to keep up with all of them, and the other couple will be a lot older when those two little ones get into their teen years. Now, I want you to stop your fretting, fetch your coat, and let's go to the courthouse before Daniel wonders what happened to us."

When she didn't move, Adam said, "Samantha, last night we put those children in the Lord's hands, didn't we?"

The question brought her up short. Heat flooded her cheeks. "Yes, we did."

"And you think He doesn't care about these children even more than we do?" She hadn't thought of that before, and paused to consider. She shook her head. *Of course He does.*

"And so you can trust Him to handle the situation?"

"Yes, Adam, I can. I'll get my coat."

Twenty minutes later Adam was escorting Samantha across the marble entry of the Minneapolis Courthouse. Samantha's heels clicked crisply against the smooth cream-colored marble, and she cringed at the intrusion in an otherwise rather formal, whispers-only environment. They paused in the middle of the two-story foyer, its twin-spindled staircases leading to double balconies above. Samantha was counting the doors that lined the balconies over her head when Adam tapped her on the arm.

Daniel was walking toward them from a hallway between the stairs. "Sam, Adam." He held out his hand in a formal manner, then gave Samantha a quick squeeze and kiss on the cheek. His arm around Samantha's shoulders, he began guiding them back down the hallway. "The Vanderhavens are here already, and the hearing will begin in about ten minutes. It will be simple—the judge will have each lawyer introduce the prospective parents and give brief background information. Then the judge may ask each adoptive couple a few questions." He gave Samantha an encouraging smile. "No reason to be nervous about any of it."

She tried for a smile herself, then said, "Easy for you to say, Daniel. But thanks."

Daniel stopped before the rich mahogany doors, released Samantha, and straightened his tie. He grinned at the pair. "Here we go." He turned the brass knob on the right, pushed it open, and motioned them inside.

Samantha stepped over the threshold and froze, awestruck by the beautifully appointed room. Beneath her feet, a highly varnished parquet oak floor shone like a mirror. Richly stained paneled walls boasted gilt-framed oil paintings centered within egg-and-dart trimmed insets. The ceiling repeated the floor's pattern, and a large brass-and-crystal chandelier hung from a brass-plated chain directly from the center of the soaring height. Spindle railings separated the judge's arena from the spectators' gleaming benches, and decorative carvings graced the ends. Although there were no windows in the large square room, evenly spaced electric lights in globes extending from the walls at shoulder height lit the area. Samantha had never seen a more beautiful room, and she felt totally out of place.

A murmur of voices caught her attention. Three people—two men and one woman—sat at a table on the far side of the railing at the front and visited with the judge who sat on a raised platform behind a tall, paneled desk of mahogany. He leaned on its top with his arms crossed, chuckling at something one of the men had just said. His gaze shifted to the doorway, and a smile broke across his face. "Ah, Mr. Klaassen. You're here. Come on in.—You know the procedure."

Samantha flicked a startled glance at Adam, then Daniel. She would have expected stiff formality and perhaps an amount of sternness in a room such as this. The judge's friendly, casual bearing didn't seem to fit any better than she did.

Daniel put his hand under Samantha's arm and propelled her forward, Adam trailing them. They paused at the second table in the front. "Judge Simmons, this is Adam and Samantha Klaassen from Mountain Lake." Daniel said, with a nod at the judge, then at the two.

The judge nodded back, smiling widely enough to show a gold tooth. "Mr. and Mrs. Klaassen," he acknowledged, then gestured to the table on the opposite side of the tall desk. "Lester, introduce everyone at your table, please."

A small, wiry man rose and squared his shoulders. With a confident sweep of his hand, he indicated the well-dressed, early-forties' couple who remained seated. "Mr. and Mrs. Klaassen, may I present Dr. and Mrs. Herbert Vanderhaven of Minneapolis."

"It's a pleasure to meet you," Adam said confidently. Samantha, unable to peel her tongue off the roof of her dry mouth, offered a tentative smile.

"Likewise," Mr. Vanderhaven responded with a slight nod. Mrs. Vanderhaven bobbed her head, then turned her attention back to the judge.

"All right, everyone, sit down, sit down." Judge Simmons reached into his breast pocket and withdrew a pair of wire-rimmed spectacles. He snatched up a file from the corner of his desk and rustled through the contents as he continued, "We all know why we're here this morning. Both the Klaassens and the Vanderhavens"—he acknowledged each couple as their names were pronounced—"are petitioning to adopt the orphaned McIntyre children." He pulled a sheet from the file with a satisfied "ah!" Holding the paper at arm's length, he read as if by rote, "Lucille Elizabeth McIntyre, age six; Henry Rollin McIntyre, Jr., age five; William Everett McIntyre, age twenty-nine months; and Ellen Marie McIntyre, age three and half months."

Samantha listened eagerly to this brief snippet of information, mulling over the names and ages. Adam glanced over at Samantha with a little smile.

The judge dropped the paper on the desk, interlaced his fingers on top of it, and addressed the Vanderhavens' lawyer, "Do I understand that Dr. and Mrs. Vanderhaven are expressing interest in adopting William Everett and Ellen Marie McIntyre?"

Lester nodded briskly as he stood to his feet. "That is correct, Your Honor."

"Fine, fine, but please let's just stay seated, or you'll all be worn out before we're finished in here, Lester," Judge Simmons said.

Samantha's eyes got wide, then she swallowed a grin at the judge's informal manner.

The judge now turned to Daniel. "And the Klaassens are expressing interest in the older two children?"

Samantha sat up straight, her heart pattering. Beside her, Adam also gave a start. They looked at each other and then at Daniel. He started to rise, then apparently thought better of it. "No, sir," he said quickly. "No, Mr. and Mrs. Klaassen are petitioning to adopt all four of the McIntyre children. They wish to keep these children together in the same home. . . ." His voice trailed off.

Judge Simmons turned his attention to Adam and Samantha, looking steadily at them through his round spectacles. "Mm-hmm," he murmured to himself. He examined the paper again for a few minutes.

With the judge focused on the contents of his file, Samantha sneaked a glance at the Vanderhavens. The woman was dressed in an impeccably styled navy blue velvet suit, and the jabot of her white silk blouse lay in a perfect flurry of ruffles across her bodice. Her hair, in a sleek French knot, was set off with a matching navy velvet cloche in the latest fashion. She wore a choker of pearls with an opal and sapphire pendant, matching opal and sapphire clusters dangling from her ears. Her attire undeniably spoke of elegance and wealth, culture and good breeding.

Samantha, with her simple outfit and youthful face, couldn't help remember the children's fable she'd just read to her niece, Laura Beth—about the city mouse and its country cousin coming for a visit. . . .

She gave her head a single shake and turned her attention back to the judge in time to see him lift his head.

He cleared his throat and set the paper aside. "Very well, then. Let's proceed."

Chapter Twenty-Four

*H*ere we go. . . . Adam fidgeted in his seat as Lester rose, swept his hand through his hair, then extended a palm toward the couple seated at his table. "Dr. and Mrs. Vanderhaven, as you well know, are respected members of the community. Dr. Vanderhaven has been in medical practice for almost twenty years, earning a reputation as a fine physician as well as a caring humanitarian. He and Mrs. Vanderhaven both donate extensive time and not a small amount of financial support to various charities."

He went on to describe their lengthy list of philanthropic endeavors, as well as their spacious home in one of the finest neighborhoods in the city. "You will find letters of reference in their file from many community leaders who verify their kindness and generosity, as well as their ability to more than provide financially for the McIntyre children."

The judge sat with one hand propping his chin as the Vanderhavens' lawyer spoke on their behalf. He raised a hand. "May I ask a question?"

"Certainly," Lester replied.

"Dr. and Mrs. Vanderhaven, I reviewed your file earlier today and took note of your—shall we say—impressive financial position. It seems as if you would have the means to support all of the children. I'm wondering, then, your reasons for choosing to adopt only the two youngest."

Samantha groped for Adam's hand, and he clutched it. Was the judge reluctant to separate the children? His question seemed to indicate so.

Lester began, "Well, Your Honor—"

"Excuse me," Judge Simmons interrupted, "I really would prefer to hear from Dr. or Mrs. Vanderhaven."

Dr. Vanderhaven pushed back his chair and stood, looking rather regal in his carefully tailored three-piece suit, tie, and matching three-point pocket square. "Your Honor, my wife and I have three children at home," he began in a deep, cultured voice. "Our oldest, Nathaniel, is fourteen years of age, Rachel is eleven, and Michael is nearly ten. We believe that adopting four additional children would put an undue strain on our financial budget, but even more importantly, this larger intrusion on our family would be difficult for our natural children to accept.

"I think you'll notice in our paperwork that originally we had only planned to adopt the infant. After some consideration and juggling of figures, we decided perhaps we could make room for the next youngest as well. While we realize this may create some temporary unhappiness on the part of the older two siblings, we also believe they will have a better chance of being adopted if there are fewer than four children involved in the undertaking. Assuming the care and upbringing of four children would be a tremendous responsibility for any family, especially ours since we already have three of our own."

"And your reason for selecting the youngest two?" the judge pressed.

Now Mrs. Vanderhaven responded, remaining seated. "That was my decision, Your Honor. As my husband pointed out, although our own children are far from grown, they are well on their way to adulthood. I greatly miss having a baby in the house. And, in all honesty, I feel it will be much easier to bond with an infant than with a child who has strong memories of another mother."

After listening to the Vanderhavens' refined speech and comfortable manner, Adam wondered if he'd have the courage to open his mouth during the proceedings. But he took a deep breath and told himself it wasn't about social standing, this was about four youngsters who needed love and each other far more than money and the right address.

"Thank you, Mrs. Vanderhaven, I appreciate your honesty." Judge Simmons removed his glasses, massaged the bridge of his nose briefly, then turned to Daniel. "Mr. Klaassen, the floor is yours."

"Thank you, sir." Daniel sat in his chair with a comfortable ease that further soothed the edges of Adam's nerves. "Your Honor, Adam and Samantha Klaassen cannot boast of high-paying positions or membership in clubs or organizations. They are a farm couple from Mountain Lake, Minnesota, where the only 'clubhouse' to which they can belong is the community church—and there they are members in good standing."

The judge chuckled and nodded, further relaxing Adam, and Daniel went on. "Adam and Samantha have been married for five and a half years. Adam is a wheat farmer, making his living on land that has been in the Klaassen family for half a century. His income, although certainly not extensive, is adequate to meet the needs of the children, should adoption be granted. They own their home, which was built two years ago by Adam with help from his family. It has four bedrooms, thus ample room for the children. I'm sure one of your questions to the Klaassens will be why a young couple wants to adopt four children."

The judge nodded, and Adam could see Lester and the Vanderhavens turn as one to look at him and Samantha.

"You see, Your Honor, Adam and Samantha both desire a large family. Adam is one of nine children. Samantha was raised almost as a single child, as her only brother was not in the home most of her growing up years. For different reasons, each looked forward to raising many children. But due to injuries sustained as a child, Samantha is unable to bear children. Thus they are interested in adoption—this group of four children in particular. I might add they met Esther, the mother of the McIntyre children, briefly on a previous visit to Minneapolis. Upon hearing of the death of both Esther and Henry McIntyre, they felt immediate and deep sympathy for the children."

Samantha's fingers clamped hard on Adam's, and he gave a reassuring squeeze. "Adopting the children would serve two purposes," Daniel continued in an easy manner. "Not only would it fulfill their desire to have a family, it would also provide a home where the children could stay together. Mrs. Klaassen, especially, feels strongly that this would be best for these children."

The judge aimed his gaze at Samantha. "Mrs. Klaassen, Daniel has indicated you have a strong belief that the children remain together, is that right?"

Samantha's hand began to tremble within Adam's. "Y-yes, sir."

"Is there a particular reason this is important to you?"

Samantha looked to Adam, and he offered an encouraging smile. Samantha took a deep breath and pushed to her feet, her hand still gripped in Adam's. "Your Honor, when I was a little girl, my older brother left home for . . . personal reasons. We were out of contact for eight years. I spent every day of those eight years wondering where he was, how he was, if I'd ever see him again. . . ." She paused, swallowing. "I wouldn't wish such heartache on any child. I realize the baby girl and the littlest boy probably won't remember their older brother and sister if they're separated now, because they're quite young. But the older boy and girl, Lucille and Henry, will certainly always remember they have a little brother and baby sister someplace. My memories from the age of six are very strong. I can't imagine Lucille's would be less."

The judge's head was angled so the lights reflected from his spectacles. Adam wished he could see his eyes and know what he was thinking.

Samantha finished meekly, her voice nearly a whisper, "They've already lost their mother and father. It hardly seems fair that they should lose one another too." She slowly sat down, her heart beating like it would leap out of her chest.

The judge nodded and turned his attention back to his papers. The group maintained a respectful silence as the gray-haired man on the platform withdrew into private thought.

A pendulum clock on the wall counted minutes while the judge rustled through the papers before him, tapped his nose thoughtfully, and made little sounds like "mm-hmm," and "ah-ha." Adam glanced around, inwardly praying for favor. Samantha's face was pale and her fingers gripped his hand so tightly the nails cut into his flesh. Daniel, apparently accustomed to such proceedings, leaned back in his chair, crossed an ankle over the opposite knee, and waited.

At the other table, Lester took a pose similar to Daniel's. Adam saw Dr. Vanderhaven lean and whisper something in his wife's ear, and she turned to look at Samantha, then whispered something back.

At long last the judge stacked the papers together, slapped them into a brown folder, and set them aside. He pulled off his spectacles and cleared his throat. Time seemed to still in spite of the clock's relentless ticktock, ticktock. Adam held his breath, aware that the judge's next words would affect them—all of them, both the Klaassens and the Vanderhavens—for the rest of their lives.

"I don't want you folks to think the decision I'm about to announce is made lightly. I spent a great deal of time last evening looking over the information in this file"—he tapped it with his spectacles—"and today's hearing was mainly to give me a chance to put faces to the names in here." He leaned forward. "I can see for myself that both of you are fine couples, and both have a lot to offer the children in question."

Turning to the Vanderhavens, he said, "Dr. and Mrs. Vanderhaven, I have no doubt you would care very well for the children. You have the means to support them and provide many privileges to which others are not privy. Since you've already raised three children, I'm sure you have the know-how to raise two more."

He turned his attention to Adam and Samantha. "Mr. and Mrs. Klaassen, I appreciate your convictions in wanting the children to remain together. I can see that you sincerely want what's best for those youngsters. Farming is honest work, and you would surely meet the needs of the children in that vocation." Adam tried to follow the judge's choice of verb tenses, but he could make out nothing firm from what he was hearing.

Beside him Samantha trembled so that the little watch pinned at her shoulder quivered. Tossing aside any concerns about court protocol, Adam slipped his arm around her shoulders and held tight.

Judge Simmons sighed. "What I have here are two fine couples both willing to assume responsibility for someone else's children, children who have been tragically orphaned. My first priority is to do what is best for the children, but I also am thinking of you folks, as well." He linked his fingers and leaned his elbows on the desk, looking fully at Samantha and Adam. Adam detected a hint of sympathy in his eyes, and dread settled over him.

"Mr. and Mrs. Klaassen, let me assure you I have the greatest admiration and respect for you. You've come a long distance to indicate a heartfelt concern for the children of a woman you met only briefly. Not many people would have such caring. You are to be commended. But I would be less than honest if I said I had no reservations. For one thing, you are quite young and, although it's certainly no fault of your own, you have no parenting experience."

Adam's pulse pounded in his ears. *No, oh, please, no* . . . Samantha pressed her fist to her lips.

The judge spoke softly, apologetically, yet firmly. "Taking on four children would be, as Dr. Vanderhaven stated earlier, quite an undertaking for even an experienced parent. For two young adults . . . well, I want you to understand I'm not finding fault with you personally. I think you're fine people, and I'm sure in a few more years you'll be ready for the large family you both want. I'm just not sure you're ready for it now. Therefore, I cannot, in good conscience, grant you custody of four children. I could, however, consider allowing you to assume custody of two of the children. If you are willing, I would like to speak to you following the hearing about the possibility of your adopting the older two McIntyre children."

Samantha ducked her head, and Adam offered the judge a weak nod in acknowledgment.

The judge returned his spectacles to his nose. "Dr. and Mrs. Vanderhaven," he said, peering over the top of his eyewear, "I am granting you custody of William Everett and Ellen Marie McIntyre. I will instruct the authorities at the Foundling Home to expect you next Monday morning by nine a.m."

Dr. Vanderhaven rose. "Thank you very much, Your Honor."

Samantha lurched to her feet. "Your Honor?"

Everyone swung startled gazes in her direction. Adam started to rise, but Daniel caught his arm and held him in place. Samantha braced her hands against the wooden tabletop and aimed her tear-stained face at the judge. "Your Honor, I'm not trying to tell you your job. I'm just the wife of a farmer, and I haven't had that much schooling. But, sir, I don't understand how you can make a decision that will hurt those children for the rest of their lives."

The Vanderhavens' lawyer leaped up. "Now, Mrs. Klaassen, we know you're disappointed, but—"

Judge Simmons held up his hand. "Hush, Lester. Let the lady talk."

Samantha's body quivered and her head drooped—from heartfelt conviction or simply nervousness, Adam wasn't sure. But pride in her swelled as she lifted her head and again addressed the man behind the desk. "I never knew my mother. And my father was . . ." She hesitated, and Adam placed a hand over hers. After a grateful smile to him, she continued. "My father was less than loving. My great-grandmother lived with us and did a wonderful job as surrogate mother, but she died when I was six. After that, the only person I really had to depend on was my brother, David. But as I told you earlier, he had to leave home, and I didn't know where he was for a very long time.

"I can't describe how much the loss of my brother affected me. If I'd had a loving parent, perhaps David's leaving wouldn't have been so hard. But he was all I had, and when he was gone, my whole world was turned upside down. Right now, all Lucille, Henry, little William, and baby Ellen Marie have is each other. I'm not trying to take anything away from the Vanderhavens— I'm sure they're good people, and they have valid reasons for not taking all of them. But, Your Honor, taking the little ones away from the older ones is bound to be hurtful. Haven't they already been hurt enough? Even if you don't let us adopt them, at least give them a chance to stay together with another family. Maybe the Vanderhavens will change their minds and take . . ."

She stopped, glancing around at her audience. Adam's gaze followed hers across the faces, noting the various reactions to her impassioned plea. Daniel's eyes reflected admiration; the judge hid whatever he was thinking behind his spectacles; Lester's face wore an expression of disdain; and the Vanderhavens stared straight ahead, seemingly oblivious to her pleas.

"I'm sorry, sir, if I was impertinent." Samantha bit down on her lower lip, lowering her chin.

"You were not impertinent." At the judge's kind tone, Samantha looked at him. "There's no law against a person speaking her mind. But I will tell you I've made a decision based on my own strong feelings of what is best for all concerned."

Samantha nodded and sank into her chair, her shoulders slumped. Adam put an arm around her again, and she leaned into his embrace.

"Dr. and Mrs. Vanderhaven, you are free to leave," Judge Simmons said. The Vanderhavens thanked him in solemn tones before preceding Lester to the double doors. Adam watched them go, his chest aching. When they reached the doors, Mrs. Vanderhaven paused to look back at Samantha. Adam blinked, puzzled—what did the woman's pained expression mean? She'd won. She should look thrilled. Her husband ushered her out the door, and the judge began speaking again. Adam turned his attention forward.

"Mr. and Mrs. Klaassen, would you be willing to consider adopting Lucille and Henry, Jr.?"

The consolation prize? He pushed the cynical thought aside. Any child was a gift, and he would welcome it. "Yes, sir, but we would like a chance to discuss it. Could Daniel—Mr. Klaassen contact you some time tomorrow?"

"That would be fine. I'll look for you tomorrow, Daniel." Then to Samantha and Adam he added, "It was nice meeting both of you. I'm sorry I couldn't grant your request."

Adam held Samantha's arm, and they followed Daniel to the hallway. Outside the courtroom, Daniel expelled his breath and said, "I'm sorry, you two. I wish—"

"It's not your fault, Daniel." Adam put a hand on his brother's shoulder. "You did your best."

Samantha lifted a pale face to Adam. "Adam, what are we going to do?"

Adam pulled her against his side. "We're going to take Lucille and Henry, Jr., home and do our best to make them happy. We can't just leave them, can we?"

Samantha shook her head. "No, we can't just leave them here. I just hope . . ."

"What?" Daniel prompted.

She sighed. "I hope we can be enough to replace what they will lose."

Chapter Twenty-Five

*R*ose picked at the food on her plate. She'd prepared a fine meal, hoping it would be a celebratory supper. But everyone's sad countenance cast a pall over the meal. Christina, Katrina, and Camelia, young as they were, seemed to sense the melancholy mood of the grown-ups and curbed their usual dinnertime chatter. When the girls finished their meal and had been excused, Rose spoke the words that had hovered in her mind since Daniel had taken her aside and shared the outcome of the court visit.

"Adam and Samantha, I am so sorry I sent you that letter."

Adam's head came up, and Samantha's jaw dropped. Samantha asked, "Why would you be sorry?"

Rose confessed, "I knew if I wrote to you, you'd come for those children. And that's precisely what I intended. If only I had talked to Daniel first, I would have known the Vanderhavens had petitioned for the two younger ones, and I could have saved you a lot of heartache. I am so very sorry I dragged you into this mess." Tears stung her eyes.

Adam swiped a napkin across his mouth, shaking his head. "Don't apologize, Rose. And we don't see this situation as a mess. Of course, Samantha and I are disappointed that the judge has chosen to separate the children, but we are going home with a son and daughter. That's a reason for rejoicing."

"Then why are we all sitting here with glum faces?" Rose asked, lifting her shoulders in a shrug.

Samantha grimaced. "I'll tell you why. I feel guilty. The minute I got your letter, my heart told me to come after those children. But my stubborn pride held me back. If I had asked Adam immediately instead of waiting—"

"Sam, I felt the same way about them, but I didn't say anything right away either," Adam said. "So don't feel guilty for not bringing it up sooner. I could have spoken up just as easily as you."

Daniel waved a hand at them all. "I'm not sure even if you had petitioned earlier the outcome would have been any different. After all, the judge felt you were too young and inexperienced to take on four children at once."

So it was back to Rose again. She sighed. "I still feel I should have kept the information to myself."

Samantha rose and began clearing dishes. "I'm not worried about myself right now. What concerns me most is how Lucille and Henry are going to feel when we take them away from their baby brother and sister." She paused, gazing out the window onto the snow-covered side yard.

Adam crossed to Samantha and wrapped his arms around her. "Sammy, somehow we'll help Lucille and Henry understand. It may be hard for them at first, but they're young. In time, with love and patience, they'll adjust."

Samantha looked up. "Will they, Adam? I never did. I missed David every day of every year that he was away from me. I never stopped wishing he was close to me. I know how it feels, and I'm not sure it's something you ever adjust to."

Rose sent Daniel a helpless look. Samantha's anguished tone cut at her heart. No matter what anyone said, she'd played a leading role in this drama, and now she only wanted to make things right. *But how?* She beseeched Daniel with her eyes, however he only shrugged in reply. Her heart sank even further. There was no solution.

Adam said, "We aren't miracle workers, Sammy. All we can do is our best. That's all any parents can do. I don't know how many times I've heard Ma say, you do the best with what you've been given and pray it will be enough."

Rose hurried around the table to her brother- and sister-in-law. "I'm sure Lucy and Henry will be upset that they must leave Will and Ellen Marie behind. But"—she hesitated, wondering if sharing her deepest concern would do more harm than good—"more than that, they no doubt know the Vanderhavens didn't ask for them. They must be feeling very unwanted and insecure right now."

Samantha turned from Adam's embrace. "I'll make sure they know they are very wanted by us. They'll never have to question that." Her voice held conviction.

Adam nodded. "That's right. We may not be able to do anything about the separation from their little brother and sister, but we can make sure they feel secure and loved."

"Well!" Rose clapped her hands together, determined to turn this evening into a happy occasion. "Right now, Samantha, you and I are going upstairs to sort through Christie and Katie's outgrown clothes. I'm sure there are some things in there your Lucy can use."

A smile lifted Samantha's lips. "My Lucy . . ." She closed her eyes for a moment, seeming to savor the words. Then she opened them with a hesitant expression. "But, Rose, shouldn't you hang on to those things for Cami?"

"Nonsense." Rose took hold of Samantha's elbow and aimed her for the stairs. "By the time Cami grows into them, they will be hopelessly out of style. Styles do change, you know! So let's just leave the dishes until later and go have some fun."

Adam let out a huff of laughter. "Go on, Sammy. And maybe by the time you two come back down, the Good Fairy will have visited and taken care of this mess."

"Sounds like you're volunteering my services too, brother," Daniel said, rolling his eyes. "Well, let's get to work," he added, rolling up his sleeves.

Samantha giggled, making Rose smile too. The two women went up to the little room tucked under the eaves where they spent a cheerful half hour digging through the attic trunks. Samantha chose two nightgowns, underclothes, and a pair of black patent slippers with a tiny strap that buttoned across the instep.

"Are you sure you want to part with these dresses?" Samantha held up a sweet frilly frock of dotted Swiss.

"Please, take them." Rose added it to the stack of calico dresses and ruffled pinafores. "These will be perfect for Lucy to wear to school. And as I said, it will be a long time before Cami can wear them anyway." Samantha still looked doubtful, so Rose leaned forward and patted her arm. "If it makes you feel better you can always ship them back when Lucy outgrows them."

"That's true," Samantha mused, smoothing a hand across the row of lace ruffles on the pale pink dotted Swiss dress. "This one will be Lucy's church dress, and I'll put her hair in pin curls like Christie and Katie's."

Rose smiled, delighted to see Samantha making plans for her daughter. She reached the bottom half of the large trunk, and her breath caught. "Oh, Sammy, look. I'd forgotten about this."

Samantha gasped and reached to take the baby gown from Rose's hands. She traced one finger across the embroidered roses dancing across the unbelievably small bodice and tapped each pea-sized pearl button. A tiny white satin bow graced the neckline. Samantha fingered the bow, her expression wistful.

"Oh, Rose, this is so soft and sweet. It says, in the most innocent of ways, *baby*."

Rose accepted the gown from Samantha's outstretched hands. Memories of her girls as infants, clean and powdered after a bath, flooded her. She impulsively pressed the gown to her face, burying her nose in the little garment. Only the smells of cedar that lined the trunk and mothballs that Rose used to discourage insects hung in the folds of the fabric, but she imagined she caught the scent of baby powder. She lowered the gown to her lap and shifted her gaze to Samantha. Rose could see the tears shimmering in her sister-in-law's eyes.

"Rose . . . will I ever have my own little baby?"

Pain stabbed at Rose's heart. How could she have been so unthinking . . . again? She set the gown aside and captured both of Samantha's hands and squeezed—hard. "You will, Sam. Daniel might not have told you this yet, but once you adopt through the courts, your name stays on record. If you decide later to adopt another child, it is simply a matter of paperwork, because you've already been approved by the court. You know Daniel will keep his ears open for news of any babies who need a family and will contact you at once. Give yourselves time to settle Lucy and Henry into your home, then come back and try again. You'll have a baby someday, Sam. I just know it."

Samantha nodded, her throat convulsing. "I'm sure you're right. . . ."

"Rose? Samantha?" From downstairs, Daniel's voice interrupted. "Would you two come here, please?"

The women brushed away their tears, set the clothes aside, and descended the narrow attic stairs to the landing. Daniel stood at the foot of the stairs looking upward with an unreadable expression on his face. "There's someone here who wants to speak with Samantha."

Samantha looked at Rose, but she just shrugged. Samantha and Adam didn't know anyone else in Minneapolis. Samantha headed down the stairs first, pausing when she reached the bottom. Daniel gestured toward the parlor.

Samantha came up short right inside the parlor's arched doorway. Seated on the settee was none other than Dr. and Mrs. Vanderhaven.

⌒♾

Samantha froze in place, uncertain what to say or do. Her gaze found Adam, who sat on the edge of a side chair nearby. His face reflected the bewilderment she felt.

The doctor rose, holding out a hand as if he were host. "Please, Mrs. Klaassen, come in."

Hesitantly Samantha entered, and settled herself in a Queen Anne chair near Adam. He stretched his hand across the small table between the matching chairs, and she clasped it. *Lord, whatever this is, please help us. . . .*

Dr. Vanderhaven sat back down as his wife angled herself to face Samantha. "Mrs. Klaassen, I have spent the entire afternoon thinking of you. What you said in the courtroom earlier today, concerning your own troubled childhood. . . . I must say, your words were quite . . . well, quite upsetting to me."

Samantha glanced uncertainly at Adam before answering. "I didn't intend to upset anyone. I apologize, Mrs. Vanderhaven."

"Don't apologize, please." The older woman twisted a pair of kidskin gloves in her hands. "Your heartfelt speech made me look at things from a quite different perspective than I had before. You see, my husband and I are accustomed to getting whatever it is we want or need. We have been blessed in many ways—perhaps too blessed," she added, glancing briefly at her husband. "It's been too easy for us to lose sight of what others want and need."

Samantha nodded, but she didn't know what to say. Surely the couple hadn't come across town on this snowy night just to say that her words had touched them. She sat silently, holding Adam's hand as if it were a lifeline, waiting for the other woman to continue.

"Herbert and I have been talking, and—" Her shoulders pulled up, and a single sob broke out. Her husband pulled a handkerchief from his pocket and offered it to her, putting an arm around her shoulders and patting her gently. She held the handkerchief to her lips. "I'm sorry, I was determined not to break down like this."

Sympathy rolled through Samantha's breast. "It's all right, Mrs. Vanderhaven."

She shook her head, speaking through her tears. "No, Mrs. Klaassen, it is not all right. What my husband and I have intended to do is most certainly not all right—not for the McIntyre children."

Samantha's heart began thumping. She could feel the pressure of Adam's hand on her own increase.

Dr. Vanderhaven spoke. "Mr. and Mrs. Klaassen, my wife and I have planned for several years to adopt a baby. It had always been our intention that when our own children were of an age to be somewhat self-sufficient, we would open our home and hearts to an unwanted baby. We firmly believed we would be giving a secure home to a child who would otherwise grow up alone and unloved. When we petitioned the courts to adopt the McIntyre baby and toddler, we honestly felt we were doing the right thing. Neither Lorraine nor I believed anyone would be willing to take on four children at once. We truly felt that by separating the children, we were giving the older two a better chance at finding a suitable home. I hope you will believe that."

The man's tone and expression left no doubt in Samantha's mind concerning his sincerity. Not to mention the tears of anguish that continued to roll silently down Mrs. Vanderhaven's pale cheeks.

Adam said, "We understand, Dr. Vanderhaven. Samantha and I hold no ill feelings toward you or your wife." Samantha swallowed and nodded her agreement.

The doctor offered a grateful smile before continuing. "Now that we've had time to see things, as it were, from a different perspective, we have had a change of heart." He paused, taking in a shuddering breath. "We have concluded that we cannot in good conscience separate the children."

Mrs. Vanderhaven added, "It would be cruel to ask them to grow up apart from one another. Even our own children substantiated it for us when we asked their feelings on the matter. As much as I want the baby, I just can't—" She stopped again, her face crumpling. She lifted the handkerchief to cover her mouth.

Dr. Vanderhaven put a bolstering arm around his wife's shaking frame. "We have withdrawn our request for adoption of William and Ellen Marie."

Samantha's heart lifted wildly in her chest. But then just as quickly she remembered the judge's words—he could not grant custody of four children to a young, inexperienced couple. The children would be separated anyway if she and Adam were to go through with the adoption of Lucy and Henry, Jr. Her spirits sank once more and her stomach whirled as if she'd just ridden a tornado. She'd gone from hoping for four children, to fearing they'd be given no children, to being granted two children, and then back again to no children, all in the space of one day.

She pressed her palms to her quivering belly, willing the fearful churning to calm.

Adam spoke softly, as if reading Samantha's thoughts. "Then the children must remain at the Foundling Home until another family is willing to take all four is found."

"No, Mr. Klaassen, you misunderstand." Dr. Vanderhaven looked from Adam to Samantha. He patted his wife once more, waited for her nod of approval, then said, "Lorraine and I visited with Judge Simmons at his home before coming here this evening. We withdrew our petition only on the condition that all four children remain together in your custody. After seeing you in court and hearing your expressions on their behalf, we truly felt, despite your young years, you could best provide the kind of home the children will need. Judge Simmons agreed to a six-month probationary period, after which a simple hearing will take place. If all has gone well, final adoption will be filed." He paused, looking as if he'd overstepped his boundaries. He added hesitantly, "That is, if you are still interested in adopting all four children."

Samantha was out of her chair and halfway across the room before she was aware she had moved. She held both hands out to the other couple. "Oh, Dr. and Mrs. Vanderhaven, yes, yes, we're interested. It's what we prayed for all along!"

Adam was beside Samantha in an instant and placed his arm around her waist. "We don't know how to thank you."

Mrs. Vanderhaven looked up, her eyes still shimmering with tears. "Take good care of those children. Love them. You will, won't you?"

Samantha took the older woman's hand and squeezed it. "I promise you, we will love them as our own."

Mrs. Vanderhaven nodded, drew in a great breath, and rose. She lifted her chin, taking on the regal bearing she'd carried in the courtroom. "Purchasing clothing and furniture for four children will take a substantial amount. I had already secured several items for the two youngest children. I want you to take them." Samantha opened her mouth to protest, but the other woman held up her hand. "I would consider it an honor to contribute toward the children's new beginning with you. Please allow me this small pleasure."

Samantha, in her usual way, looked at Adam, and he smiled his assent. She turned to Mrs. Vanderhaven. "Thank you, ma'am. We appreciate very much your generosity. For everything."

Dr. Vanderhaven stepped forward. "I am sure you will have your hands full on the train handling the children, so we will have the items shipped to your home. Will that meet with your approval?"

"That would be fine," Adam said. "Thank you."

The four of them stood in the center of the room, uncertain of what to do next. Then Samantha impulsively took one step toward Mrs. Vanderhaven and opened her arms. The other woman had moved, too, and they found themselves sharing a brief embrace. In that moment, as Mrs. Vanderhaven clung unashamedly to her, Samantha recognized the amount of love it took for Mrs. Vanderhaven to let go of the baby she truly wanted and entrust the child into Samantha's hands.

As they stepped back, Samantha said, "When Ellen Marie and Will are old enough, I'll show them the things you bought for them and tell them how much they were wanted by another mother."

Mrs. Vanderhaven touched Samantha's cheek and offered a quavering smile.

The doctor said, "The papers must be signed at the courthouse Monday morning, and then you will pick up the children. I'm sure Mr. Klaassen—" he turned to Daniel, standing with Rose near the door, "—will be able to help you through those details."

"Yes, sir," Adam said, his voice full of excitement. "We'll be there."

"Very well then. Good evening." The doctor took his wife's arm and guided her toward the door. The instant the door closed on the couple, Adam swept Samantha off her feet in a rib-crushing hug and swung her around.

"Thank You, Lord!" Samantha rejoiced, holding to Adam's neck. She laughed and cried at once. Her dreams had come true.

Chapter Twenty-Six

*T*he Vanderhavens' amazing visit occurred on Friday evening. Adam and Samantha couldn't pick up the children until Monday morning. The weekend stretched endlessly before them. They made good use of the time—and Daniel's telephone—first, with calls home to tell the family the wonderfully good news. They also began the search for simple furnishings to fill the long-empty bedrooms at their home.

Si and Laura promised to haul Daniel and Frank's old iron bed over for the two boys to share. Laura's voice trembled just a bit over the telephone when she told Adam of her joy at "getting four more grandchildren all in one swoop!" Priscilla told them her parents had a maple bed and dresser Lucy could use. Jake and Liz offered the loan of a cradle, and Becky and Teddy volunteered to round up a supply of used toys from the various children in the family.

Hulda and Hiram too were overjoyed when they heard the news, and immediately they insisted on providing rugs for each of the bedrooms, including the master bedroom. Frank said he'd burn the midnight oil and make toy boxes for the children's belongings. Stephen and Josie thought there was an old bureau in the attic at Stephen's brother's place—if so, they'd bring it over for the boys' room.

So getting the home ready for the children became a group effort. And even though Samantha and Adam were miles from home, they heard that the rooms for their children were taking shape. Their excitement mounted ever higher with each tick of the clock drawing them closer to the moment of meeting—the moment of culminating their dreams of a family of their own.

On Monday morning, Rose prodded, "Samantha, please, you must eat something."

Adam glanced up from his own breakfast. Sure enough, her plate was still untouched. Samantha held her fork, but instead of carrying food to her mouth, she only used it to push the scrambled eggs, bacon, and fried potatoes back and forth.

"I can't eat." Samantha put down her fork with a shaking hand. "I feel as if there are bats flying around in my stomach. There's no room for food."

Katrina gazed, astonished. "You have bats in your tummy, Auntie Sam? How'd they get there?"

Christina rolled her eyes and nudged her sister none too gently. "Auntie Sam just means she's nervous."

Katrina looked to Samantha. "Is that true? You're nervous?"

Samantha nodded, a hand against her belly. "Yes, sweetheart, that's exactly what I mean."

Katrina sighed with relief. "Whew! I'm glad you don't really have bats in your belly. That would be a very bad thing!" She turned to Daniel. "Daddy, would having bats in your belly be as bad as bats in your belfry?"

Daniel sputtered on his coffee.

"Well, 'member you said Mr. Rooney down the street had bats in—"

Rose exclaimed, "Oh, Katie!" while adults burst into laughter.

"What's wrong?" Katrina looked at them in confusion.

"Never mind." Daniel shook his head. "Just finish up so we can get you off to school."

Katrina shrugged, obviously thinking, *Grown-ups!*, and dug into her scrambled eggs. But she'd barely taken two bites before she turned to Samantha again. "Auntie Sam, why are you nervous?"

Samantha brushed Katrina's bangs to the side with one finger. "Today is the day Uncle Adam and I meet the children we are going to adopt."

The little girl wrinkled her nose. "But I thought you *want* to meet them."

Adam tried to explain. "We do want to meet them, Katie, but it's kind of like going to school the first day. It's very exciting to begin something new, but at the same time it makes your tummy feel funny because you don't know just what to expect."

Katrina looked thoughtful. "Yeah, I guess that makes sense," she finally conceded. "But, Uncle Adam, don't worry. You're just meeting four little kids, and when I went to school there was lots more kids than that. I did okay, and you will too."

"Thank you for the words of encouragement, Miss Katie," Adam said, his lips twitching. "I'm sure Auntie Sam and I will be just fine, like you said."

Samantha, still chuckling, picked up her fork and went to work on her own breakfast.

⌒つ

Promptly at nine o'clock Samantha and Adam stood before Judge Simmons in his office—which Daniel called his chambers—and signed the papers that gave them temporary custody of Lucy, Henry, Will, and Ellen Marie McIntyre.

Adam pressed the pen so hard a spurt of ink shot above the first letter in his name. When Samantha took the pen, her hand shook so badly the signature was barely recognizable. But it didn't matter—the signatures, made in front of the judge and a witness, Daniel, were legally binding. They were officially embarking on their voyage as Mother and Father.

"Now, Mr. and Mrs. Klaassen," Judge Simmons told them, slipping his spectacles off and smiling, first at one, then the other, "Daniel will accompany you to the Foundling Home. The nuns were informed that you'd be coming, and they will have the children ready. Just give them this"—he handed Adam a brown envelope—"and then you will be free to take the children. In six months' time, we will meet here a second time. If all has gone well, at that time we will complete the necessary paperwork to make the adoption final."

Samantha pressed two trembling hands against her ribs and beamed at Adam. He returned the smile with one equally brilliant, then turned to Judge Simmons. Adam shook the judge's hand. "Thank you very much, Your Honor."

"Yes, thank you," Samantha seconded, placing her hand on Adam's arm. "We appreciate very much your concern for the children. You have our word that we will do our very best for them."

"Good luck to both of you," the older man said.

Samantha smiled. "We don't need luck, sir. We have God's blessings, and that's better than any amount of luck. We'll see you in six months."

She walked out of the judge's chambers with an eager, confident step. But then when they reached the rock-paved walkway leading to the doors of the Minneapolis Foundling Home, suddenly a wave of something she couldn't identify—panic? nervousness? apprehension?—struck. Samantha slowed down and pulled on Adam's arm.

"Sammy, what is it?" Adam asked.

Samantha clung hard to her husband's sturdy arm. "I don't know, but I—I think I might faint!"

Daniel reached over and began fanning her with the thick envelope the judge had given them. "Calm down, Sam. You're going to be fine. I can't ever remember anyone fainting from becoming a parent."

"Are you sure?" Samantha gasped in puffing breaths.

Daniel gave a short laugh. "Yes, my dear, I'm sure."

"That's good to know," Adam said, panting himself, "because I think—" he blew out a breath, "I think I'm feeling faint too."

Samantha continued to gasp for breath. "Give me a minute to calm myself. I can't meet our children for the first time while I'm so . . ." But she didn't finish as the reality of the moment tumbled over her like a load of bricks. Such an awesome responsibility, the raising of a child. From this day forward, a separate, living soul—four of them, to be specific—would depend on her and Adam to meet all needs from physical to spiritual. She'd wanted it, had longed for and prayed for it, and now here it was, ready for the taking. A gamut of emotions rolled through her— exhilaration and fear, apprehension and anticipation, all at once.

"Sammy, you're not having second thoughts, are you?" Adam peered at her in concern.

"Oh, no, Adam, it isn't that at all!" She looked into his eyes. "You know how much I want to take those children home. They are our dream—yours and mine! It's just . . ."

Adam squeezed her shoulder with a smile of understanding. "It's just that it's right here looking us in the face, and it's all a little overwhelming."

Samantha nodded. "Yes, that's exactly it!"

"The worst part is over, Sammy—the waiting is done," Adam said kindly. "Right through that door are four little children who have been entrusted to us. And I am ready to meet them and let them know how very much we have wanted them. I think you're ready, too."

Samantha pressed her hand to her stomach and took a great breath. "Yes, Adam. I'm ready. Let's go meet our children." He held out his arm in gentlemanly fashion, and she took it like a true lady would. They exchanged one last long look of silent wonder, and then they moved forward.

Daniel held the door open, and the pair entered together, stepping into a square foyer of sterile white. A short, round nun with smiling face and apple cheeks came forward to greet them. "You must be the Klaassens," she said in a voice soft as eiderdown.

"That's correct," Daniel answered for them, offering his hand.

The older woman accepted it, squeezing it briefly as she introduced herself. "I am Sister Mary Catherine, and I have had the privilege of looking after Lucy and Ellen Marie." She dropped Daniel's hand and took the papers that would officially release the children. She glanced through them, tapped lightly on the official seal of the court, then set them aside on a desk.

Turning to Samantha and Adam, she reached out a gentle hand. Samantha clasped it at once. "We are all so very pleased that our little ones will remain as family. So worried little Lucy has been that someone would take her sweet baby sister from her." Her clear green eyes went from Samantha to Adam, then back again. "They are dear children, but very frightened. You will be patient as they learn to know and accept you as their new parents?"

"Oh, yes, we will," Samantha assured the elderly woman. But a part of her hoped it wouldn't take too long—she was so anxious to be mama!

Adam said, "We're looking forward to meeting the children and getting them settled in their new home."

"Ah, of course you are, Mr. Klaassen, of course you are." Sister Mary Catherine gave Samantha's hand one final squeeze. "The children are being readied now for their journey. If you would please wait here"—she gestured to four wooden chairs in a row next to the wall—"I shall bring the children down directly."

"Thank you," Samantha said. So they were forced to wait a little longer as the nun moved silently up the staircase. Daniel and Samantha sat—Samantha on the edge of the seat with her hands pressed, palms together, between her knees—but Adam paced back and forth, his gaze glued to the spot at the top of the stairs where the children would descend.

They waited, listening to the grandfather clock that stood sentinel next to the staircase. Somewhere in the building, school was in session, for addition instructions could be heard over the sounds of chalk scratching against a blackboard. Traffic noises intruded from the street outside, and once a sparrow perched on the windowsill and pecked at its own reflection in the window.

And then came a creaking at the top of the stairs.

Adam immediately stopped, his face aimed upward. Samantha rose slowly, her gaze, like Adam's, focused above. Her breath caught in her throat and held. The staircase was built with a half wall of plaster rather than a railing, so the first view of their children was merely the tops of two heads—one brown, one blond—moving quite slowly in the way small children, place both feet on one riser before stepping to the next. Sister Mary Catherine carried the baby in her arms, and Samantha strained to see, but the littlest one also was hidden by the nun's starched habit and the shielding stairway wall. So they had to wait until the little group reached the bottom and came around the corner.

Samantha's fingertips flew to her lips and tears flooded her eyes at the first full sight of Lucy, Henry, and Will. Lucy was holding the toddler's pudgy hand securely in her own small hand. The little girl had fine brown hair that fell straight to her shoulders with a few wispy bangs softening the severity of the cut. Her eyes, large and velvety brown, were surrounded by long lashes.

Both little Will and his big brother were towheads, Will's baby hair curling into soft ringlets behind his ears. Henry's hair was close-cropped on the sides with the top a bit longer, and one strand flopped across his forehead. A spattering of copper-colored freckles sprinkled his nose. Both boys had hazel eyes. The children stood in a silent line, their solemn, unsmiling faces and unblinking eyes looking back at the strangers in front of them.

Sister Mary Catherine stopped behind the three, and the baby squirmed in the nun's arms. The woman turned the baby against her shoulder and patted her back. "I had to wake the wee one, so she is likely to be a bit cranky," the Sister explained. She turned her attention to the children and said, "Children, I want you to meet Mr. and Mrs. Klaassen. They are the nice couple I told you about, who want to take care of you." The Sister touched the back of Lucy's head. "Lucy, can you say hello?"

Whisper soft, Lucy offered, "Hello."

Samantha moved forward slowly, dropping to her knees in front of Lucy and holding out her hand to touch the little girl's arm. "Hello, Lucy. I'm so glad to meet you. You and Will and Henry. Your baby sister, Ellen, too." She smiled at each in turn.

Lucy pointed at Henry. "He's Buddy."

Samantha asked, "What, honey?"

"He's not Henry, he's Buddy. Our papa is Henry. He's Buddy."

Samantha smiled brightly at Henry—Buddy. "Buddy . . . is that what you like to be called?"

The little boy nodded soberly, his hair bobbing against his forehead.

"Then Buddy it is." She turned and touched a soft blond coil behind Will's ear. "And I'll bet you get called Curly sometimes."

Will rewarded her with a bashful smile before hiding his face in his sister's dress front, but neither Lucy nor Buddy smiled. Both wore narrow-eyed expressions of wariness and fear. Samantha couldn't blame them. She rose as Adam also knelt to greet the three older ones who stood stiff and sober.

Holding out her arms, Samantha asked the nun, "Please, may I hold the baby?"

The nun nodded with a tender smile. And then Samantha's arms were filled with the sweet weight of Ellen Marie—her own baby whom no one would ever take away. She pressed the baby girl's dimpled cheek against her own, breathing in the scents of milk and talcum. She closed her eyes, savoring the wonder of the moment. Ellen Marie fit just right in her arms—a round, warm bundle of perfection—and holding her, Samantha felt complete.

Perhaps in her joy Samantha unwittingly held the child too tightly, and Ellen Marie planted a tiny fist against Samantha's chin and pushed, beginning to protest. Adam reached for her. "Let me hold her, Sam." But the baby gave him the same treatment—flailing arms and unhappy squalls. Reluctantly, he handed her to Sister Mary Catherine. Ellen Marie settled down in the familiar arms of the nun, and the woman offered a sympathetic look over the baby's head.

"Do not be discouraged. The wee one is just confused by all the changes. Be patient." Her gaze dropped to the children who now huddled in a tight group, Lucy's arms around her brothers. "It may take some time, but all will be well. You will see."

Samantha nodded, taking Adam's hand. She vowed to do whatever it took to erase the looks of fearful uncertainty on the children's faces. Soon her arms would be the ones the baby preferred over all others.

She moved away from Adam and leaned forward, propping one hand on her knee, stretching the other, palm up, toward the sober-faced children. "Come, children. Let's go home."

At the word *home*, little Will released his sister's skirts and placed his chubby hand in Samantha's. Her fingers closed around it as she straightened, sending a smile of success to Adam. He returned it with one of his own, then turned to Lucy and Buddy.

"Yes, children. It's time we take you home," he said.

Lucy looked up to Sister Mary Catherine, and the nun gave her a nod of encouragement, her face wreathed with gentle smile lines. Hesitantly Lucy placed her hand in Adam's, and Buddy followed her lead, taking Adam's other hand.

"The children's bags are beside the door," Sister Mary Catherine told Daniel. "The little basket holds sandwiches and fruit and canned milk for your trip."

"Thank you," Adam said, "that's very thoughtful of you."

"It is the least we can do to send these little ones off on a good start," the nun said.

The little entourage headed out the door, Daniel in the lead, the battered cardboard suitcases bumping against his leg. Sister Mary Catherine followed next with Ellen Marie who protested loudly at being covered with a layer of shawls. Samantha followed, carrying Will, and Adam brought up the rear with the small hands of Lucy and Buddy curled in his palms. Daniel tossed the suitcases into the rumble seat, then helped Samantha crawl into the backseat, and Sister Mary Catherine handed a still-complaining Ellen Marie to her. Will and Buddy climbed in beside Samantha, and Adam and Lucy shared the front seat with Daniel.

"God bless you all," the Sister said warmly before Adam closed the door. And they were off to the train station to begin their journey home . . . and the even longer journey toward becoming a family.

Chapter Twenty-Seven

*T*he moment they arrived at the train station, Lucy turned stubborn and refused to leave the automobile. Adam finally picked her up and carried her onto the passenger car. Although he asked her repeatedly what was wrong, she refused to answer, only stared at him with her chin quivering and her eyes clearly displaying her distrust.

Little Will kicked his feet, swung his fists, and cried out, "Mama! Mama!" in a high-pitched wail so heartrending it made Adam want to cry too. Buddy obediently huddled in the seat Adam pointed out for him, but tears rolled down his thin cheeks, dripping from his chin.

And Ellen Marie screeched in an ear-splitting fashion until she was hoarse. She fought against being held, but they couldn't put her down anywhere. She wouldn't take a bottle, but she sucked her fist until a purple spot showed on the back of her hand. She cried and cried and cried. She finally fell into an exhausted sleep, her little chest still rising and falling in shuddering breaths. Adam couldn't help questioning if maybe the judge had been right all along. Maybe four children all at once was too much for them.

Aware of glares from irate passengers, Adam did his best to soothe Will. Samantha, her arms busy cradling Ellen Marie, could offer no help. At last a buxom matron with fuzzy apricot hair and several chins apparently took pity on them. Without a word of warning, she scooped up the wailing Will and pressed him against her ample chest. She ordered the two men occupying the seat nearest Adam and Samantha to trade with her, and they did, too startled to argue. She plunked herself down and began moving back and forth against the seat's padded back, patting Will's bottom in rhythm with her rocking.

To Adam's great relief and appreciation, Will, too, fell asleep, his head drooping back against the woman's heavy arm. "Should I take him now?" Adam whispered.

The older woman shook her head. "Nah, I'll hold 'im till he wakes." She grinned and added, "I've rocked more'n my share of li'l 'uns. M' arms'll hold up."

"Thank you, ma'am," Adam said, and he meant it. The whole train car seemed to breathe a sigh of relief. With Will and Ellen Marie sleeping, the atmosphere was quiet at last.

Adam settled back next to Buddy and placed an arm around the boy's narrow shoulders. The blond hank of hair that hung down across Buddy's forehead swayed with the motion of the train. His hands were planted against the seat to hold himself erect as the train pitched and rolled with the rails. The tears had stopped running, but two drops still hung on the little boy's lashes. Adam used a thumb to brush them away.

"Buddy, I'm sorry you're sad," Adam said. "I'd like to help you, if you'd tell me what's troubling you. I hope you aren't afraid of me, son."

Buddy hunkered into his jacket.

Adam gave the boy's shoulder a light pat. "Please, won't you talk to me, Buddy?"

The child clamped his lips closed and leaned away from Adam. Rebuffed, Adam shifted his attention to Lucy, who sat on the other side of Buddy. "Lucy, can you tell me what's bothering your brother?"

Lucy flicked a quick, resentful look in Adam's direction then turned her face to gaze out the window. Buddy leaned into his sister's shoulder as far from Adam as he could go without leaving the seat. Adam waited for several minutes, but neither of the children acknowledged him in any way.

With a sigh, he looked across the small expanse and met Samantha's eyes. He sent her a weak smile, which she returned. When she yawned, his heart twisted in sympathy. *She must be exhausted—she'd been holding the baby for almost two hours now.* He would offer to take the little one, but he didn't want to risk waking her and creating a new disturbance.

So he sat in silence with a tired wife, two sleeping children, two uncommunicative children, and a heart filled with mixed emotions and more questions than he could answer.

~⌒๑

By the time the train rumbled into the Mountain Lake station, Samantha's arms ached so badly from cradling the baby she was sure they would fall off. Her ears hurt from listening to Ellen Marie's wails and Will's screaming tantrums, both resumed about the same time as they awakened. Her neck and calves ached from bracing herself against the seat and holding her body as still as possible to keep from jostling the baby. But mostly, her heart hurt.

She hadn't been naive enough to expect the children to love her instantly, but she had anticipated some small measure of cooperation. The children were so obviously upset and unhappy, it was impossible not to experience empathy pangs on their behalf as well as disappointment for the negative response. The first few hours of being a mama were far from what she'd hoped for.

Lucy and Buddy had finally fallen asleep with their heads against the windowpanes. While Adam now retrieved the crying

Will from the helpful matron, Samantha wiggled Lucy's knee with her fingers, coaxing, "Lucy . . . it's time to wake up." She tapped Buddy's knee and added, "Wake up now, children, we're home."

Buddy roused first, twisting his shoulders high and wriggling sideways in the seat. He lifted his fists to clear his eyes, then reached out blindly with a foot and clunked his sister on the shin. Drowsily the little girl lifted her head and tried to focus. She scowled for a moment, looking at Samantha blearily, as if trying to figure out who she was.

"Children, we're home now," Samantha repeated gently, smiling at the pair.

Lucy's features smoothed, and she turned to the window. She pressed her palms and her nose to the glass eagerly. Buddy knelt on his seat and did the same. "Hey!" Buddy flung himself away from the glass. "What's this place?"

Thrilled that he was finally showing some interest, Samantha answered brightly, "This is Mountain Lake, Minnesota, Buddy. This is home."

Lucy turned a fierce scowl on Samantha. "This ain't home! I knew you was fibbin'. To get home we never took a train. Only needed a trolley car. Or we could walk."

Fresh tears rolled down Buddy's freckled face. He pointed an accusing finger at Adam, who stood in the aisle with Will clinging to his neck. "That man lied, too. He called me 'son.' An' he ain't my papa. I want my papa! I wanna go home!" Buddy threw himself into Lucy's arms. She glared at both Samantha and Adam over her brother's shoulder.

Ellen Marie began crying again, no doubt upset at her brother and sister's distress. Samantha bounced the baby and sent Adam a baffled look. Hadn't anyone explained to the children their parents were gone, and they would be going to a new home?

Adam dropped down on the seat next to Lucy and Buddy. "Children, did the Sisters at the Foundling Home tell you about your mama and papa?"

Lucy's lower lip thrust out belligerently, and Buddy blinked against tears. Lucy answered in a near-whimper, "They said Mama and Papa went up to heaven."

Adam nodded and reached out an arm to draw the pair against his side. "That's right. Your parents went to heaven. And that means there is nobody at your house to take care of you anymore. When Samantha and I heard about you, we knew we wanted to take care of you. So we talked to a judge at the courthouse, and he said it would be all right for us to be your new mama and daddy." He whisked a quick glance at Samantha before turning back to the children. "The Sisters explained that to you, didn't they?"

Slowly Lucy nodded, her brown eyes wide in her narrow face. "The Sisters said we'd be goin' home, an' *she* said"—she poked an obstinate thumb in Samantha's direction—"you'd be takin' us home. But this ain't home!"

Obviously the children had completely misunderstood what would be taking place. Oh, how Samantha wished she and Adam had asked a few more questions before removing the children from the Foundling Home.

The conductor appeared at the passenger car doorway and asked briskly, "You folks ready to light out? We've already watered the engine, and we're ready to move on."

Adam answered with a tired sigh. "Certainly. We're getting off right now."

"Noooo!" Lucy flung herself face down on the seat. "I wanna go home! I wanna go home!"

Buddy took up the cry as well, kneeling beside his sister and clinging to her as if his life depended on it. Ellen Marie screamed in body-jerking hysteria, and little Will threw back his head and started wailing, "I want Mama! Mama! Mama!"

Samantha looked helplessly at Adam, on the verge of tears herself, and then a sweet voice intruded.

"Would an extra pair of hands be useful right now?"

Samantha spun to find Si and Laura at the end of the aisle, and her shoulders wilted with relief. "Oh, Mother and Papa Klaassen . . . thank heaven you're here!"

Laura came forward and lifted Ellen Marie from Samantha's arms, taking a moment to pat Samantha's cheek lovingly. "Now you get the other little girl and come on outside."

Lucy had curled her fingers around the seat, but Samantha managed to unloose them and lift the still sobbing Lucy and help her walk to the door. Si scooped up Will and the suitcases, Adam lifted Buddy, and they made their way to the boardwalk. Minutes later, the train chugged around the bend.

Si raised his voice to be heard over the children's wails. "I told the rest of the family not to come meet the train. Figured the little ones would be confused and upset and a huge gathering would overwhelm them."

Samantha, looking down at Lucy's belligerent face, heaved a sigh of relief that the entire family hadn't been there to witness their less-than-happy plunge into parenthood. She said, "The children thought we'd be taking them back to their old house, where they lived with their parents."

Laura's face softened in sympathy as she cuddled the still crying Ellen Marie. "The poor little things . . . how difficult this must be for them! And how disappointing for you, too," she added, sending Samantha a sympathetic smile. "This isn't quite the homecoming you'd imagined, is it?"

Adam and Samantha exchanged looks, and Adam stretched his eyes wide. Suddenly it all struck a funny chord inside

Samantha. The emotional roller coaster of the past few days played briefly in her mind—the hopeful rush to Minneapolis to claim the children, the crushing disappointment of the courtroom scene, the victory of the judge's changed verdict, the excitement of meeting the children, then the hugely depressing train ride. To think that they'd hoped and prayed to bring these children home only to have those same children wailing in despair because they'd been brought home! Whether it was tiredness or hysteria or simply a means to cope, Samantha felt her shoulders start to vibrate with soundless chuckles. Then an amused, very unladylike snort erupted.

Adam looked at her in surprise as she burst into full laughter. She took in his shocked expression and laughed all the harder. Si and Laura looked from Adam to Samantha to each other, their eyebrows raised high in silent query while Samantha continued to laugh and the children continued to wail and the station-master stuck his head out of the train depot to gawk curiously.

"Sam, what on earth—?"

"I'm sorry!" Samantha managed through giggles. "It's just—it's just we wanted kids so much! And now—now we've got 'em, but they aren't too happy about it!"

Adam's lips twitched, and then he started laughing as well. Si and Laura stood by, indulgent smiles creasing their faces. Then Laura nudged Si and pointed—Lucy had stopped crying and was peering up at Samantha and Adam with her mouth open and her eyes wide. Buddy had calmed, too, clutching Lucy's hand and staring at the two laughter-crazed grown-ups.

With Lucy and Buddy quiet, Will seemed to decide there wasn't any more reason to be upset, so his tears ceased as well. Only little Ellen Marie continued to sob softly in Laura's arms while Adam and Samantha struggled to get their amusement under control.

Adam finally said, "Why don't we head for home before we all turn into snowmen out here?"

"Yes, we'd better," Samantha agreed with one more giggle. "The spring thaw is a ways off yet."

They shared one more round of laughter before Adam looked down at the now-silent children. "Are you ready to go?"

Buddy surprised them by announcing, "I'm hungry."

"Then we'll feed you the minute we get there," Adam promised. He mouthed to the others, "Don't say 'home' for a while till they get adjusted."

"Come on," he raised his voice and motioned to the children. "Ever been on a hayride?" Adam asked Lucy as he lifted her into the back of Si's high-sided wagon bed spread thickly with yellow hay. Lucy simply shook her head silently.

"Then you're in for a treat," Adam told her. "Snuggle down and pull the hay around you—it will keep you warm. Buddy and Will, you, too."

The children buried themselves in the hay while Samantha settled in a corner with Ellen Marie. When everyone was ready, Si gave a chirrup to the horses, and they started for home.

⁓৩

Samantha saw Lucy reach for Buddy's hand under the cover of the hay, and he gripped it back. He leaned over and whispered loudly, "They act kinda funny, don't they?"

"Uh-huh." Lucy kept her gaze fixed on Samantha while Samantha cuddled Ellen Marie and hummed a lullaby, pretending she didn't notice. "She looks awful fond o' Ellen Marie."

Buddy shivered. "Reckon we'll be all right?"

Lucy nodded hard. "I'll take care o' you an' the little guys. Don't worry."

Buddy leaned against his sister. She pulled her arm out of the hay and placed it around his shoulders. "I'll make sure we're fine." Her narrowed gaze never wavered from Samantha.

Samantha's heart melted as she remembered another girl, older than Lucy but just as frightened and uncertain, who arrived in Mountain Lake. She'd discovered healing in the folds of the Klaassen family's love, and she'd make certain Lucy experienced the same place of belonging no matter what it took.

Chapter Twenty-Eight

*A*dam kept his first promise to Buddy. The moment the newly formed family arrived at the farm, he seated the children around the table and fed them a quick supper of bread, cold sausage, and canned peaches while Samantha gave Ellen Marie a bottle. Buddy ate as if he'd never seen food before, but Will turned fractious, rubbing his eyes and whining, too tired to eat. Although Adam suspected Lucy was hungry, she only pushed the food around on her plate with a stubby finger, a scowl on her face.

When Ellen Marie finished her bottle, Adam reached for her, eager to share in the baby's caretaking. "Let me rock her to sleep."

For a moment, Samantha held tight, but then she nodded. "Very well. I'll give the others a spit bath."

Buddy turned up his nose. "Spit bath? Ick!"

Samantha chuckled softly. "I promise . . . there's no spitting involved. I don't know why it's called that."

Adam sank into the rocking chair with the delightful weight of Ellen Marie in his arms and watched Samantha line up the three older children for a wash. He couldn't stop a smile from growing. Mothering seemed to come awfully naturally to her.

Will stood complacently in his diaper and socks, yawning widely as Samantha ran a warm, wet cloth over his pudgy little-boy body. After drying him with a length of toweling, she slipped a nightshirt over his curls, manipulating his droopy, uncooperative arms into the sleeves. He then leaned against her leg with a finger in his mouth while she subjected Buddy to the same treatment. Buddy proved more challenging as he hunched into himself, apparently trying to hide. The moment she finished with him, Buddy thrust himself into the offered nightshirt and sat back down at the table for cookies, while Samantha reached for Lucy.

"Uh-uh." Lucy stepped away from the dripping cloth and folded her arms across her skinny chest. "I can do it myself. You don't gotta wash me."

Samantha glanced at Adam, her expression uncertain. Adam thought back—he'd bathed himself at the age of six, and no doubt Samantha had, too, since she had no one to help her. But in his wife's eyes he recognized the desire to connect with Lucy in some way. His heart ached for both new mother and child as the pair squared off, one reaching and one resisting.

At last Samantha nodded. "All right, Lucy. After you're washed and dressed, come upstairs. I'll read you a story and tuck you in."

"You don't gotta," Lucy repeated, taking the washcloth and moving a safe distance from Samantha.

Samantha maintained a low, kind tone. "I know I don't have to, Lucy, but I would like to. I'll take the boys up now, and you can join us when you're in your nightie, okay?"

Lucy paused, the dripping washcloth clenched in her fist. Indecision marred her brow, but at last she shrugged. "All right." She turned her back before beginning to undress.

Samantha scooped up Will. "Come on, tired boy, let's get you tucked into bed." Will rested his head on her shoulder, and Adam's heart leaped, witnessing the trusting gesture. She turned to Buddy. "Are you finished with your cookie, Buddy?" When he nodded, she added, "Good, let's go upstairs then." Samantha held a hand out to him, and after only a moment's pause, he took it and together they climbed the stairs.

Ellen Marie was sleeping soundly, so Adam decided to give Lucy some privacy. He ascended the stairs and looked into the bedroom where Samantha sat with Buddy and Will on the bed, the pair of blond heads tipped toward a picture book, her animated voice reading the tale. Adam wished for a camera to capture the scene, but he knew the memory was burned into his mind.

He carried the baby to the nursery, but he discovered he wasn't ready to relinquish the warm, soft body to the cradle yet. He stood near it, gently rocking and watching Ellen Marie pucker her little lips in sleep. A shuffle at the door alerted him, and he spotted Lucy in the doorway. Her hair stuck up at her forehead where she'd swished the cloth across her face, and she held her locked hands behind her back. He smiled. She maintained a stoic face.

"Want me to put Ellen Marie to bed?" Lucy asked.

Adam tipped his head, wondering if that had been one of her responsibilities. "Sure, that would be nice, Lucy. She's already asleep, but you come over here—" Adam kept his voice low to avoid disturbing the baby, "and I'll put her in your arms. The cradle is all ready for her."

Lucy quickly came and stood in front of him, her hands outstretched. Adam carefully placed the infant in Lucy's arms and watched the girl's expression soften. He tipped the cradle, and the little girl laid her baby sister down and patted her a few times. Adam and Lucy both tucked the blanket around baby Ellen and stepped back.

"Why don't you go in with Will and Buddy and listen to the story? They're across the hall."

Lucy nodded silently, her eyes on Ellen Marie. She stood for several seconds before finally turning and heading away on bare feet. Adam, curious, decided to follow.

The moment Lucy stepped into the bedroom doorway, Samantha lifted her head and offered a warm smile. "Come on in, Lucy. There's room for one more."

But Lucy remained frozen in place. "I just came to say 'night to Buddy an' Willie."

Samantha caught Adam's eyes. The yearning in her face encouraged him to touch the back of Lucy's head and coax, "Go ahead. I'm sure you'll enjoy the story too."

Lucy jerked away from Adam's touch. "No." She waggled her hand. "'Night, Buddy. 'Night, Willie. Sleep tight, don't let the bedbugs bite."

Will held his chubby arms toward his sister. "Gimme hug, Woosy."

Without a moment's hesitation, Lucy ran to him and scooped him clear off the bed with her exuberant hug. She kissed his apple cheek twice before plunking him down. The little boy scrambled back into his spot close to Samantha, and Lucy spun and raced out the door, taking care to stay as far from Adam as she could.

Adam flicked a quick look at Samantha and the boys, sending his wife an encouraging nod before once again following Lucy. The little girl hovered against the wall as if uncertain what to do next. Adam pointed, "Your room is right here." Lucy scuttled into the open doorway across the hallway from the boys' room without a backward glance and closed the door in Adam's face.

Irritation mingled with concern. He needed to talk to the child, but he decided he needed to pray for patience first. Lucy had lived through an unspeakable loss, had been snatched away by people she'd never seen before—people who had held out the promise of "home." It would take some time for her to settle in.

He returned to the boys' room in time to see Samantha trying to disengage herself from the pair of sleeping boys. He tiptoed forward and shifted Will from her lap. She helped Buddy slide down until his head rested on the pillow. Tenderly, she tucked the covers up to their chins, pausing to bestow a light kiss on each forehead before turning out the lamp. Then, hand in hand, they crept to the doorway. There Samantha paused, looking back with a small smile creasing her face.

She whispered, "Don't they look innocent?"

Adam nodded, his heart lifting. The two lay with their blond heads tipped toward each other. Will's lower lip puckered out in a sleepy pout, and Buddy already snored softly. *Our boys* . . . The thought filled him with joy. Then he looked toward the closed door across the hall, and apprehension churned again through his middle.

Lucy was going to be the difficult one, he knew. Adam had always gotten along well with children. All his nieces and nephews adored him, just as they did Samantha. For the first time, Adam had found himself uncomfortable in a child's presence, and he knew Lucy's aloof behavior was also creating a sense of insecurity on Samantha's part. Somehow, they had to find a way to assure Lucy she was safe here. And loved.

"Let's tuck Lucy in now, shall we?" he said. With Samantha's hand in his, he stepped toward Lucy's door and tapped lightly. "Lucy? May we come in?"

After a long silence, Lucy's flat voice could be heard. "I don't care."

Adam opened the door and ushered Samantha through. Lucy lay in bed, the coverlet pulled clear to her chin. Her huge brown eyes watched warily as Samantha approached and perched on the edge of the bed.

"You're all tucked in," Samantha commented, smoothing a hand across the cover, leaving it rest on the far side of Lucy's stiff form.

Beneath the layer of blankets, Lucy shrugged. Adam inched to the other side of the bed, his gaze locked on the little girl's face. Resentment glittered in her eyes, but did she rely on resentment to hide her fear? He wished he could read below the expression of the child's eyes.

"We're so glad you're here, Lucy," Adam said. "Samantha and I have waited for a little girl like you for a long time. It makes us very, very happy that you've come to be with us."

Lucy lay still and wary, her eyes darting from Adam's to Samantha's face.

Adam went on quietly. "I know everything seems strange to you now. It's a different house, with a different bed and different people. But I hope you'll soon feel comfortable here. Samantha and I want to be a good mama and daddy for you and your brothers and sister."

When Lucy still didn't respond, Adam said, "Well, let's get you tucked in, shall we?"

Lucy's fingers curled over the edge of the cover. "I tucked me in."

Samantha shot Adam a helpless look. Adam forced a chuckle. "Well, now, you are a big girl then, aren't you? But we can say good night, can't we?"

"I don't care."

Samantha leaned over and placed a kiss on Lucy's forehead and stood to step aside. Adam also deposited a kiss on the child's brow, but then he sat on the edge of the bed, praying silently for guidance. "When I was a boy your age," he said quietly, "before I went to sleep, my ma and pa always came to tuck me into bed and listen to my bedtime prayers. It made me feel safe, to have a kiss and a prayer before I fell asleep. I'd like to say a prayer with you now, Lucy. Would that be all right?"

He watched Lucy's expression for any signs of softening. None were seen, but she didn't refuse. Adam placed a hand on Lucy's chest and closed his eyes. "Now I lay me down to sleep . . ." he recited the simple prayer offered by thousands of children nightly. At its completion, he added his own postscript. "Thank You, God, for bringing Lucy, Buddy, Will, and Ellen Marie here safely. Help them to understand how very much they are wanted and loved by us. Give them happy dreams to take them through this night. Amen."

When he opened his eyes, he found Lucy's gaze pinned on him, a puzzled scowl on her face. He smiled and said once more, "Good night, Lucy. *Schlop Die gezunt.*"

"What did you say?"

Adam grinned, pleased to have finally gotten a response. "I said, sleep well."

"Didn't sound like sleep well."

"It's *Plautdietsch*—the language my family speaks besides English," Adam said, "and it's what my mother always said right before she left my room."

Lucy stared at him unblinking. "My mother always said 'Sleep tight, don't let the bedbugs bite.'"

Samantha asked, "Do you want me to say that to you at bedtime?"

"No. You're not my mother." Lucy rolled over, pulling the covers over her ear, effectively closing herself away from them.

Samantha put trembling fingers over her mouth and reached for Adam's hand. He took it, and together they left the room. The moment he closed Lucy's door, Samantha leaned into his chest.

"Oh, Adam."

Adam stroked her hair. "Sammy, be patient. Both of us will need to practice lots and lots of it. Remember, when you came to our family? You wore belligerence like a shield too." She sniffed and lifted her head to look at him with wet eyes. "But love and a whole lot of patience eventually broke through those barriers," he continued. "She'll come around. She's the oldest, so her memories are the strongest. We just need to make sure she knows that we aren't trying to replace her birth parents, but give her a secure, loving, new home."

Samantha looked toward the closed door. "She's so . . . distant."

"Yes, but expecting instant acceptance isn't realistic." He spoke to himself as much as his wife. "Give her time."

Samantha sighed, nodded, and then her eyes flew wide. "Ellen Marie hasn't cried in over an hour."

"I know," Adam said proudly. "Come here." He led Samantha to the nursery. Lifting a silencing finger to his mouth, he opened the door and guided her inside. On her tummy in the borrowed cradle, Ellen Marie slept peacefully. Her lower lip drooped open, her nearly transparent eyelids quivered, and one tiny fist curled sweetly against her cheek.

Samantha's fingertips rested on the edge of the cradle. "Oh, Adam . . . our baby."

Adam laid his hands on her shoulders and squeezed. "She drank the entire bottle, burped like a sailor, then gave me the biggest smile. I changed her, then rocked her, and she fell asleep in my arms."

"When she wakes, it will be my turn," Samantha said.

Although Adam would have cheerfully met the baby's needs, he knew how much Samantha longed to care for the infant. "Fair enough. But right now, let's let her sleep. Come on." They crept from the room on tiptoe.

On the way down the hall, Adam said, "I should tell you that Lucy came in before I put Ellen Marie down, and she wanted to put her sister in the cradle. I saw a tenderness that was very moving, and I saw a very careful little girl with her baby sister. And for just a minute or so, she and I made a connection."

Samantha looked up at Adam, hope in her eyes. "Oh, Adam, that is so good to hear after the day we've had."

Snug in bed, her head nestled in the crook of Adam's arm, Samantha sighed. "Do you feel any different?"

Adam forced heavy eyelids open. "Different how?"

"Well, we're parents now." Samantha quiet voice held a note of wonder. "From now on, we will be responsible for four children. They'll depend on us for everything. It's exciting, but it's scary too."

Adam gave a brief chuckle. "You know, Sam, I had those exact same thoughts as we were walking up to the Foundling Home."

She twisted her head a bit, and he sensed her gazing at him in surprise. "You did?"

"I sure did." How alike they'd become—as one, just as God intended. The thought warmed Adam.

She went on in a subdued tone. "I hope I'll be able to do it right. When Lucy said what she did, about me not being her mother, it made me think about the fact that I never had one. Will I know how to be one?"

"Of course you will." Her question almost made him laugh. Adam shifted, drawing her closer. "All you have to do is remember the way your gran treated you. Imitate her, and you'll make a wonderful mother. And if you need specific advice, my ma has been known to have an answer or two up her sleeve."

Samantha nodded against his shoulder. "Yes, I can do both those things. The loving part will be easy. I already feel the beginning of love stirring in my heart. It's hard not to, when faced with such worried little faces. And I know what else I can do."

Conviction steeled her tone. "I can let them be children. I had to grow up so fast, I never really got the chance to be carefree and unburdened. I'm going to make sure my children have lots of time to play and just have fun."

Adam gave her arm a little squeeze. "Did you hear yourself? You called them 'my children.' You already sound and look and act like a mother."

"I do want to be a good mother," she whispered. "I know you'll be a good daddy. You were so good with Lucy tonight, and with Ellen Marie."

"Wait and see, Sammy. By the time we go back to the judge to make the adoption final, all four children will be calling you Mama and loving you nearly as much as I do."

Samantha rolled sideways and pressed her lips against Adam's neck. "I love you, Adam."

"I love you, too," he replied. He yawned and pushed his pillow under his head. "Good night, little mother."

"Good night, new daddy."

Chapter Twenty-Nine

The first few weeks of parenthood were exciting and rewarding, yet an exhausting time for Adam and Samantha. Especially for the "little mother." Although she allowed Adam to give Ellen Marie her evening bath and bottle, Samantha insisted on performing all of the other duties surrounding the baby's care both day and night. After a few days Ellen Marie was adjusting nicely to her new home, and she thrilled her fledgling parents with her sunny disposition and cuddly nature. But even so she awoke twice nightly for bottles, each feeding taking up the better part of an hour. Consequently Samantha got much less sleep than was normal for her.

Additionally, little Will was still in diapers, so washing two dozen flannel squares had to be fit into the daily schedule. Samantha found the best time to tend to laundry was during Will and Ellen Marie's afternoon nap. Adam encouraged her to rest when the little ones were doing so, but Samantha felt it was more difficulty than it was worth to be filling tubs with water and washing soiled clothes with Will under her feet.

To her undisguised delight, Will became her little shadow. She proudly informed her brother, David, that if she took a step backward, she would step on Will—he was always there. The curly haired toddler was the first of the children to begin calling Samantha and Adam "Mama" and "Daddy." The words were music to their ears, and each time the little boy reached for Samantha and uttered that wonderful word—*mama*—Samantha's heart leaped from happiness.

Buddy, in turn, became a true little buddy to Adam. At first Adam brought the youngster along for chores simply to ease a bit of Samantha's care for the children. But before long he took the boy along just for the pleasure of his company. Buddy was a bright, inquisitive little fellow, curious about everything.

His questions were endless. What do worms eat? How come some clouds are fat and some clouds are skinny? Why do horses have manes? Will that little seed really grow into a big ol' wheat stalk? and so on. Adam answered every question with patience, thrilled with the interest Buddy took in all aspects of farming and animal care. He bragged to anyone who would listen about his "little farmin' buddy."

The only cloud in an otherwise sunny sky was Lucy. After a week, Samantha took the little girl into town and enrolled her in school. Samantha had wanted to keep her home until the next term, but Adam felt it would help Lucy realize this home was a permanent one and give her a sense of stability. Lucy's teacher said she was a better-than-average student, but very withdrawn and uncommunicative, preferring to sit alone rather than join the other children. Adam and Samantha could believe that—although she smothered her brothers and baby sister with affection and attention, the only time Lucy talked to her new parents was to let them know she didn't need their help with something or other.

Samantha did everything she could think of to let the little girl know she was loved and wanted. Lucy had all the freedom Samantha's childhood had never included. Samantha made her bed, picked up her toys, laid out a clean dress and apron for her each morning, and combed her fine brown hair into perfect pin curls held away from her forehead with bows to match her dresses. Samantha pampered her, read to her, tried to cuddle her. But Lucy did her best to keep Samantha at arm's length.

Often she would look up from some chore to find Lucy's narrowed, resentful gaze boring a hole in her. Samantha despaired at ever getting through to the child.

Samantha and Adam privately discussed Lucy's aloofness with Si and Laura, hoping their extensive child-rearing experience would help steer a course toward a solution. They advised normalcy—to simply treat Lucy no differently than the others and hope, in time, she would come to accept them as her brothers and sister had.

So Samantha and Adam established routines to create security, including Samantha's favorite—the bedtime routine. She loved the nightly baths when she would make the boys laugh, blowing bubbles through her fist, cuddling together on the bed while she read a Bible story, and saying a prayer with them before tucking them under the covers and delivering a kiss. Both Will and Buddy relished this nighttime ritual as well. Lucy listened to the stories and allowed Samantha and Adam to pray with her and tuck her in, but the child never smiled—only observed everything with the closed, wary expression that had become all too familiar.

As the weeks passed with no improvement in Lucy's demeanor, their concerns grew. The six-month probationary period was closing in more quickly than they could have imagined. What would they do if, when the time came to make the adoption final, Lucy was still so unhappy? Would the judge still grant them permanent custody of the children? The worry became a dark cloud hanging over their heads.

Winter melted away to a beautiful spring. Crocuses and daffodils bloomed, the songbirds returned, and Adam and his Buddy spent every minute they could outside, taking advantage of the warmer days to ready the fields and repair snow-broken fences.

Samantha appreciated the sunshine too. Now she didn't have to lug all that wet laundry to the attic where it freeze-dried—laundry hung outside on the lines captured the sweet, outdoorsy fragrances, and Will played peekaboo with her between the sheets and long johns. Having him make games out of the chores made the work load move along more quickly, and Samantha appreciated each moment with Will's cheerful presence.

Baby Ellen Marie enjoyed being outside as well. One of the items the Vanderhavens had provided was a wicker pram. At first, Samantha had wondered what on earth they would do with the ungainly thing on the farm, but once the weather was warm enough to be outdoors, she was grateful for the gift. Samantha could push the baby to the side yard when she hung laundry, to the backyard when she worked in the garden, and to the front yard when she sat on the porch to catch up on darning or other handwork. Ellen Marie sat happily in the pram, chewing on a rattle and watching from her vantage point.

One rainy afternoon in mid-May, Adam was attempting to talk Buddy into a nap with his brother.

"Aw, Daddy, do I hafta?" Buddy's green eyes pleaded. "I'm not a baby."

Adam ruffled the boy's hair, then crouched down to his level and smiled. "I know you're not a baby, son. That's why I know you'll understand that I need to talk to Mama alone for a little while."

Buddy looked at Samantha, who was cutting potatoes into wedges to plant in the garden, then back at Adam. "You need to talk to Mama? All by yourself?" His head tilted. "What about?" Another question, not surprising.

Adam couldn't help but grin. He shrugged, feigning a nonchalance he didn't feel. "Just grown-up talk. Sometimes grown-ups need to do that. So I'd like you to lie down for a bit with Will, then when you are done, we'll go to Uncle Frank and Aunt Anna's and take a look at the new calf they've got in their barn. Doesn't that sound like a good plan?"

Buddy wrinkled up his face, three freckles disappearing in the creases on his nose. At last he sighed. "Okay, I'll take a nap. But it won't be a real long one, will it?"

Adam laughed. "No, not too long. Now head on upstairs, and try not to shake the mattress too much when you climb in. Will is already asleep."

"Yes, Daddy." Buddy plodded upstairs with a disgusted slump to his shoulders.

Samantha smiled after him, shaking her head. "I think you just used bribery."

Adam slid into a chair across from Samantha, chuckling. "It didn't hurt anything, did it?"

"No." She dropped two more chunks of potato into the bowl. "My brother might not approve of such methods, but I prefer that approach to commanding the children. They obey you because they know you love them." Tears glittered in her eyes for a moment. "You're a good daddy, Adam."

Adam was touched by her words, and to cover the rush of emotion he affected a haughty pose. "Why, thank you, ma'am. I think so, too."

Samantha snorted. "And you're modest to go with it," she said as she threw a potato wedge at him.

He caught it and plopped it into the bowl on her lap. Then he sat, his chin in his hand, observing her as she continued her task. A meal required a lot more potatoes now that they had four children in the house, and they rarely shared a quiet moment alone together during the daytime hours. He enjoyed sitting, feeling the peacefulness in the cozy kitchen while raindrops spattered against the windowpanes, Lucy was off at school, and the other three drowsed upstairs.

In time Samantha raised her gaze from the potatoes. "What did you want to talk to me about?"

Adam sighed and ran a hand through his hair. "As you might guess, Lucy."

Samantha set aside the bowl of potatoes and knife and gave Adam her full attention.

"I'm worried, Sam," Adam admitted. "I'm afraid Lucy is never going to settle in here. Do you realize it's been four months? And she is no closer to accepting us as her new parents than she was the day we pulled into the depot, and she accused you of lying to her."

Samantha bit her lower lip. "I know. But what can I do, Adam?" She quietly confessed, "I don't think Lucy likes me very much."

The same thought had crossed Adam's mind more than once, but he wouldn't hurt Samantha by telling her so. Instead, he caught her hand and squeezed it. "I don't think Lucy likes being here. I think somehow she blames us for taking her away from her mother and father."

"But surely she understands that her parents are dead and can't care for her anymore. And we certainly can't be blamed for that."

"Of course not," Adam said, "but she's just six, remember. I still get the distinct impression she's angry with us. We took her away from Minneapolis and everything that was familiar. Even though the death of her parents is none of our doing, we are responsible for pulling her even further away from the home she knew with them. In her young mind, we've taken her away from her mother and father."

Samantha's eyes grew wide. "Do you really think so?"

Adam shrugged. "I don't know how else to explain her defiant attitude. She's harboring a strong anger, and somehow we have to help her get past that."

"But how? We've done everything your parents suggested. What else can we do?"

Adam shook his head. Feeling the bleakness of the situation nearly overwhelm him. "I don't know, Sam. I just don't know . . ." He reached across the table and took Samantha's hand. "Lucy doesn't like being here, and time is running out. The only thing we can do is continue to pray. I hope she settles in soon. Because I still think it would not be good to separate those children. If we can't adopt all of them and have them happy here, I'm thinking we should not go through with adopting any of them."

Samantha pulled her hand free, staring at him in alarm. "What are you saying?"

"I'm saying we have two months to hope Lucy understands we want her to be part of our family. If we can't do that, then it's possible all of the children should go back to the Foundling Home—maybe another couple can make it work where we have not been able to do so."

Tears flooded his wife's eyes, nearly breaking Adam's heart. She choked out, "What would our—our children think if we sent them back? We can't do that!"

"I don't want to send them back, Sammy, surely you know that." Adam moved around the table and dropped to one knee beside her. "But I'm at a loss! It isn't fair to Lucy to make her stay with us if she isn't happy here. If after half a year she hasn't accepted us, I wonder if she ever will. It just doesn't seem right to me that we adopt the three younger ones unless Lucy lets us know that she wants to be here, too."

"I . . . I agree they need to stay together. I'm not arguing against that, Adam. But . . ." Samantha clung to Adam's hands. "You know it would tear my heart out to let them go now."

Before Adam could reply, the quiet was interrupted by the sound of Ellen Marie waking from her nap. Samantha's hands were mucky with potato starch, so Adam rose. "I'll get her." He mounted the staircase, his heart heavy. When he peeked over the edge of the crib, Ellen Marie broke into a smile of recognition and babbled merrily. She stretched her chubby arms to him, begging to be picked up. And when Adam reached for her, the baby's jabbers suddenly formed, "Da-da-da-da. Dada."

Adam's hands stilled on the baby's ribs. Had he heard correctly? Had the baby really said—?

"Da-da," Ellen Marie said again, following it with a stream of gibberish.

Adam swept the baby from the cradle and down the stairs with the child bouncing in his arms. "Sam! Sam! Listen to this!"

Samantha met him at the base of the stairs looking alarmed. Adam turned the baby to face Samantha, and prodded, "Come on, Ellen Marie. Dada—say Dada."

"Adam, she's not old enough—"

"Yes, she is! She just said it when she looked up at me." He jostled the baby a bit. "You can do it, Ellen Marie. Say Dada for me." And to Adam's delight, the baby obliged her daddy.

"Da-da," she chortled, her face wreathed into a two-chin grin. "Da-da. Da-da."

Samantha squealed in surprise, startling Ellen Marie. Adam danced the baby around the kitchen until she giggled. "What a big girl! Daddy's so proud of you! But now we need to teach you 'Mama.'" He stopped and looked hopefully at the baby. "Can you say, 'Mama,' Ellen Marie? Huh? 'Mama, mama,'" he coached.

But Ellen Marie just gave him a wet grin of appreciation at all the attention, then jabbered senselessly, ending with the clearly recognizable "Da-da."

Buddy and Will appeared at the top of the stairs, Will rubbing his eyes sleepily while Buddy demanded, "Hey, what's goin' on down there?"

"We're celebrating Ellen Marie's first word." Samantha waved the boys down. "Naptime is over. Come join us."

Buddy took Will's hand and the boys hop-skipped down the steps. "Is this her first word?" Buddy gazed at Ellen Marie in wonder. "She's talkin'?"

"Yep." Adam stooped down and settled Ellen Marie on his bent knee. "Show off for your brothers, Ellen Marie. Say 'Dada.'"

Ellen Marie waved her hands wildly. "Da-da!"

Will clapped his hands and Buddy cheered, "Hey! That's great, Ellen Marie!" He beamed at Adam. "She's really smart to know you, huh, Daddy?"

Samantha dropped an arm around Buddy shoulders. "She's a real smarty pants, for sure."

"Boy, her first word." Buddy grinned up at Samantha. "Won't Lucy be surprised!"

Adam was brought back to reality, imagining Lucy's reaction, but he managed to give Buddy a smile. "Oh, I'm sure she will be."

"This calls for a reward of some sort," Samantha said, turning to the boys. "Up to the table for cookies and milk in honor of Ellen Marie's first word."

Buddy boosted Will into his seat before clambering into his own chair, asking over his shoulder, "Then can we go see the baby calf, Daddy?"

Adam chuckled as he put Ellen Marie in her high chair and reached for a bib. "Sure, Buddy. Right after Lucy gets home from school. Maybe she'd like to see the calf, too."

Buddy nodded, his mouth full of Samantha's homemade applesauce cookies. When he was finished with the bite, he observed, "Maybe the little calf will make Lucy smile. I'd like that."

Adam sent a startled glance in Samantha's direction. He hadn't realized Buddy was aware of Lucy's sullenness. But the simple comment made it clear that he and Samantha weren't the only ones who were concerned. They had to find a way to gain Lucy's trust.

Samantha placed a cup of milk in front of Buddy. "I'd like that too, Buddy."

Buddy turned a thoughtful look on Adam. "I'm really glad Ellen Marie knows who you are. An' I hope she gets to keep you."

Adam's nose stung as he battled his emotions. Buddy's innocent comment indicated the little boy still mourned his birth parents and, in his sweet way, he wanted his baby sister to avoid such pain. Adam wished he could promise none of them would ever lose him, but he wouldn't make a promise he might not be able to keep. A lot depended on Lucy and the next two months.

He stood behind Buddy, tipped the little boy's head back, and planted a kiss in his tousled hair. "I love you, Buddy," he said. "Let's go see the calf."

Help us, Lord—we can't send any of them back. Help Lucy. . . .

chool let out the end of May. Lucy was glad to see it over for the summer. Oh, she enjoyed the lessons, especially reading. If they'd let her, she'd read all day long, books were so fun. But being in a roomful of strange children made her nervous. She missed her brothers and her sister, and it bothered her that she wasn't home to take care of them the way she'd promised Buddy she would do. She was ready to spend her days with them again.

But she quickly discovered that Buddy wasn't around much during the day. Their new daddy took him away every morning and often didn't bring him back until suppertime. Her brother returned filthy dirty and tuckered out from chasing the plow around the fields, but he was always happy. Lucy envied him that happiness. It also made her feel something inside she didn't like. Why was he happy and not she?

At least Will and Ellen Marie stayed at the house all day. Ellen Marie was getting to be fun too. She could sit up and scoot herself around the floor and was even trying to talk! Her hair was finally coming in—blonde curls, just like Will's. Sometimes Lucy toyed with the soft ringlets fluffing out behind her baby sister's ears and wished her own hair was curly so she didn't have to sleep on those lumpy rags her new mama insisted on every night. Maybe if her own hair was blonde and curly like Ellen Marie's and Will's, her new mama would like her better.

Because, she was sure, her new mama didn't like her nearly as much as she liked Ellen Marie, Will, and Buddy. Her new mama insisted on doing everything for them herself, as if Lucy would hurt them if she touched them. She was sure her new mama didn't think too much of Lucy at all. And she knew why; she was too old. Lucy had heard the Sisters at the Foundling Home whispering about how hard it would be to find new parents for her. People only wanted babies and little kids. Lucy believed it, too. Lots of people had come and looked at Ellen Marie at the Foundling Home, but not once did somebody come in and say, "I'd like to meet Lucy, please."

The Sisters' worries about Lucy's age made her sure she really hadn't been wanted at all. These people only took her to get her brothers and baby sister. The day they picked them all up at the Foundling Home, she knew they were taking her back home where she had lived with Mama and Papa and the little ones. But they'd brought her here on a long, scary train ride. She'd known right away that it wasn't going to turn out like she'd thought it would.

Ever since, they treated her like she was some itty bitty kid who couldn't do anything. Every time she thought about it, anger welled.

If Lucy got something out to play with, her new mama put it back before Lucy was done with it. If she pulled a dress from her wardrobe, her new mama said, "Let's wear this one today, honey," and picked something else. If Lucy tried to help Will cut up his green beans, her new mama took the fork away and did it herself. If Lucy started pulling weeds in the garden, her new mama told her, "Why don't you go on and play?" It was clear they didn't want a big girl around. All they wanted was babies and little kids.

On a hot June day, Lucy sat on the porch steps and watched her new mama wheel Ellen Marie to the side yard in her pram. Will trotted along behind with a windup tin goose in his hand. Lucy watched while her new mama dragged a big basket of wet laundry to the line and began hanging wash to dry. Lucy squinted. Were her dresses in that basket? Curious, she scuffed over to look.

Sure enough—her favorite pink-and-white checked dress lay crumpled among Will's and Buddy's things. She shook out the wrinkles and reached for the little bag of wooden picks nailed to the post.

Her new mama held one of their new daddy's shirts in her hands, clothespins at the ready. She looked a question at Lucy.

Lucy pointed to the line. "Gonna hang my dresses up there."

Her new mama came over to Lucy, a smile on her face. "Oh, sweetie, that's nice of you to offer, but you don't need to do that. Why don't you go over and play on the swing?"

Lucy pressed her lips into a grim line. Couldn't she even be trusted to hang her own dress? Fury built inside, and she threw the wet dress back into the basket, whirled, and stomped away in the direction of the barn.

"Lucy, dear, what's the matter? Where are you going?" her new mama called, but Lucy pretended not to hear. When she reached the corner of the barn, she looked back at her new mama for a moment. She stood with her forehead all puckered up. She didn't look happy, but Lucy didn't care. Why should she care if she upset her new mama? Her new mama upset Lucy all the time.

She ran around the corner and ducked into the toolshed. There! Let her new mama do everything herself. Lucy didn't want to help that dumb lady anyway.

                                   ✺

Samantha sighed, shook her head, and went back to her hanging. But between each shirt and pair of pants, she turned her head to search for Lucy. Some unnamed uncertainty, even fear, held her captive. Should she go after the little girl? But she couldn't leave Ellen Marie and Will unattended while she hunted. Worry continued to plague her, and finally she stepped to the end of the clothesline, cupped her hands by her mouth, and called, "Lucy? Lucy, would you come here, please?"

She waited, but Lucy didn't appear.

Again she called, panic rising. "Lucy! Where are you, Lucy?"

"Good morning, Samantha!"

Samantha whirled around to find Priscilla, with Joey and Jenny in tow, standing in a splash of sunshine in the yard. Focused on Lucy, she hadn't even heard their buggy arrive. "Oh, Pris . . . And Joey and Jenny—hello." How disheartening to be caught in such a state of failure. She doubted either David or Priscilla would ever lose track of one of their children. She leaned down to receive Joey's boisterous hug and kiss. The instant she let him go he dashed across the grass to join Will, and Samantha reached for Jenny to give her a cuddle.

Priscilla headed straight for Ellen Marie's pram. "I told David I had to come out and compare notes with you. Jenny cut her third tooth last night! It's such fun having children the same age!"

"Mm-hmm," Samantha said absently, her gaze aimed at the barn. *Where was that child?*

Priscilla looked over her shoulder and frowned. "Are you looking for something?"

Samantha drew a deep breath. "I think so. Lucy. She took off for the barn a little while ago, and she won't answer when I call. I can't leave the others to look for her."

Priscilla poked a playful finger at Ellen Marie. "Are you worried?"

Samantha smiled ruefully. "I've been worried about Lucy for months."

"Then go after her." Priscilla flicked her fingers, shooing Samantha away. "I'll keep track of the other two for you."

"Are you sure, Pris?" Samantha handed Jenny to Priscilla, impatience to find the errant Lucy tightening her stomach.

"Of course." Priscilla grinned. "You won't be able to relax and visit with me until you've located her, so just go."

"Thanks, Pris." Samantha took a moment to hold Will's face with her hands and instruct, "Be a good boy for Aunt Prissy, Will. Stay here and play nice with Joey, okay?"

Will nodded, pointing at his cousin. "Wiw pway wif Joey."

"That's right, sweetheart. I'll be right back." She planted a kiss on Will's soft curls and took off at a trot for the corner of the barn where she'd last seen Lucy.

⁓♡

Lucy huddled in the corner of the dark toolshed. Their new daddy had told them to never go in the toolshed; he said there were dangerous things in there that could hurt them. Lucy had never even wanted to go inside. The shed didn't have any windows so it was dark, and it smelled musty. She didn't like being in here with shadows all around her and funny smells making her nose twitch, but her new mama wouldn't find her in here. She didn't want to be found. Yet she didn't want to be alone, either. Tears stung, and she sniffed. The sniffing made her sneeze. Loud. Two times.

After the second sneeze, the hinges on the door squeaked and sunlight spilled across the floor, shining all the way to Lucy's bare toes. Her new mama stood in the doorway. Lucy pulled her feet back and buried her face against her knees, hoping she wouldn't be seen, but her new mama must have seen her.

"Lucy, you know that you are not to be in here. What are you doing?"

Lucy could have said, "I'm hiding," but she decided not to talk. She hunkered in a tighter ball.

For a long time, her new mama stayed across the room. Then Lucy heard footsteps, and a hand touched her head. "Lucy, why did you run off? I was very worried about you."

Lucy knew her new mama wasn't worried about her. People only worried when they really, really cared. With her face against her knees, Lucy said, "Go away an' leave me alone."

The hand on Lucy's head pulled away, but even though she listened for footsteps, none came. Instead, her new mama said in a very soft voice, "I'm not going to leave you alone, Lucy. I don't think that's what you want." Lucy dared to peek. Her new mama knelt in front of her. Her face looked kind. "I remember lots of times when I was a little girl and all alone. What I wanted was someone to come and hold me."

Lucy gulped. How did she know that Lucy did wish for a hug? Her new mama caught hold of her beneath her armpits and pulled. Lucy tried to resist, but she ended up in her new mama's lap anyway. It felt so good to be there she started to cry. She didn't make any sound, but her body shook. Her new mama held her tighter, but Lucy still couldn't stop crying.

Her new mama rocked back and forth, the same way she rocked Ellen Marie or Will. "Honey, I know you're unhappy. Won't you please tell me what I can do to help you smile?"

Lucy remembered why she'd run off. She remembered all the other times she'd wanted to run off. All of the hurts from the past weeks piled on top of her until she couldn't hold it in. She wriggled to free herself. "Let me go home again."

Her new mama's mouth dropped open. "Lucy . . .?"

Lucy pushed hard against her new mama. "Let me go *home*. You don't want me. You don't need me."

"W-what—?"

"You don't need me!" Lucy scuttled backward until she reached the corner once more.

She crouched, holding herself tight, and glaring at her new mama.

"Lucy, how can you say such a thing?"

Lucy let out a huff and spat out, "My mama, she needed me, but not you. You only need *babies*." Her new mama reached for her, but Lucy hunched her shoulders. "I wanna go home."

For a long time, her new mama sat there with her hands outstretched. Finally, she dropped her arms. She looked very, very tired. Very sad. "Sweetheart, you can't go back to your old home. There's no one there to take care of you."

Lucy sat up straight. "I can take care of me. I did it before. I dressed me, an' fed me, an' I even dressed Willie and Ellen Marie. Sometimes I fed 'em. An' Buddy, too. An' I swept, an' made beds, and did lotsa' stuff. I can do it. I can take care of all of us."

Her new mama hung her head. "Oh, Lucy . . ."

"Buddy, he gets to be the new daddy's helper." Lucy tried to sound accusing, but she didn't feel as angry as she had before. Instead, her chest hurt. The way it had hurt when the nuns said Mama and Papa were never coming back. She sniffed hard. "But *you* don't need a helper. You just need the babies, not me."

"Lucy, please come here, darling, before I cry."

Lucy was suspicious. "Why're you gonna cry?"

"Because I've made you sad, and that's the last thing. . . ." Her new mama held her arms open. "Please, Lucy, come here. I want to tell you a story."

Lucy saw tears in her new mama's eyes, and it made her feel funny. And even though she was still a little mad, a story did sound nice—better than being all alone. Hesitantly she scooched across the floor on her bottom. When her hip bumped against her new mama's legs, at once she folded her arms around Lucy, holding her securely, and that felt kind of good, too. She relaxed a little bit.

Her new mama smoothed Lucy's hair away from her damp forehead and smiled. A tender smile. "Lucy, I'm going to tell you a story about a little girl." Lucy stared into her new mama's face. "This little girl's mama died when the girl was born, so she never had a mama at all. But she had someone else—a grandma. She called her grandmother 'Gran,' and Gran took care of the little girl, the girl's brother and their pa, and the girl's house. Gran did all of the cooking and cleaning and—well, all of the things that a mama would do for her family."

She paused for a moment, shifting her arms a bit more snugly around Lucy, and Lucy rested her elbow in her new mama's lap. "When the little girl was six years old—"

"Same as me?" Lucy interrupted.

Her new mama smiled. "Just the same age as you. When she was six years old, her Gran also died. The little girl was very sad and lonely, because she had loved Gran so much and now Gran was gone forever."

"Like Mama and Papa." Lucy could feel her chin quiver, and she put her hand up to hold it still.

"That's right, honey."

Lucy leaned her head against her new mama's shoulder.

"After that, the little girl and her brother and pa were alone. There wasn't a grown-up lady in the house to take care of things, so the little girl had to be the lady. She had to cook and clean and wash clothes. . . . There wasn't time for playing like the other children did because there was always work to be done. All the work was very hard for her, and she promised herself that when she grew up, if she was lucky enough to have little girls of her own, she would let them play all day and never make them do any chores at all. She wanted her own children to have fun instead of having to work, like she had to do."

Lucy leaned fully against her new mama. "What was the little girl's name?"

For a little while, Lucy thought her new mama wasn't going to answer. But then she said, very quietly, "Her name was Samantha."

Lucy sat up to look fully at her new mama. "You?"

She smiled, but somehow she still looked sad. "Uh-huh, I was that little girl." She took hold of Lucy's chin and looked straight in her eyes. "All I ever wanted was to be a mama and let my children do all the things I never got to do. I wanted my children to be able to play and sing and laugh the day away, and never have to fuss with washing dishes or making beds or any kind of work at all. I wanted my children to have fun."

She stroked Lucy's cheek. Her fingers felt soothing to Lucy. "My own childhood wasn't fun, Lucy. I've wanted yours to be different than mine. I've wanted you to be happy and carefree, not overwhelmed with responsibilities. Do you understand?"

Lucy thought about the story. She felt sorry for her new mama, now that she knew how sad she had been as a little girl. Her new mama hadn't wanted Lucy to be "overwhelmed with responsibilities," she'd said. Lucy stared at her new mama. Maybe she really did love Lucy. Maybe she'd been sent off to play because her new mama was saying she loved her.

"Do you . . . do you and the new papa want me to be here too?"

The new mama made a little choking sound, then wrapped both arms so tight around Lucy she thought she couldn't breathe. But it felt good too.

"Oh, Lucy dearest, I can't tell you how much Daddy and I want you. . . ." It sounded like the new mama was crying, and Lucy wriggled free to look at her.

Lucy said, "I want . . . I want you too." Her throat sounded kind of choked up, but she was starting to feel real good inside. "It would be fun . . . for me . . . to be your helper," Lucy said. "I liked bein' Mama's helper. I didn't hafta do everything that Mama did, but I did some things. An' since I helped her, Mama had more time to play with me. I liked that."

"Oh, Lucy, I would like that too."

For the first time Lucy reached to wrap her arms around her new mama. Her new mama hugged her back, and Lucy closed her eyes. She liked being held this way. The hug made her feel like she was loved after all. She held tight for a long time, then she let go to snuggle down into her new mama's lap.

Her new mama stroked Lucy's hair. "Would you hang up the clothes with me, Lucy? With your help, it will get done quickly, and then maybe we can bake some oatmeal cookies."

Lucy scrambled up. "Oh, yes, Mama! Let's do that"

Mama wiped her tears, stood up, and took Lucy's hand. "Let's go then. We've got a lot to do."

Lucy skipped under the sunshine, swinging her mama's hand as they crossed the yard to the clothesline.

Chapter Thirty-One

Buddy laughed boisterously as Adam swung the boy onto his shoulders. "Watch your head!" Adam warned as they pushed through the front door of the farm home. From the kitchen the sounds of cheerful children's voices could be heard. Light spilled through the kitchen doorway, creating a golden shaft of welcome. The welcoming glow and pleasant murmurs of his beloved family drew Adam like a magnet.

Samantha was stirring a pot on the stove, a smile on her heat-flushed face. In the high chair, Ellen Marie banged a tin cup against the tray. Will stood beside her making her squeal by pretending to grab her cup. Lucy circled the table, carefully placing enamel plates in front of each chair.

Adam called out in a playful voice, "What's for supper, Ma?"

Lucy put down the last plate and ran around the table. She threw her arms around Adam's waist, surprising him so much he nearly dropped Buddy on the floor. "Daddy, guess what?" Lucy enthused, her arms holding Adam's middle and her head thrown back. "I helped Mama hang the clothes today, an' then we made oatmeal cookies with pecans. I chopped the pecans, too. Mama says we can have 'em for dessert if we eat all our supper."

Adam swallowed three times, rapidly, before he could say, "Well, then, we'll have to be sure and eat all our supper, right?"

Lucy released him and danced back to the table. "I'm settin' the table, Daddy, see?" The pride in her eyes was unmistakable.

"An' then I'll put out the spoons an' forks. Mama and I figured out things I can do to help." She returned to her task with all seriousness.

Adam put Buddy on the floor, nearly weak with shock. He crossed the kitchen to stand beside Samantha who smiled at him, her eyes shining with everything she wasn't saying. Adam gestured toward Lucy who had shooed Buddy away from the table so she could put out the forks. "She just called me 'Daddy'—and she referred to you as 'Mama,'" he said in a low voice. "She's actually smiling. . . . What happened?"

Samantha shrugged, but the smile on her lips was a bit tremulous. "We had a talk, Lucy and I. And we decided that since you had a helper—namely, Buddy—I should have one, too. Lucy was the obvious choice since she's hardly a baby and quite capable of being a big assistance to me."

Then she laid the spoon down and admitted in a whisper, "Adam, I made such a dreadful mistake! By doing everything for her, I made her feel as if she wasn't needed. She felt unimportant. She didn't think we really wanted her, and that's why she was so angry inside." She sighed. "Oh, Adam, I of all people should have understood her need to be needed. . . . I'll never forget the weeks I spent working for Liz and Jake—filled with some of the hardest work of my life, yet they were the most rewarding because Liz and Jake genuinely appreciated my help. Their appreciation gave me a sense of worthiness and belonging. In my shortsightedness, I was robbing Lucy of feeling needed and worthy."

Adam placed a hand on Samantha's shoulder. "But it's all right now?"

Samantha nodded, her gaze on Lucy. She was tying a bib around Ellen Marie's neck and chattering away to the baby. "I think things are going to be fine now." She looked into Adam's eyes, wonder blooming across her face. "Do you realize all four of them are calling us Mama and Daddy now? They really have become our children."

Joy exploded through Adam. He swung Samantha up in his arms and danced her around the kitchen. The children watched in silence for a moment, then they all joined in the laughter.

"Mama and Daddy are funny, aren't they?" Lucy told her siblings.

As Samantha spooned oatmeal into bowls, the telephone jangled. Lucy sat straight up, her face hopeful. "Can I answer it, Daddy?"

Adam waved a hand toward the telephone on the wall. "Go ahead, daughter. Remember your manners."

"Yes, sir." Lucy dashed to the phone. She tucked her hair behind her ear, lifted the earpiece, and placed it against her ear. Raising up on tiptoe, she spoke into the mouth horn. "Hello, Klaassen residence. This is Lucy." After a moment's pause, a smile of recognition broke across her face. "Hi! Yes, Daddy's right here. Just a minute, please." She turned, holding out the earpiece to Adam. "It's for you, Daddy. It's Uncle Daniel."

"I'll bet it's about the hearing," Adam murmured to Samantha as he pushed away from the table. Samantha stirred milk into Ellen Marie's oatmeal while she listened closely to the one-sided conversation.

"Hello, Daniel . . . Fine, thanks. How's everyone there? . . . Good . . . Yes, we know it's that time. We're ready for it. . . . Friday at ten? Yes, I think that will work with us if we come in on Thursday evening. . . . Are you sure? There are six of us now, you know."

Samantha smiled, hearing the pride in Adam's voice.

"Well, then, we'll see you Thursday. Thanks a lot, brother." Adam replaced the telephone and returned to the table. "The hearing's set for ten o'clock on Friday," he told her quietly.

Samantha filled Ellen Marie's eager mouth with another bite. "We'll all be ready."

Buddy looked up from his breakfast, a milk mustache on his freckled face. "What's a hearing, Daddy?"

"Betcha I know." Lucy sent a wise grin around the table. "It's when you go hear somebody say something you want to hear."

Adam and Samantha chuckled, and Adam tweaked the girl's nose. "You're not far from the truth, Lucy. A hearing is when you talk to a judge, and he makes a decision for you."

"What kind of dish—decision?" Buddy, of the many questions, wanted to know.

Samantha answered. "Lots of different kinds of decisions, Buddy. But this time he will decide—" She paused, looking to Adam for support. At his nod, she continued, "He will decide whether you and your brother and sisters will stay here as our children from now on."

"Forever and ever?" Buddy asked, green eyes wide.

"Forever and ever," Samantha echoed, reaching to smooth his cowlick into place.

Buddy nodded. "I like it here with you, Mama and Daddy."

"I'm sure the judge will ask you if you're happy here, and if you want to be our son." Adam turned to Lucy. "The judge will talk to you, too, Lucy. And we'll want you to tell him the truth. You know, whether or not you want to live here and be our daughter."

Lucy's face puckered. "Daddy, I—" She bit her lower lip.

Over the past several weeks, Lucy had settled into the home, opening up and becoming as affectionate as her younger siblings. Her sudden apprehension made Samantha's heart flutter. Adam said, "What is it, Lucy?"

She looked from Samantha to Adam, her eyes holding the wariness they thought had disappeared for good. "It's just . . . Well . . ."

"Come here, Lucy." Adam held out a hand to the child. She came around the table, leaning between Adam's legs as he put an arm around her. "Tell me what's troubling you."

Within the secure circle of Adam's arms, Lucy apparently discovered her courage. "I like being here with you an' Mama, an' I want to live here." She paused, picking at a button on Adam's shirt. "But I still remember my real mama an' papa. Sometimes . . . I still miss them." She hung her head as if ashamed.

Buddy observed his sister. "Me, too," he said softly, his mouth quivering a little. Samantha caught his hand and gave it a squeeze of understanding.

Adam hugged Lucy, then stretched out one hand to place his fingers on the back of Buddy's neck. "We hope you don't ever forget your first mama and papa. Your memories of them are a very important part of you, and someday, when Will and Ellen Marie are old enough, you'll want to tell them about them. You can go right on loving them, thinking about them. It is just fine with your new mama and me."

"Really?" Lucy stared into Adam's face.

Adam hugged her again. "Really. We can't take the place of the mama and papa you were born to, but we love you, and we believe you are learning to love us, too." He lifted her onto his knee. "You see, Lucy, God made our hearts in a very special way. A heart seems very small, but there's always room to hold love for one more person."

Lucy pulled back and examined Adam seriously. "I do love you an' Mama. I want to be your daughter."

Adam smiled and placed a kiss on Lucy's temple. "I'm very glad to hear that."

Samantha nearly wilted with relief. "Me, too."

"Will our name be Klaassen like yours after the hearing?" Lucy asked.

Adam nodded. "Is that all right with you?"

Lucy tapped her chin with one finger. "Lucy Klaassen. Lucille Elizabeth Klaassen." She grinned. "That sounds pretty good, I guess."

Buddy said, "What about me? What will I be?"

Samantha poked his ribs. "You will be Henry Rollin Klaassen, known affectionately as Buddy. And your brother, William Everett Klaassen. And this little kitten"—she tapped Ellen Marie's nose with a gentle finger—"will be Ellen Marie Klaassen. All of us will be Klaassens."

Buddy shrugged, grinning.

Adam shifted Lucy from his lap with a gentle push. "Well, now, Klaassens, breakfast is getting cold, so let's finish up."

Will, who had continued eating throughout the conversation, looked up brightly and announced, "B'eakfass aw gone!"

Lucy rolled her eyes. "What a piggy." She and Buddy giggled, and Will joined in, waving his empty spoon. Ellen Marie jabbered and joyfully waved hers too.

Adam and Samantha smiled across the table at each other. Laughter and children . . . It was theirs now, too.

Chapter Thirty-Two

*E*llen Marie dozed in Samantha's arms, and Will hummed happily beside her on the seat of the passenger car. The little boy galloped a tin horse across his knees, and in the seats facing her, Lucy and Buddy crowded in beside Adam, sharing a book. Gazing at the contented children, Samantha remembered the train ride she and Adam had taken with the children only six months earlier.

She almost wished some of the passengers who had glared and bellyached about them the last time could be here to see them now. They wouldn't have a thing about which to find fault—the children were clean, healthy, quiet and well-behaved, and happy instead of sullen. Another prayer of gratitude winged from her heart for the little family she and Adam had been given.

Adam finished his book and handed it to Lucy. "Help Buddy find all the letter A's on the first two pages of this book. If you count them all correctly, I'll buy you a licorice when we reach Minneapolis."

"Yay!" the children chorused. Lucy took the book, and the two little heads bent over the page. Will hopped down from his seat and stood between their knees, poking his head in the way. Lucy shifted him back just a bit, and they began counting.

Samantha clicked her tongue on her teeth, shaking her head.

Adam grinned at her. "What's that for?"

"You and your enticements," she said with a chuckle. "David would be appalled."

"No need to tell him," Adam retorted.

Samantha laughed, startling Ellen Marie. She gave the baby some soothing pats then lifted her face to Adam's once more. "What time is it?"

Adam raised one eyebrow. "Five minutes later than the last time you asked. You aren't anxious about anything this time, are you?"

"Don't tease me, Adam. You're just as anxious as I am, and don't even try to deny it. I've seen you checking out the window every few minutes to see where we are, and if Minneapolis might be around the next bend."

Adam shrugged and ran a hand through his hair. He yawned. "Maybe the time would go faster if we napped."

"I'm too excited to sleep, but go ahead if you want to," Samantha said.

Before Adam could slouch in the seat and close his eyes, Lucy patted him on the arm. "Daddy, there are twenty-one A's—see?"

Adam sat up and reached for the book. "Show me," he said, and watched as Lucy recounted each A with Buddy adding his assistance. When they were finished, he said, "Good job! You've earned your licorice."

Lucy's eyes twinkled. "If we find all the B's, will we get another piece?"

Adam laughed, dropping an arm around Lucy and pulling her tight against his side for a brief hug. "Here's a little girl after my own heart—sweet tooth and all!"

"Will we, Daddy?" Buddy screwed his face up in concentration.

Adam laughed a "maybe" and scooped Will up and settled the little boy on his lap. He pointed to the book and said, "Let's count all the letters and see which one is used the most."

The various games kept them occupied until supper. They ate the sandwiches and cookies Samantha had brought along, then the children gave in to the gentle rocking of the train. Will slept contentedly in Adam's arms, while Buddy and Lucy leaned together and napped. Before they knew it, the screeching of brakes announced their arrival in Minneapolis.

Samantha drew in a breath, anticipation speeding her pulse. "We're here." She shared one brief, glowing smile with her husband—*this is it!*—then readied the children for departure. Lucy took Will by the hand; Buddy grabbed the small valise; Adam handled the larger suitcase; and Samantha carried Ellen Marie.

Adam spotted Daniel at the end of the walk, and soon they were rolling along the cobblestone streets, everyone laughing and talking at once. They made one stop at a corner store to purchase the promised licorice—five cents' worth so they could share with their cousins—then headed to Daniel's home.

The evening passed in pleasant conversation between the adults and companionable play between the children. Eventually Samantha tucked Ellen Marie, Will, and Buddy into their pallets on the floor of the guest room before tending to Lucy's pin curls. As she combed the hair into careful coils, securing them with strips of cloth, Lucy fidgeted.

Samantha said, "If you sit still, Lucy, we'll get this done a lot faster."

Lucy sighed. "Mama, why do we do this?"

Samantha paused, surprised. "You don't like your hair in curls?"

Lucy shrugged, toying with the hem of her nightgown. "It isn't a matter to me if my hair's curly or not. But maybe"—she peeked over her shoulder at Samantha—"you like curly hair better than straight hair? I know you like Will's and Ellen Marie's little curls. . . ."

Samantha pulled Lucy snug against her, wrapping her arms across the child's stomach. "I put pin curls in your hair, because it gives me a chance to spend a bit of just-us time with you. But if you don't like them, I can brush your hair out at night and leave it down. It's up to you."

Lucy tipped her head until her temple encountered Samantha's cheek. After a few thoughtful minutes she said decisively, "Gimme curls, Mama."

Samantha looked into Lucy's face. "Are you sure , Lucy?"

Lucy grinned impishly. "Yes. We gotta use all those bows you made to match my dresses."

Samantha laughed and delivered a kiss to Lucy's cheekbone before finishing the job.

In the morning, Samantha combed Lucy's hair into perfect sausage curls, complete with a huge bow of pure white organdy at the crown. She dressed each of the children from Lucy down to Ellen Marie in their Sunday best. Samantha took as much care with her own attire, and Adam wore the suit he'd worn to the first court hearing back in February.

As they stood together in the home's foyer before leaving for the courthouse, Rose gave them the once-over. "May I make a suggestion?"

Adam said, "Of course."

"After your hearing, stop into one of the photography studios on Main Street and have a family portrait taken. It would be the perfect remembrance of this day."

Samantha was delighted. "That's a wonderful idea, Rose. Can you recommend a good one?"

Rose gave them the name of a photographer their family had used, and then Daniel stuck his head in the door. "The motor's running. Let's get moving, all you Klaassens."

Daniel brought the car to a stop at the curb outside the courthouse. "Hop out. I'll go park and be right back."

Adam herded his crew inside, his heart banging against his ribcage. It seemed as though years passed while they waited inside the doors until Daniel joined them.

They made their way to the same room in which they'd met before. Judge Simmons was already behind his desk, and he raised a hand of greeting when Daniel swung the door open and stuck his head in. "Come in, come in!" the judge called in a jovial tone. "Oh, good, you've brought them all. Hello, children."

Will chirped an unconcerned, "Hewo." But Lucy and Buddy, suddenly shy, remained speechless. Adam prompted them forward until they stood in a row in front of Judge Simmons, their heads tipped back to see him behind the tall desk, eyes wide with awe. Adam and Samantha stood directly behind them, Samantha holding baby Ellen Marie.

The judge smiled. "So have you used these past months to get acquainted?"

Buddy fidgeted, and Adam placed his hands on the boy's shoulders. He immediately stilled. "Yes, sir. The children have settled into their new home. We've all adjusted well, I think."

Judge Simmons leaned on his forearms to peer over the edge at the children. "Is that right, children? Have you settled into your new home?"

Lucy looked up at Adam. He winked, nodding for her to go ahead and speak. She straightened and turned to face the judge, shoulders back. "Yes, sir. We like our new home just fine."

The judge nodded, then turned to Buddy. "What about you, young man? Do you like your new home?"

Buddy nodded, blinking rapidly. "I like the farm, an' the animals, an' bein' in the fields with Daddy."

Judge Simmons smiled. "Thank you, Henry."

Will looked around. "Who Henwy?"

The judge turned to Buddy. "Why, isn't your name Henry?" He consulted his notes.

Will shook his head and pointed at his brother with a chubby finger. "He be Buddy."

The judge leaned back in his chair and chuckled. "I stand corrected." He leaned forward again and asked Will, "Are there any other name changes about which I should know?"

Will turned shy and inserted his favorite finger in his mouth. Lucy spoke up. "Yes, sir. Me, Buddy, Will, an' Ellen Marie—" she pointed to each in turn—"we all are gonna change our name to Klaassen like Mama and Daddy."

"Is that what you want?" The judge was very serious now.

Lucy matched his solemnity. "Yes, sir."

"Then we shall do just that." Judge Simmons reached for a pen and a paper. "Before we sign this legal document," he said, his eyes roving from person to person, "I'd like to say a few words." He leaned back in his chair, interlaced his fingers and rested them on the paper.

Adam scooped up Will, perching the little boy on his broad forearm, and slipped his other arm around Samantha's waist. They turned attentive gazes on the judge.

"I look at an adoption much like a marriage. When two people wed, they vow to care for one another in all circumstances, to honor and respect one another. Mr. and Mrs. Klaassen, by assuming responsibility for the McIntyre children, you are making a similar commitment. Parenting is a twenty-four-hour-a-day obligation, every day of every week of every year for the remainder of your lives. When you sign this paper, you are saying you want the responsibility, and you will take it seriously. Do you understand the commitment you are making?"

Samantha replied promptly. "Oh, yes, Your Honor. We understand, and we make that commitment with our whole hearts."

The judge then focused his attention on Lucy and Buddy. "Children, I want to be certain you understand that from now on, Adam and Samantha Klaassen will be your legal guardians. They will be"—he smiled—"your daddy and mama. By accepting them as your parents, you are telling me you will respect and obey them. Can you do that?"

Lucy took Buddy by the hand. "Yes, sir. We won't ever forget our real mama an' papa, but we've got room to love this mama an' daddy, too." She turned a grin on Samantha and Adam, then faced the judge again. "They're good parents, an' we'll be good children."

"Very well, then." Judge Simmons lifted the document and slid it to the edge of the desk. "Shall we make things legal?"

Adam put Will down and picked up the pen. His hand trembled slightly as he realized the finality of this act, and he paused, savoring the moment—the official bond that would meld them together as a family. Then the pen touched the paper, his signature emerged, and he took Ellen Marie in his arms so Samantha could sign.

Buddy tipped this way and that, trying to see what they were doing. "Do we sign it, too?"

The judge sat up straight, apparently taken aback. "Well, son, I suppose you could, if you really wanted to."

Buddy crinkled his nose. "Don't know how yet. But I'm learnin' my A's."

The judge's laughter joined that of Adam and Samantha, and Adam affectionately rubbed his hand over Buddy's head.

Lucy waved her hand at the judge. "Are we all Klaassens now, Mister Judge?"

Judge Simmons swallowed his chuckles to answer Lucy with all due solemnity. "Yes, Miss Lucille Elizabeth Klaassen, you are all officially Klaassens now."

Her eyes wide and guileless, Lucy stated sincerely, "Thank you very much."

Epilogue

Adam tiptoed from room to room, checking one last time on his children. He took a moment to tuck the sheet up beneath Will's chin, pulling the ever-present finger from the boy's mouth at the same time. He removed the truck that Buddy held in the crook of his arm. The child mumbled and rolled onto his side, curling into a ball beneath the covers. In Lucy's room he smoothed the wispy bangs from her face and placed a gentle kiss on her forehead before moving quietly out. He stood for a long time at little Ellen Marie's crib, smiling down at the funny way her lower lip poked out in sleep. He watched the rise and fall of her little chest, listening to her soft breaths.

Satisfied that all were well, he headed downstairs. He paused to touch the frame on the family portrait which had stood prominently on the entry table for the past three months. Although they would certainly take more family portraits in the years ahead, he intended to always leave this one on display as a symbol of God's great gift to him, to Samantha.

He spotted his wife's silhouette through the lace curtain over the oval glass in the front door. She leaned on the porch railing, her face toward the sky. He couldn't help his smile. She was star-gazing again. His mind skipped back in time, to another porch and another star-studded night when he'd stood beside Samantha and peered skyward. He'd barely known her then, but she had turned a wistful gaze upward and made a wish on a star, forever imprinting her image on his heart. How young they had been back then, how full of hopes and dreams . . .

The desire to share the moment with her propelled him forward, and he stepped outside and stood behind. He wrapped his arms around her and pulled her firmly to him. She stacked her arms over his, tipping her head back to nestle next to his chin. She sighed contentedly as they stood in the darkness, enjoying the pleasant night sounds, the earthy scents of burgeoning fall, and the sky full of shimmering brightness. Suddenly, above their heads, one star streaked across the velvet backdrop of sky.

"A falling star!" Adam pointed. "Make a wish, Sammy."

The star burst into tiny pieces and disappeared into the expanse of black velvet and glittering diamonds.

Samantha held her breath, then let it out, and turned within his embrace to wrap her arms around his torso. The smile she offered warmed him from his head to his toes.

Adam tucked a strand of hair behind Samantha's ear. "So what did you wish for, my sweet?"

Her smile turned secretive. "No wishes, Adam."

"No wishes? What does that mean?"

The tenderness in Samantha's eyes brought a lump to Adam's throat as she answered softly. "I have no need for wishes anymore. I have everything my heart could desire right here—a God who loves me, this home, our children sleeping upstairs, and you."

Adam lifted her face upward and bestowed a long kiss on her smiling lips. They held each other, Samantha's face pressed into the curve of Adam's shoulder, Adam's cheek against her hair.

"Adam, remember when we found out I couldn't have children, and I told you it seemed as if my heart was crying?"

How could he forget? It was one of the most heartrending moments of his life. Instead of answering, he tightened his grip around her.

"My heart was crying, Adam. It was begging for the chance to be a mother—to have a child to love. Of course, at the time I only wanted that to be a child we created together."

"Do you still regret not being able to have a baby, Sam?" Adam asked.

She sucked in her lips for a moment, her expression thoughtful. Finally she shook her head. "No. Regret can mean bitterness. I let go of the bitterness long ago. And I've come to realize something. . . . When a heart cries, Someone listens and answers."

Pulling away a bit, she continued. "Oh, I didn't get the answer I thought I was looking for. But God had something better in mind for us. For them. If God had given us a child back then, we never would have brought home Lucy, Buddy, Will, and Ellen Marie. They are the window that was thrown open when the door to motherhood was slammed shut. To think I could have lost them! Adam, I simply can't imagine not having them in our lives. They are every bit ours. And I think they love us as much as if we had conceived each one."

Adam drew in a deep breath, pulling her beneath his chin once more. "Yes, Sammy, you're right. We've been given more than I could have ever imagined. We are blessed, aren't we?"

From her spot, Samantha offered a reply that filled Adam's heart to overflowing. "Oh, yes. We have been blessed fourfold."

APPLESAUCE CAKE

3 cups flour

3 tsp. baking powder

2 tsp. baking soda

½ tsp. salt

2 tsp. ground cinnamon

½ tsp. ground nutmeg

⅛ tsp. ground cloves

4 eggs

2 cups white sugar

1½ cups vegetable oil

2 cups unsweetened applesauce

1 tsp. vanilla extract

Whipped cream, sweetened (optional)

Preheat oven to 350°. Grease and flour a 9- x 13-inch pan. Sift together the flour, baking powder, baking soda, salt, and spices into a large bowl. Make a well in the center and pour the eggs, sugar, oil, applesauce, and vanilla. Mix well and pour into the prepared pan. Bake in the preheated oven for 40–50 minutes or until a toothpick inserted in the center of the cake comes out clean. Serve warm with whipped cream, if desired.

HULDA KLAASSEN'S BUBBAT

4 eggs
2 cups milk, scalded
1 tsp. salt
½ cup water
5 cups flour
1 tbsp. instant yeast
4 cups ground sausage, cooked and drained*

Scald milk and add salt. Set aside and cool until steam no longer rises. Add ½ cup water to milk. Blend flour, salt, and dry yeast. Beat eggs well, add to liquids, and then stir in the flour with a wooden spoon. Stir in sausage or ham. Spread into a greased sheet pan (13- x 18-inch, with 1-inch sides) or use one 9- x 13-inch pan and one loaf pan. Cover with plastic and let rise one hour. Bake at 350° for 45 minutes. Slice and serve. Wonderful with baked apples!

*May substitute cut-up cooked ham for cooked sausage.

Acknowledgments

As always, I want to thank my parents, Ralph and Helen Vogel, for their steadfast support and for being such models of Jesus for me. Their beautiful legacy of faith lives on through my brother and me.

When I originally wrote *When a Heart Cries* and dedicated it to my daughters, they were all still living under my roof. Now they're grown and raising children of their own (where does the time go?). Kristian, Kaitlyn, and Kamryn, I pray daily for you to follow God's will so your children will grow to understand the importance of seeking a relationship with Him. I love all of you—daughters and grandbabies—so very, very much.

My amazing critique partners and prayer warriors are always there for me. You bless me with your friendship, your encouragement, your sisterhood. Thank you!

To Carol Johnson and the staff at Hendrickson, thank you so much for giving the Mountain Lake stories new life. I so enjoyed revisiting these very first, straight-from-my-heart stories. Bless you for your ministry.

Finally, and most importantly, gratitude and deepest honor to God for being ever available to me. When my heart has cried, He has given comfort, peace, and strength. He gifts me beyond my deservings. May any praise or glory be reflected directly back to Him.